# An Oracle Walks into a Bar

## The Misadventures of a Paranormal Post-Relationship Personal Effects Repossession Specialist, Book One

### Scott Burtness

# FREE Short Story

Get *Five Stars,* a FREE demonic horror comedy short story, when you sign up for **The Paranomedy Pint**, Scott's once-a-month email featuring a great book to read, a fun show to watch, something terrific to drink, and a little paranormal weirdness to enjoy!!

*For Liz.*
*Every possible future with you is a good one.*

# PRAISE FOR AN ORACLE WALKS INTO A BAR

"The writing is sharp and funny—think the 'Hitchhiker's Guide,' only paranormal. If you read only one book about a shape-shifting Post-Relationship Personal Effects Repossession Specialist this year, make it 'An Oracle Walks Into a Bar.'"
-- Andrew Shaffer, NYTimes bestselling author of "Hope Never Dies: An Obama Biden Mystery"

# CONTENTS

# SOMEWHERE IN MINNESOTA...

*An Oracle walks into a bar.*

*"I've had a vision," she says, clearly shaken. "The end of the world is nigh, and I really need a drink."*

*"You want to start a tab?" the bartender asks.*

*"... Sure," the Oracle replies. "And I'll have a bottle of your most expensive whiskey."*

# Chapter 1

*Ope! It's your horoscope, Sagittarius!*
*Your future's like a basket of pull tabs. Sure, there's a chance that you'll be the big winner,*
*but the odds stink.*

NOT TO BRAG, BUT I'm a bit of an expert on glass. I've gone through enough windows, bounced off of enough windshields, been hit over the head by enough vases, and broken enough mirrors to know a thing or two. Like the plate glass window I was currently shattering. A large, single pane that framed the front yard's maple like a living picture dominated the ranch-style home's living room wall. The window was obviously original to the home, which meant it was a good seventy-plus years old. Homes from that era still used drawn sheet glass made using the Fourcault process. I've always liked that glass. The thickness varies a bit throughout and makes for some interesting distortions. Nothing obnoxious. Just enough to add a little character. Sadly, the Fourcault process fell out of fashion in the 1950s and was replaced by the float glass method. Sure, those windows might offer a near-perfect view of what's on the other side, but, as a highly imperfect being myself, I've never been too enamored with perfection. So, yeah. I like the older windows in the older houses, especially when I'm getting thrown through one. Having gone through the more modern and hard-to-shatter types, one learns to appreciate a good, old-fashioned, and—most importantly—thin pane of glass.

The front lawn rushed up to meet me. Shifting mid-flight, I hit the ground as a thick-pelted wolverine. Swathed in my now much-too-large sweatshirt and leather jacket, the sharp shards from the shattered window posed little risk. I heard my boots thud and my suddenly empty jeans flap, followed by a sharp jangle. I had clipped my keys to a belt loop with an old carabiner, a nice trick I'd learned after losing them more times than I cared to admit. Losing keys is easy. Losing pants is harder. Not impossible, just harder, so at least I had that going for me.

With an annoyed growl, I crawled free of the rest of my human-sized clothes and trundled over the light dusting of snow and remnants of the window. Jagged chunks of the broken window glowed with reflected moonlight; the effect muted by my new form's poor eyesight. The wolverine was a useful shift–the damned things were nearly indestructible–but they couldn't see for shit. Deciding it was safe enough for my now-bare feet, I shifted back to my human form with a familiar twinge of despondency. Wolverines are badass. Scrawny, over-the-hill, naked white dudes on a chilly April night? Not so much. While one hand made a vain attempt to preserve my modesty, the other gave a well-practiced middle finger to the hulking silhouette inside the recently ruined window.

"Overreact much?" I cursed. "It's just a stupid CD. No one even likes Oasis. Not really."

"Who sent you? Him? You tell that worthless little prick that he might've bought the concert tickets, but I bought the CD and got it signed by Liam Gallagher. It's mine."

Her lament was surprisingly understandable. Werewolves don't have the best diction. It's tough when your mouth is stretched into a muzzle and stuffed full of extra teeth. More surprising than her elocution, though, was how quickly she'd turned. The plan had been simple enough: Wait for the full moon to crack the horizon, sneak in and grab the CD while she was preoccupied with the whole going-all-wolfy thing, and get out before you could say Kibbles 'n' Bits. The spare key had worked. The CD was right where Dylan had said it would be. Easy peasy and then–boom!–an upright wolf with the strength of a rock troll was throwing me through a window.

Shifting always took a toll, and my brief stint as a wolverine had left me woozy. Despite my best efforts not to, I still managed to step on a bit of glass while pulling on various items of clothing. Tugging on a boot and wincing at the new pain in my sole, I hollered back, "Yeah, well Dylan's got a hundred bucks that say otherwise, and that means he gets this."

I finished pushing a second arm through the sleeve of my motorcycle jacket: a black, shiny Schott Perfecto that somebody in my tax bracket had no business owning. It had been a gift a few years back. Maybe not for me exactly, but I'm sure whoever had shipped it would have been warmed by how much I'd appreciated the surprise when it landed at the wrong address. I loved that jacket, and thankfully it hadn't been hurt in the dust-up. Retrieving a CD case from its front pocket, I held it up in the moonlight with a flourish before trudging back to a dinged-up cafe racer that in no way deserved to be paired with the expensive jacket. A flick of my wrist added the CD to a small collection of crap piled on the sidecar's seat, all generally worthless except for the sentimental value a mixed bag of jilted lovers had invested in it. Swinging a leg over the bike's cracked saddle, I stomped on the kick start and was rewarded with a satisfying cough-turned-rumble. The smell of burnt oil mixed with the werewolf's furious howls, and I was off.

The next morning, I slid the repo'd CD across my desk and held out a hand for the agreed-upon payment. Rather than a relieved smile and one-hundred bucks, the recently divorced wolf in a human suit only gave me a scowl.

"The case is cracked."

*Unbelievable*, I thought, with no small amount of rancor. Some people were just rude.

"Gosh. Sorry," I offered, the words dripping insincerity. "Must've happened when your ex threw me through a goddamned window."

Something in the guy changed. The smile I'd hoped to see suddenly appeared, but it wasn't for me.

"She sure is something, isn't she?" the werewolf asked. "Beautiful. Tough as nails. An absolute animal in the sack. When they say things go bump in the night, they really go bump in the night. Amiright?"

His hand lifted in eager anticipation of a high-five. I looked at it, looked at him, looked at the hand again, and sighed.

*Un-flipping-believable.*

"One-hundred bucks like we agreed, unless you want a high-five. Those cost extra because they're stupid."

I was surprised when he produced a crisp one-hundred-dollar bill and slapped it down on my desk. I wasn't surprised when he took the CD without another word and left my office.

Yeah, I have an office. Not a nice one, and it was a bit of a stretch to call it mine. Hell, it was a stretch to call it an office, but being a post-relationship personal effects repossession specialist wasn't exactly a lucrative business. Interesting, sure–especially given my paranormal niche–but not a cash-cow. Satisfied clients gave me a pass on my humble digs. Unsatisfied ones called it what it was: a janitor's closet fit for a really small janitor. An old metal desk took up most of the space. The rest was occupied by a squeaky desk chair, a dinged-up wooden chair, and four sturdy safes. A still-functioning floor sink lent the room a musty smell, and light came from a single naked bulb dangling precariously from the concrete ceiling. Its harsh glow was a stark contrast to the otherwise dark ambiance provided by yours truly.

"Hey, August. Another happy customer?"

Jay's head cleared the door's jamb. Haphazard, multicolored smudges on his cheeks and forehead showed the artist had been hard at work. He'd even managed to get paint into his thick dreads despite tying them back with a handkerchief. The closet I conducted my totally legitimate business from was in the studio he leased in an old, converted casket factory.

"Benjamin here says yes," I responded with a smile to match his own. "But, holy hell, do werewolves have terrible taste in music. Oasis? Seriously?"

"I thought "Wonderwall" was pretty good."

"Everyone thought "Wonderwall" was pretty good," I countered. "Doesn't mean Oasis was good."

Jay shook his head, conceding the battle in our much larger and wide-ranging war around pop-culture, and headed back to his current project. I turned my attention to the digital answering machine next to my rotary phone, where a red '1' blinked impatiently. A finger hovered over the play button, and then my hand dropped tiredly to the top of my desk. Who would it be this time? A pissed-off mermaid? An angsty leprechaun? Or worse, a human hipster? I hated hipsters.

"I'm gonna grab a bite," I decided loudly. "Want anything? Maybe Uncle Sid's?"

"I'm still vegetarian," Jay called back.

"And I'm still a bad influence," I answered as I slung my jacket over a shoulder and pulled my office door shut. "You sure you don't want anything?"

The artist rocked back on his heels and rested his elbows on his knees. "I want the FDA and the animal agriculture lobbyists to stop colluding. I want them to stop convincing us that we need to eat twelve servings of meat every day. I want them to stop trying to give us colon cancer, so we have no other option but to use Big Pharma's so-called cures."

"So, you don't want anything."

Jay leaned toward his project again and lifted a brush. "I guess grab the Metro Pages on your way back."

I promised, but silently shook my head in bewilderment. Metro Pages was the city's local free paper. It had the usual stuff: ignorant attempts at social commentary dressed up as amateur journalism, high-browed critiques of culture written by kids too young to even know how to spell culture, much less critique it, and other hard-to-read crap. In the back:

missed connections written by people who were the type most folks would intentionally try to miss, ads for everything from legal herbal supplements to almost-illegal personal escort services and–finally–horoscopes. Jay loved reading the horoscopes.

*Which is almost as bad as being a vegetarian,* I thought, while making my way to the parking lot behind the building. *Poor guy needs an intervention.*

A few minutes later, I rocked my bike back onto its kickstand and stepped into the Northeast Minneapolis staple. A few minutes after that, all five of my senses were completely engaged in my meal. Sid's lacked charm, but damn if they didn't have the best hotdogs in the Twin Cities, possibly in the entire state. I took another bite, sighed contentedly, and let my attention wander. The little restaurant was slow, probably because not many folks considered hotdogs to be breakfast food. Their loss. The only other patrons were the two halves of a too-cute hipster couple: Him with his pomaded hair and overproduced beard, tight jeans and expensive-looking flannel, and work boots that had obviously never seen real work. Her with twin braids and a trendy prairie dress that would've been commonplace in the late 1800s and had somehow found its way back into fashion. Hipster-boy was playing videos of capybaras on his phone. I knew because the girl had squealed, "Capybaras!" at least seven times in three minutes.

"They are the chillest little guys on the planet," he proclaimed.

"We should get one," she decided.

Making the rare decision to do a little marketing, I finished my dog, took a final swig of pop, pulled out a business card, and leaned over to place it on their table. Instinct made me nudge it closer to the guy.

"For later," I advised. "Rates are reasonable, but repo'ing exotic pets costs extra."

The girl scowled while her boyfriend lifted the card and read out loud, "August Shade. Post-relationship personal effects repossession specialist. Some pets. No kids. Satisfaction not guaranteed, but at least you'll have that special whatever back." He scratched his beard, and the patient I-deal-with-weirdos-a-lot smile turned a bit more genuine. "Oh. Cool. Thanks... August. Very cool."

I nodded and made for the exit, one hand idly lifting a copy of the Metro Pages from a wire rack before I pushed open Sid's door. A burgeoning argument about why he'd kept the card replaced the couple's earlier levity, and I didn't want to be around when it went nuclear. Life is all about supply and demand. Stirring up a little demand every once in a while might not be the most ethical thing to do, but I could at least maintain a professional distance after being a meddling little jerk.

The rest of my day didn't hold much in the way of things that needed doing, so I decided to take a drive. It was wet and chilly. In typical April fashion, winter and spring were still arguing over whose turn it was, and winter was stubbornly refusing to back down. All in all, it was a typical Minnesotan day, which also meant a terrible day to be on a motorcycle. Exercising my usual good judgment, I decided a trip down the river parkway was in order and kicked the old bike's engine to life. A memory of a blinking red '1' on my ancient answering machine nagged for a sec, but soon the damp, cold air whistling past my helmet had blown it from my mind.

"Want another one?"

The cute bartender eyeballed my empty pint while I eyeballed her full tank-top and tried to do math at the same time. Multi-tasking wasn't really my thing, so math took a back seat and left me unsure of how much money I still had. I'd read once that leadership was the ability to make tough decisions with limited information, so I answered her question with a hearty thumbs-up. Besides, even if I came up short when the tab was due, I figured I'd land on her good side. I'd recently helped the succubus get a few rare herbs back after she'd dumped a moody warlock named–I swear to god–Tony.

Beer refreshed, I winked at the bartender and returned my attention to the small stage where three pierced-up and tattooed women were pounding out covers of Nirvana. Kurt Cobain had died a quarter-century before that week, and suddenly every band in town was reimagining "Smells Like Teen Spirit" and "All Apologies." Some, like the one I was listening to, did a decent-enough job, while others I'd heard made me cringe. Kurt's death had been tragic, but at least he'd never have to experience a Midwestern K-Pop band doing a dance version of "Heart-Shaped Box."

The beer, whichever number it was, had filled my head with a pleasant fog, and the all-female rendition of "Come As You Are" in screaming three-part harmony was surprisingly good. I had just made the mistake of letting myself think it was a nice night when the commotion started. Nobody noticed at first–ear-splitting grunge made everything sound like a commotion–but when the first people did notice the darkly swirling cloud growing up from the center of the dance floor, their screams got loud enough to make more people take note. When more people saw the cloud sprout thick legs, muscular arms, a stubby head, and a couple of redly glowing eyes, their screams drowned out the music.

I watched the scene unfold from my barstool; nascent good mood blown away like a fart in the wind. Some jackass had summoned an air elemental, and dark magic had a way of spoiling even the best of times.

"Tony!" I heard the bartender scream as the band's music awkwardly disintegrated. "What the fuck?"

*Tony,* I mused to myself. I'd heard that name before and struggled a bit to remember where. *Ah, right. Her ex. The warlocky dude.*

I'd been in his place once, and he hadn't been too happy about it.

*What was her name, though?*

I remembered thinking it was a cute name for a succubus, something unexpected, like Alice or maybe Juniper. I was terrible with names, but Tony had stuck. What a dorky name for a warlock.

A warlock that maybe remembered me, too.

"Shit," I muttered, sobriety resurfacing scant seconds before a translucent hand as big as a watermelon grabbed my head. A second hand grabbed my shoulder, squeezed, and pulled me from my barstool. With the ease of a tornado tossing cheap lawn furniture, the air elemental sent me sailing over the dance floor and into a stack of speakers. I wasn't exactly in top form and hadn't thought to shift, which meant that the me that hit the speaker's heavy wood casing was entirely human, and so was the pain that erupted in my shoulder. I landed flat on my back, stars swirling below the black ceiling above.

"Are you sleeping with him, too?" I heard an angry voice yell.

"A girl has to eat, right? Curves like these don't just happen," she said with a slap on a nicely rounded hip. "You said that was cool when we got together, but no. Turns out you're just an insecure little prick."

Tony's heartbroken wail was almost enough to make me feel bad for the guy. Almost. Something about being attacked by his pet elemental made it hard to muster much sympathy. I rolled to the side and felt a whoosh of semi-solid air slam the floor where my chest had been a moment before. Making it to my feet, I sprinted from the dancefloor and launched myself head-first over the bar like all the action heroes do in all the action movies. Regrettably, I wasn't an action hero. What was supposed to be a dive and roll ended up being more of a bellyflop and crumble. I took out a couple of rows of glassware, broke some liquor bottles, upended the little tray full of olives and sliced limes, and finished my stunt soaked in booze with my back on the floor and ankles resting on the top of the beer cooler. The bartender stared down slack-jawed, more shocked by the destruction I had wreaked than by the giant tower of pissed-off magic air on the dancefloor.

"We haven't slept together," I protested, pushing myself upright and pulling bits of smooshed olive from my hair.

"Yet," she agreed. "I've been busy, but you're on my list."

That revelation set me grinning like an idiot while I tried to think of a clever repartee. Unfortunately, Tony's minion interrupted our romantic little tête-à-tête when it reached over the bar, grasped my shoulders, and dragged me back into the ring. My boots kicked a few more bottles and broke off one of the beer taps along the way, and then I was sliding face-first toward a wall. This time, adrenaline had sobered me up enough to shift. There aren't many occasions where it makes sense to turn into a three-hundred-and-fifty-pound gorilla, but I've always wished there were more. Nothing makes you feel like more of a badass than starting a belly-skid across a barroom floor as a milquetoast middle-aged guy and finishing it as a gorilla. Yeah, my shirt and jeans were ruined, but still...

So. Goddamned. Worth it.

I pushed myself up to all fours, tore the remnants of my clothes free, and leaned menacingly forward, fists clenched and shoulders hunched. Fully embracing my borrowed nature, I stood up on my hind legs, thumped my chest a couple of times, and roared. In response, the air elemental swelled and took on a shape not unlike my own.

*Copy-gorilla*, I complained, the sour thought furrowing my massive brow over my beady eyes.

Badass gorilla or not, I knew I didn't stand a chance against the elemental. The only option was to go for the guy controlling it. I didn't need to be King Kong to do that–honestly, the whole gorilla thing was more to impress the bartender than anything else–but what the hell. I lunged forward and threw a shoulder block at the murderous cloud. It was the same shoulder that had slammed into the speaker, and it still hurt like hell. Sharp pain aside, the move worked like a charm. The elemental was solid enough for the blow to rock it back a bit. Seizing the opportunity, I leaped for the warlock. My gorilla-sized fist grabbed the front of his dorky black fur vest–I'm not kidding, Tony was wearing a fur vest–and lifted him from his feet. My other gorilla-sized hand wrapped around his neck and squeezed just enough to stop the magic mumbo-jumbo from escaping his lips. His bulging eyes looked like a couple of peeled grapes, and his face went purple. A moment later, a sucking sound behind me ended in a loud pop, and the air elemental was gone.

"You are in so much trouble," the bartender spat. "You know the rules. If I lose my job, I'm killing you dead. More than dead. I'm killing you and banishing your soul to the lowest circle of hell, and then I'm going to kill a whole bunch of really awful monsters and send them your way so they can rip you apart for the rest of eternity."

Chagrinned, I dropped the warlock and took a few heavy steps back. She was right. Us not-human folks were supposed to keep a low profile, even in the friendlier spots around town. Minneapolis, Minnesota wasn't like New York City or Los Angeles or New Orleans. Only decent, modest monsters up here in da Midwest, don'cha know. I'd made a big mistake. Plus, I couldn't shift back. Being a naked gorilla in a dive bar was one thing. Being a naked human? That'll get you arrested.

While I pouted and tried to look like a very contrite gorilla, Tony coughed and massaged his bruised throat. Puppy-dog eyes looked over my hairy shoulder, and I realized the bartender had been talking to him, not me.

"But I love you," he finally wheezed. "We're meant to be together."

The bartender—I wish I could've remembered her name—came out from behind the bar and crouched down, cold eyes skewering her ex's.

"We are not. I am not meant to be with a controlling, immature asshole. I never want to see you again. If I do, he's going to finish what he started."

It took a moment to realize that this time she was talking about me.

"Hey..." I protested, my gorilla mouth making it sound more like, "Hwarr," but they weren't listening anyway. No one ever listened to me.

"Now you're going to leave, and you will never come back," the succubus continued. "Clear?"

Someone opened the floodgates behind Tony's eyes, and he started to bawl. Shuddering sobs wracked his frame as he pushed himself to his feet and stumbled toward the door. He turned back and gave me one helluva stink-eye, but I flexed my gigantic gorilla arms, and he took off at a run.

*That's right, douchebag. Badass gorilla.*

Tony the warlock's pathetic exit meant the dingy bar was empty except for a fired-up succubus and moi. Naked, naked moi. I glanced around and saw what was left of my clothes. Thankfully, I'd left my jacket on a stool at the bar. Swinging a meaty fist, I grabbed its collar and held it strategically in front of me while shifting back to my human form. I chalked being naked in public two nights in a row up to my usual rotten luck, then decided that maybe I could make lemonade out of this particular lemon.

"Got anything like pants back there?" I asked playfully.

"No."

"Maybe a towel?"

"Yes, but it's really dirty."

*Huh. That was... interesting,* I thought. Throwing caution to the wind easy as an air elemental throwing people, I raised an eyebrow and crooked up one corner of my mouth.

"I like dirty."

Whatever late-night adult movie I thought someone had suddenly cast me in turned out to be a rerun of August Swings and Misses. The bartender's glare could've melted all the ice in the North Pole. With a disgusted huff, she threw a bar rag at me and crossed her arms across her chest. I caught the rag–fingers instantly confirming that it was, in fact, quite dirty–and muttered, "Thanks."

A long moment stretched.

"Sorry about all that," she finally offered. "You all right?"

"Shoulder hurts," I complained, sounding petulant even to myself, "and I broke my pants."

The bartender batted her eyelashes. "But you're my hero. You saved me."

I gave up on the bar rag and turned my coat into an impromptu kilt with the back in front. Recollections of hospital gowns tried to surface, but I shoved them right back down. My ass could feel the breeze for a bit. Didn't mean I had to go traipsing down memory lane. As dressed as I was able to be, I clothed the rest of me in a tightly woven suit of curmudgeonly cantankerism. It didn't take much effort to be surly. My earlier shift had left me with a low-grade headache that was threatening to upgrade. It was one more pain piled onto a host of others, their combined weight squashing anything even remotely resembling a good mood.

"Well, your hero needs a cab because your hero isn't going to ride a motorcycle home naked, and your hero isn't paying for it either." There weren't many cabs left in the cities, but I did my best to keep them in business. Ride-hailing apps had taken over the coasts and were making incursions into my town, but I'd be damned if I'd give in. You had to have a smartphone to use them, and I preferred my technology to be as dumb as its owner.

The succubus smiled and slid a phone from her back pocket. Of course, it had a case with a naked pin-up picture on it. The girl was on-brand in every way; I'd give her that.

"I like you, August," she decided as she dialed.

Figured that she'd remember my name. It made my own local amnesia that much worse. I found the denim shreds that used to be my jeans and pulled my wallet free. With a cavalier toss, I sent it skittering across the bar.

"My address."

Phone balanced between her shoulder and ear, the succubus flipped the wallet open and pulled out my driver's license. Her eyes skimmed the plastic rectangle, and then she raised an eyebrow. "You could walk from here."

I glared. She ignored me.

"Hi, sweetie. There's a weirdo here that needs a cab," she said when someone picked up. "No, no. He's not violent. Not anymore, anyway. Yeah, I promise. He's naked," she added in a loud whisper, "but he's got a jacket. Oh, sure. One sec."

She asked if I still had the towel. I said no, and she threw me a clean one. A clean one that had been back there the entire time. The whole damned time.

*Unbelievable.*

"Yeah, he's got a towel to sit on. Not far. He lives right off of Second and Broadway. My tab. Yeah, I know, but he's broke, and it's a long walk when you're naked. 'K. He'll be out front."

After disconnecting, she pulled out my cash and thumbed through it, although there wasn't much to thumb through. I'd broken a twenty at lunch and had a five and a few singles left over. That hundred I'd earned earlier had gone into a coffee can at home. I didn't carry large bills when I went out drinking. I'm dumb, not stupid.

"Geez, you weren't gonna pay for any of your beers, were you?" she accused as she set my wallet's meager contents aside and peered into the empty fold of leather as if decent-sized bills might magically appear. Before I could answer, her hand flipped the empty wallet in my direction and then pointed at the door.

"Cab will be here soon. Sorry again about Tony. Have a nice night, Go-Go-Gorilla."

"She called you Go-Go-Gorilla?" Jay's laughter was an annoyingly bright ray of sunshine on what was supposed to be a dark and cloudy story. "That's cute. I like her."

"Me, too," I grudgingly admitted.

The artist had taken a break and joined me in my office. He'd stopped by the liquor store on his way into his studio and grabbed a case of Grain Belt Pilsner–my favorite–just because. Sometimes, an occasion merits a beer. Sometimes, beer is the occasion.

"Any new clients?" he asked as he pulled the tab on a can.

I shook my head, purposely ignoring the blinking '1' on my answering machine. "Nah. After the last couple of nights, I need a vacation. I was thinking Cancun. Want to come?"

"Can you shift into an attractive person in a bathing suit, or would it just be you?" he asked. When I glowered in response, he shrugged. "Thanks, but I'll stay right here. Besides, there's been an uptick in chemtrails over the Yucatán Peninsula. It was all part of NAFTA. They claimed they toughened industry health and safety standards. What a joke. Do you have any idea what those chemtrail chemicals can do to you?"

I didn't, so Jay illuminated me on the nefarious powers-that-be, their influence on international trade agreements, and the wholesale experimentation on the unsuspecting denizens of the Yucatán Peninsula. I countered with my assertion that–last I'd heard–people weren't exploding in Cancun or growing extra limbs, and that conspiracies were bunk because most people were simply too stupid to pull them off, especially on a global scale. In other words, we chatted for a spell about the usual stuff.


I'd finished my first beer and had taken a sip of a second when a soft knock tiptoed into the room. I mean it. Tiptoed. I don't know how else to describe it. Some knocks grab your attention, like when the neighbors call the cops at three a.m. because they don't appreciate good music, and then the cops knock on your front door. There's that kind of knock. Then there's the, 'Sorry, don't mean to bother you,' knock. Still gets your attention, but you know out of the gate that the person knocking is only bugging you because it's really important, and they also know you're the kind of anti-social curmudgeon that tends to get really annoyed when someone knocks.

This knock, though... It was like the knocker was playing a little game of cat-and-mouse and was already three steps ahead and waiting for me to catch up. Sure, the knock came from outside the office, but I found myself glancing behind me just in case.

"Come on in," Jay offered. "We're practicing for happy hour."

I glared at Jay, surprised by my sudden reluctance to meet whoever was standing outside my door. Not that I was usually a people-person. In this instance, though, my gut was screaming that I really, really didn't want to meet them. Apparently, what I or my gut wanted didn't count for shit because the knocker stepped into view. I found myself warily studying the woman in a way I usually reserved for proctologists: evaluating their competence and sure I would end up unhappy regardless. Her face made me think she was maybe my age, although I had just started the downward slide from forty while she was likely still making the climb. The rest of her made me wonder if she'd been ice fishing before stopping by my office. Her steps clomped softly on the concrete floor, and I noticed her snow boots. Brown leather uppers, sturdy black rubber lowers, worn but a long way from being worn out. Baggy wool stockings of no particular color climbed against their will up her calves and disappeared beneath a long woolen skirt a few shades of no-particular-color darker than the socks. An old fleece-lined deerskin jacket, complete with carved toggles and decorative fringes, clung to thin shoulders like someone had hung it up to dry after a snowstorm. A red and black checkered flannel earflap hat covered most of her head, but the hair I could see was brown. Not caramel or coffee or chestnut. Brown, like the eyes that stared at me from beneath that ridiculous hat.

"Mr. Shade," she said. Said, not asked, and in a toneless, resigned way like there was no other option than for me to be him despite her secretly hoping there might be. Hearing her say my name that way, I'd never been so disappointed to be me in my life, and that was saying something.

*Well, fuck her.*

"Only my friends call me that," I said, drawing a clear line in the metaphorical sand.

Creepy-girl didn't apologize. She just stared. Not to be outdone, I stared back. Jay smiled a toothy, nervous smile and cleared his throat.

"Seems like you two have a lot to talk about," he said. "I'll, um... Yeah."

And just like that, he was gone. Jerk.

The woman's boots clomped, and then she was sitting in the recently vacated seat. Her arms folded tight across her chest, and her fingers clutched the jacket's lapels. Her eyes hadn't left mine, but no words passed her thin lips.

"Look, Miss..." I led with and waited.

And waited.

"Okay," I sighed. "I've got a couple of bucks, but that's it. And don't even start with that, 'But there's an ATM downstairs,' bullshit." I pulled two singles from my wallet and set them on the desk. "There you go, crazy person. Good luck, god bless, whatever. Now..." I finished. When literally nothing happened, I cleared my throat and nodded at the open door.

The woman's eyes hadn't moved. Hadn't blinked. She was still staring directly at me, and I was about to shit my shorts. Creepy didn't even begin to cover what I was feeling. It didn't help that the answering machine's blinking red '1' was reflected in the pupil of one of those eyes. Definitely more than creepy.

"I left you a message," she finally said in a voice that was flatter than a car tire after a Minnesotan pothole.

Involuntarily, I glanced at my answering machine. The blinking '1' suddenly looked more like a nun's ruler about to whack my knuckles than a digital digit.

"Oh. Is that you? I was about to listen to that when you walked in. Sorry. I've been," I started. My eyes settled on the empty beer can sitting next to the phone. "Um, really busy."

Suddenly sweltering, I pulled at my shirt collar. Creepy lady continued with that inscrutable stare. When no other options presented themselves, I pressed play on the machine. A tinnier version of the woman's voice filled the awkward space between us, complete with the long O's and flat A's, nasal tone, and a bit of a lilt that pegged her as a true 'Sotan. If I had to guess, I'd say she hailed from way up north where you can hear Canadians sneeze and holler back, "Gesundheit!"

"Thanks so much for taking my case. I'll get you half upfront and the rest when I get my glass eye back."

A beep signaled the end of the message, and then there was silence. Not the comfortable kind or even the pregnant kind. No, this silence was just... silent.

"Oh, you're still here," Jay said, stepping into view and casting a worried look my way. "I, um. Yeah. Um."

And he was gone again, skulking little skunk. No lifeline. No, "Oh, August. Remember that really important thing we have to do right now? We should really do that thing." He just up and left. Jerk.

"Taking your case? What case? You know, lady, you really shouldn't make assumptions," I counseled. "It makes an ass out of you and umptions."

That little quip usually got a smile, but from her? Nothing. Just those resigned eyes. I blinked and felt something melt a bit, way down beneath my usual cynicism and snark. I dealt with broken hearts. People–or other things–that had found and lost love. Holding hands one day, sharing a toothbrush the next. Having someone that laughed at your jokes and actually cared when you cried. That feeling that your puzzle piece had finally found its match. Losing that was tough. Double-tough. My work was never about that favorite lamp or grandma's promise ring or who got to keep the fancy espresso machine. No. More often than not, engaging my services was nothing more than an expression of raw pain, a fierce act of self-preservation, a tourniquet around the ripped and bloody half of a heart. So yeah, I'd added a few layers to the already thick cloak of who-gives-a-damn that I'd been wrapped in for as long as I could remember. It kept me sane. Every once in a while, though, a client slipped through the cracks, sank a little hook, and tugged.

I saw the woman sitting across from me in a softer light. She'd loved someone and believed they had loved her too. Now she was here and just wanted some piece of her former self back. It wouldn't make things right and wouldn't make her whole, but it was something, and it was something I could do.

The woman nodded. A hand disappeared into the jacket and reappeared with a crisp white envelope. She placed it on the desk, rose, and left, taking my ability to breathe with her. When I saw spots, I gasped and sucked in a huge lungful of mildewy air. Fingers found the side of my neck and confirmed my heart was still beating. A minute later, Jay poked his head in again and took a seat after confirming that the coast really was clear.

"She seemed nice," he offered without a hint of sarcasm.

I snorted. For a guy that loved conspiracies about cabals of ne'er-do-wells running the planet, he was surprisingly upbeat. Jay could get along with damn near anyone, even my peculiar clientele. Paranormals didn't bother him at all. I'd asked him about that once, and his response had been, "As long as they aren't part of the military-industrial complex, they're fine by me."

Yeah, Jay was pretty great.

"That was far and away the weirdest consult I've ever had," I said honestly and watched Jay's eyes go wide.

"So, what's the job?" he asked.

For a second, I couldn't recall. A moment later, the thought, I'm a bit of an expert on glass, ran through my mind.

"Her glasses?" I guessed, suppressing a sudden chill.

The artist frowned. "That doesn't sound too bad."

"Normally, I'd agree, but her? I'm adding my standard holy-shit-this-is-creepy mark-up, plus another ten percent because holy fuck, creepy. If she comes back, I'm telling her it's a grand. One-thousand dollars. If she doesn't want to pay, she can piss right the hell off."

Just talking about her had set my hackles on end. I wasn't easily rattled. Hell, the past couple of nights had each been a nine on my one-to-that-totally-sucked scale. Werewolves and warlocks and worse. Did I lose my shit? Nope. Cool as a cadaver. The last few minutes, though, had left me shaking.

My hand reached for my beer but passed it by and grabbed the envelope instead. The lady had left it without a word of explanation. Its thickness and weight surprised me. She hadn't sealed it. Instead, the flap had been tucked neatly inside, leaving it easy to open. I flicked a glance at Jay and saw him watching with unmasked trepidation. His head gave the tiniest of nods, so I took a breath, held it, and opened the envelope.

And damned near shit myself.

It was full of twenties. I pulled the stack out and started counting them out onto the desktop.

"… four-sixty, four-eighty, five-hundred. What in the goddamned hell is this shit?"

"That is a lot of money," Jay announced, oblivious. "Geez. You could actually pay some rent for a change."

Rather than respond, I glared and pressed play on the answering machine. A second later, the woman's voice wended its way around us. 'I'll get you half upfront and the rest when I get my glass eye back,' she'd said, but not once had we talked about money, and I'd pulled that quip about charging a grand out of my sweaty ass after she'd left and way after she'd left that voicemail. When the message finished, Jay's face squished up.

"Her glass eye?" he asked.

I frowned, confused. "She said glasses."

"Pretty sure it was glass eye."

My frown went from confused to grossed out. "No. The hell, she did," I protested and then replayed the message. We strained our ears until the machine beeped.

"She definitely said, 'Glass eye,'" Jay decided.

I shook my head angrily. "That's ridiculous. She had two eyes, Jay. You saw."

"Maybe she's got a spare?" he suggested with a shrug.

"You're missing the point!" I snapped, partially to avoid conceding that he'd likely been right. "I've never met her before today. Not once did we talk about money when she was here, and yet…" I finished with a dramatic wave at the cash-stuffed envelope.

I watched Jay finally get with the goddamn program. I watched him finally feel what I was feeling. I watched him get really, really creeped out.

"How… I mean, that's not. There's no way…" he tried.

"Recent events would seem to indicate otherwise," I offered with a shaky shrug. "Psychics, seers… Everyone talks about them, especially us PN's." That's what us paranormals and other things called ourselves. Pins. I'd tried to get 'sins' for supernaturals to catch on, but, apparently, I wasn't an influencer. "They aren't real, though. Parlor tricks. Sleight of hand. Plain old cons, all of 'em. No one can see the future. At least, I don't think they can…"

The artist chewed his lip and rubbed absently at a faded spot of blue paint on his cheek. "This takes things to a whole new level. My horoscope said I'd be looking inward. Pardon me while I crawl inside myself and hide."

"Bon voyage. What are you?"

"Leo. You?"

"Sagittarius."

Jay gasped like someone emerging from a carnival dunk tank. "That's right. You are. You get whisked off your feet this month."

"Already was," I amended. "Douchey warlock. Air elemental. Remember?"

Jay blinked, then blinked again and sternly advised me to stay put.

Like I had anywhere to go. I waited while my friend rummaged through some corner of his studio or another. Half of my second beer was gone before he returned, brandishing the local free paper like a trophy.

"Your future's like a basket of pull tabs. Sure, there's a chance that you'll be the big winner, but the odds stink. Just hunker down. Focus on work to keep yourself busy 'til your number is up, and you're whisked off your feet," Jay read after turning to the back pages. "Saturn meets up with Mercury this month and sends you a message. Be sure to listen and listen good."

"What'd you say?" I asked, all innocence.

I got a look for that one, but Jay continued without retort.

"There's more. 'Things might not make sense, but they can still make dollars.' Sense: S-E-N-S-E, not cents. That's what it says. That is literally what it says."

"Okay... You have a point?"

Jay opened his mouth, about to speak, and then loudly exhaled. "Come on. The lady, the message, that horoscope."

"Horoscopes aren't real. Horoscopes are trite panaceas for sad people. Sad and lonely people."

A hint of his usual good humor returning, Jay said, "Like you."

With a grunt, I picked up the envelope and started shoving bills back inside. I'd just slipped the last few twenties in when he whooped.

"What? Christ, what?" I exclaimed, startled.

"Look at the name on the envelope."

I hadn't noticed a name on the envelope, but I hadn't looked at the front. It had been addressed like a regular old letter with careful, delicate pen strokes: my name and office address in the center and a name and P.O. Box for the return address. I really wish she'd taken the next logical step and mailed the damned thing to me, but–knowing how postal workers are–I also knew I would've received an empty envelope.

"Clarissa Steyer," I read out loud, not following. "So? Now I know her name. And...?"

Paint-stained fingers reached for the newspaper again, flipped to the back pages, and spun it around so I could read it. There, in bolded type, I saw the last flipping straw in my own personal hay bale of crazy: "Ope! It's Your Horoscope!" by Clarissa Steyer.

# Chapter 2

*Ope! It's your horoscope, Gemini!*
*You bring people together like a string between two cans.*

T HE NEXT FEW DAYS nearly drove me bonkers. I went through my routines. Picked up a few clients, repo'd a few things, made a few bucks. I drank a few beers. I ate a few hotdogs while Jay watched with tolerant disgust. I watched a movie at a local second-run theatre. I drove my old Guzzi around town just for the hell of it, shit weather be damned. And I took exactly no pleasure in any of it. All this time, I'd thought I'd been doing what I wanted to do, making my own choices. Even Jay's propensity for finding hidden meanings in every headline had never phased me. That meeting with Clarissa Steyer, though, had spun me like a top. Was I really choosing my own path, or was I nothing more than a Hot Wheel in some cosmic plastic racetrack? Did I pick the movie, or was it pre-ordained? Did I get hotdogs because I liked them or because I was fated to like them? Thinking about it made my head hurt. I'd actually gone to college once upon a time. Not often and not for long, but I had managed to show up for a couple of philosophy classes. I'd hated them.

"So, I'm taking the night off. Not gonna think about it. Hell, I'm just not gonna think."

The bartender frowned in sympathy. No, not that bartender. Not that bar. I was still too rattled to go back there. Fortunately, there were other places that catered to my exacting standards, and by that, I meant a complete lack of any.

"That's quite the story, my dude," he said after I'd shared the details of my encounter with the local rag's horoscope author. He'd called me 'my dude' six times so far, and I was seriously considering having standards.

He was right, though. It was quite the story. A silly and unbelievable story that I would've doubted myself if I didn't still have most of the five-hundred bucks in a coffee can behind my sofa. Guilt tugged my ears down toward my shoulders as I considered the money I hadn't earned, but what could I do? What I knew about Clarissa was a grain of sand compared to the desert of what I didn't know: I didn't know who she'd been involved with, or where they lived, or even what her flipping glass eye looked like. I didn't have any way to contact her to ask any of those very necessary questions. I didn't like being set up to fail, and I was really starting to resent the strange woman who had so effectively damaged my calm.

*If she's as clairvoyant as she seems to be, why can't she get her own damn eyeball back? I pondered with no small amount of rancor. She'd know when her ex was going to be deer hunting, or making seed art, or getting seconds at the neighborhood potluck. She could just wait until that foreseen moment, pop in, grab her eye and call it a day. Hell, she wouldn't even have to stress. She'd already know the moment when she'd see when they'd be gone, and she'd know when she'd have her eye back. She would simply need to do the things she'd already seen herself do in one of her visions or whatever, and she could just do those things, and oh my god, what if she's already seen me sitting here thinking all this shit and...*

"Fuck!" I suddenly screamed.

"Hey, my dude. Calm down. I don't want to eighty-six you," the bartender cautioned.

I held up my hands and offered my best sorry-it's-been-that-kind-of-a-day smile. Too worked up to sit still, I drained my beer and headed into the cool night air. I'd nabbed a parking spot down the street, but my feet went in the opposite direction. Sometimes, a night walk was just the thing to help me untangle whatever knots I'd tied myself up in.


Northeast Minneapolis–Nordeast to the locals–was a wonderfully weird 'hood. A mashup of all sorts of folks whose collars weren't just blue or white but spiked, popped, paint-spattered, and more. As my boots tread the cracked sidewalk, my eyes roamed, seeing the past laid like a translucent film over the present.

The city was born less than two miles from my apartment. In the mid-1800s, some clever fellow had set up a mill on the Mississippi River by a waterfall named after Saint Anthony. I'd assumed Anthony was the patron saint of falling. Turns out he was the patron saint of lost things, which maybe explained what had drawn me to Minneapolis in the first place. After breaking out of the hospital back in the mid-nineties, I'd begged, borrowed, and stole my way to the Midwest. It had been a question of when, not if, the psycho doctors would come looking for me, and I'd figured that flyover country would be a great place to hide. I'd been eighteen, alone, and broke when I'd washed up in the city's gutters. In no time at all, I'd become completely enamored with my randomly adopted home. There was a rawness to the city, a primal hunger that welcomed the grungy angst spilling out from the country's northwest coast and sucked it in like a flannel sponge. It had fit me better than the leather jacket that had more recently landed on my doorstep, so I'd stayed.

The coolest part of the city's history was how humans and paranormals had been living side-by-side through damn near all of it. We'd gone from being scary stories whispered in the dark to being neighbors, coworkers, even friends with the humans. I suppose every place has its own melting pot story. In the Twin Cities, that story started with–and I truly loved this part–beer. The Yoerg Brewery, founded before Minnesota was even a state, was the first place to officially employ a PN. As local legend had it, Anthony Yoerg was a fair and honest employer. If you could do the work, you got the job. He'd hired an eager gnome looking for a better life and the rest, as they say, is history.

I won't lie and say it's always been peaches and cream. More than a few PNs would happily eat humans, and there will always be humans that want to grab their pitchforks and torches and wipe out the PNs. Those simple facts have led to some truly epic debacles, like the Great Minneapolis Fire of 1893. The official account was that some kids were smoking on a hot summer day. Uh-huh. Sure. Anyway, when those flames were finally extinguished, city officials, the governor, and emissaries representing the many PNs living in the state got together. At the end of their days-long palaver, they laid down a simple ground rule: Get along or face some very unpleasant consequences. Human law governed most transgressions. The nasty stuff–like a werewolf having a schoolteacher for a midnight snack–went to the PNs to mete out our own justice. Say what you want about paranormals, but we know how to lay the smack down. Minnesotans of all types have always been pragmatic, so folks made it work. Sure, there have been 'accidents.' For the most part, though, humans and PNs had been living side-by-side for over a hundred years. When you added it all up, Nordeast Minneapolis was the perfect place for an anti-social shifter to hunker down in society's cracks. I didn't stand out. I didn't fit in. For the first time in my life, I'd been able to just be.

I looked up from my musings and realized I'd walked farther than I'd intended. The Plymouth Avenue Bridge stretched across the Mississippi River like a triple-dog-dare. I briefly considered visiting the far side, but it was late, and I didn't want to bump into…

"Wizard? That you?"

... Canute.

The craggy voice and accompanying wet snuffles clunked and trundled from the shadows where the bridge's deck and abutment joined. Dismally, I realized I was about to become one of those 'accidents' I'd just been thinking about. My mind flipped through some options: Run, shift into something with four legs and run even faster, or just deal with the fact that I was an idiot that had blundered into the domain of one of the Midwest's most stubborn and stupid trolls... again.

"Hey there, Canute. Yep, it's me. You're on the east side now? That's nice."

"My bridge. All sides."

"Of course they are, Canute. Of course, they are."

To the casual observer, it might've looked like I was talking to myself. A keener eye might've decided I was talking to a large mound of smelly trash. Either fellow would've rightfully concluded I was a bit off my rocker and hastened past, and it's fair to say they would've been the better for it.

"Future happened. No goat," the troll complained.

I resisted the urge to face-palm. Canute was more than a grumpy old troll. He was technically a client. While some jobs sucked more ass than a katakirauwa, I always finished the job. I just had no idea how to finish this one.


Oh, sorry. Katakirauwa. Demon pigs from Japan. The little pricks run between your legs and suck your soul out of your ass. Yeah, they're a thing, and if we're being honest, that was a pretty good metaphor. What I'll never be able to conjure, though, is a metaphor that even hints at the possibility of describing two trolls in love.

Love's a funny thing, and even the likes of old Canute had found it once upon a time in a land far, far away. Okay, not really. It was in Stillwater, another river town about twenty-five miles east on the Wisconsin border, but it had been a long time ago. Near as I could figure, Canute and his lumpy ladylove had gotten together back in the 1920s. They'd shacked up under the original swing bridge over the St. Croix River that connected Minnesota to her slightly older sister. The pair had spent their nights doing all the horrible, nasty, you-don't-want-to-think-about-it stuff that trolls in love do. After ninety-plus years of whatever passes for bliss with their kind, things soured. I have no idea why. All I know is that one night after closing down the neighborhood dive bar, I'd taken a walk to clear my head. I'd meandered over the Plymouth Avenue Bridge, climbed down the bank on its far side, and was suddenly confronted by a large, smelly, and sobbing pile of dirt and trash.

Literally. Trolls blend into their surroundings like nobody's business. Damned things are the chameleons of the paranormal realm. Stick one in a cave, and barely a fortnight later, you'd swear it was a moss-covered boulder. Plop it under a drawbridge, and within a week, its arms and legs would be indistinguishable from the span's rough-hewn lumber. Shove it under a bridge in modern-day, litter-prone Northeast Minneapolis and, well, you guessed it. Hell, even if you didn't guess, you'd smell it.

So, there I'd been, minding my own drunken business, and suddenly I was consoling a quarter-ton of heart-broken stupid rolled in a garbage patch. The troll had been so distraught, it didn't even try to eat me. Instead, I got the whole story. Well, as much as a troll's limited vocabulary can convey. His name was Canute, and he was in love with Urmalena, the most unlikely thing the word 'beautiful' had ever been attached to. Despite their long, happy years together, she'd given the poor sod the boot and sent him packing with only the random detritus that was stuck to his hunched and misshapen back. Usually, that would've been enough for a troll. They didn't need much in the way of worldly possessions. Their devotion to the philosophy, "Can't eat it, don't need it," was near-religious, but poor Canute had wanted one thing back from his ex.

Which brings me to the goat.

I can't think of much that a troll could ever do to show affection. Hell, just trying to envision an affectionate troll would probably land most folks in therapy. But one thing I do know: A troll not eating a goat because it wants its better half to have it... Well, there might not be a more pure and selfless expression of love in all of creation. On the fateful night of their parting, Canute had snatched up a goat, carried it back to the St. Croix River Bridge, and offered it up to Urmalena.

"Good goat," Canute had crooned. "Fat. Noisy."

Canute had been so impressed with the goat that he'd used pretty much all of his words describing it. Urmalena had apparently been impressed as well. With such a wonderful goat, she'd decided she no longer needed Canute, and the rest was history. The inconsolable troll had wandered west, found the Plymouth Avenue Bridge, and displaced–by which I'm pretty sure I mean killed–its previous denizen. Then little old me had stupidly blundered by, and the troll had dumped his tale of woe in my lap.

"I'm sorry about your goat, Canute," I had offered with something in the ballpark of sympathy.

Canute had snuffled and then farmer-blew a bucket of snot from first one nostril, then the other. Suddenly free of the sticky sludge, he'd smelled me. Like, really smelled me.

"What are you?" he'd asked, suspicious.

The question had caught me a bit off guard. I knew what I was. I was human... most of the time. It had never occurred to me, though, that I might not smell human.

There was more vigorous snuffling by the troll, and then Canute had declared, "Urmalena like you."

"No, Urmalena's a troll. I'm not a troll," I'd clarified, completely missing the point.

What happened next still soaked my nightmares in terror. Canute had grabbed me in hands like stone vices and started lumbering east. I had struggled and screamed, but all I got for my efforts was Canute's explanation that Urmalena would like me more than the goat.

"Urmalena get you. I get my goat," he'd reasoned as his bent legs gobbled up the distance between us and another big, scary troll.

"But don't you think she's already eaten it?" I'd screamed, foolishly thinking that trolls could be swayed with something akin to reason. "By now, it's probably a pile of troll poo by the side of the river. You don't want troll poo, do you, Canute?"

"Urmalena poo," he'd pined, his wet snuffles turning to sobs.

Apparently, the idea hadn't been as unappealing to him as I'd thought it would be. Yeah, trolls are pretty gross.

While Canute had trundled along, his every step jarring a fresh sob from my lungs, I'd wracked my brain for everything I'd ever heard about trolls. I knew the obvious stuff. They were big, strong, smelly, and stupid. None of those details seemed to lend me an advantage. Even if I'd shifted into a gorilla, I'd doubted I'd last more than a couple of rounds. The fact that he smelled like Satan's toe-cheese didn't help me in the least, and his stupidity was a stone wall between his perceptions and reasonable conclusions.

Then I'd realized that maybe, just maybe, I could use that last bit to my advantage.

The troll had been carrying me along a circuitous route, wending his way up alleys and down dark side streets, but his eastward path was still roughly parallel to Plymouth Avenue, although by that point, it had changed into 8th Avenue. Street names are weird that way. Anyway, I knew we were still following the main drag because we'd already crisscrossed 8th a handful of times, his heavy steps leaving small craters in their wake. People naively think potholes come from ice melting into cracks and crevices and then refreezing. Sure, that might account for some of Minnesota's terrible roads. The rest... well, let's just say a troll with wanderlust is hell on a highway.

"You'll get your goat back," I had informed the troll in a loud voice to make sure I'd be heard over his heavy breaths and the petrified-wood-on-concrete sound of his footsteps.

"My goat," he'd agreed.

I'd pitched my voice to make it clear that I was pulling back the curtain on a mighty secret. "I know because I'm a powerful wizard that can see the future."

"The future?" Canute had asked, puzzled.

"Yes, Canute. I know what's going to happen before it does."

"No, you don't," he'd pushed back, skeptical.

I'd nodded vigorously, which wasn't tough since his jarring strides were already sending my head bobbing like a life-sized bobblehead doll. "I can prove it. Go straight to the next road and then stop."

Apparently, being in possession of a bona fide future-telling wizard was enough to spark what little curiosity managed to survive between Canute's endless appetite and epic bowel movements. He'd followed my instructions and landed us at an intersection with a stoplight.

"That red light will turn green," I'd informed him sagely, secretly hoping trolls weren't red-green color blind.

It did, and apparently, trolls weren't. Canute had gasped and dropped me to the asphalt. I'd landed on my ass—not the most distinguished pose for a powerful future-scrying wizard—but the troll had been too shocked to care.

"Wizard," he'd whispered.

"Yes. A very powerful one, too," I'd agreed. "You don't need to trade me for the goat. I have seen the future. In the future, you will get your goat back, but only if I'm alive and well. And you'll find a new love, too," I'd tacked on. It seemed like a nice gesture. With a final expansive wave of my arms, I'd finished with, "As I've seen it, so it shall be."

And with that dramatic proclamation, I had run like hell.

That had been back in the fall, and I'd studiously avoided the Plymouth Avenue Bridge at night ever since. Until now.

"Future happened. No goat! No love!" the troll roared, fists like wrecking balls rising and crashing down on the concrete below. Cracks spider-webbed out, and I rocked on my feet from the force of the concussion. The garbage patch lumbered forward until Canute's snotty, pimply, hairy, and hooked nose was mere inches from my own. I held my ground—not because I'm tough or brave or anything like that—but because I knew that any movement would result in me being a pile of troll-poo by the side of the river.

"Yes, Canute," I agreed in a very calm, very steady voice. "You're right. The future happened, but someone changed it; another wizard. His name is," I intoned while wracking my brain for a name, any name, to throw the troll for a loop, "... Tony."

"Tony changed future?" Canute asked.

"That's right. Because Tony is a douchebag. You know what that is?"

The troll brought a thick finger tipped with a coarse and cracked nail up to his temple and scratched. "Douchebag?" he asked.

"Yes. Douchebags are the worst. They're mean and selfish and don't want trolls like you to get their goats back. Tony the Douchebag changed the future so you can't get your goat. What a jerk, right?"

While the sticky cogs in Canute's brain tried to turn, I quietly slid one foot backward, then another, each shuffling half-step a desperate leap for freedom. Despite their enormous size and awkward shape, trolls can be pretty damn fast. Don't believe me? You try catching a goat that doesn't want to be caught and see how quick you are. Anyway, I tried to estimate how far Canute could leap in a single bound and sought to put at least that much distance between us, one slow inch at a time. With a bit of a head start and a bundle of luck, I figured I could haul ass and most likely not get eaten. Three, maybe four more surreptitious steps, and I'd have been home-free.

And then Canute leaped.

"You douchebag! You jerk!" he screamed, his gravelly voice booming in my ears. Those vice-like hands gripped me, and my nightmares came crashing back.

"No! Tony's the douchebag!" I yelled, but it was no use. Canute was past caring about whatever I had to say. I tried to shift into anything–a gorilla, a turkey, a goddamned sparkle pony–but the pain of being squished into a human-burger patty was making it hard to concentrate. A rushing sound filled my ears. I assumed it was the Grim Reaper whooshing in to bear my soul off to wherever mediocre and generally unlikeable shifters went to when they died. Then suddenly, the troll and I were rising into the night air.

"Look down!" I screamed as loudly as my collapsing lungs would allow. "Look down, you dolt!"

"Wha...?" Canute asked, confused, and then he did.

The troll's eyes went wide, his hands relaxed, and I was free. The troll continued to rise on a pillar of dark, smoky air, but I was no longer being dragged along for the ride. Gravity reasserted its hold on me, and I started to fall. Panicked, I shifted into a turkey–don't judge, I just said I was panicked–and flapped my near-worthless wings as hard as I could. It didn't do much, but it was enough to slow my descent. I landed, splayed my tail feathers in irritation, and shifted back to my human form. I hated the turkey. Smooshing human consciousness into a bird brain always left me feeling stupid afterward. I was trying to remember how to get my clothes straightened out when a sullen voice pouted its way to my ears.

"You don't get to die yet," it said.

I spun around and saw none other than the aforementioned douchebag. Tony wasn't looking at me. His eyes were on the rising troll while his lips produced whatever string of vowels and syllables helped shape the elements around him. After another moment, his eyes flicked to mine, and he asked, "Where should I put it?"

I'm an asshole, not a murderer. "River. Canute's not all that bad."

Tony's hands flipped through a few crisp gestures, and then the troll was falling, his distraught roar ending in a loud splash.

"I hope he can swim," the warlock commented.

I hadn't thought about that, but decided it was out of my hands. More pressingly, I wanted to figure out why the warlock that had tried to kill me was now playing my knight in a dorky fur vest.

"What are you doing here?" I demanded, then added, "I mean, thanks and all, but what gives?"

The warlock crossed his arms across his chest and glared.

"I saw you. I followed you," he replied. "I don't want you to die, August Shade. Not yet. When you do, I want it to be when your spirit is broken. When all hope is gone. When everything around you is ruin and damnation. Most importantly, I want it to be by my hand."

I squinted. "You saved me so you can kill me?"

"Exactly."

"You're weird."

I didn't mean it as an insult. It was more of an observation that my inside voice should've kept inside. Unfortunately, my inside voice was prone to overstepping its bounds.

"You're an abomination!" he screamed. "Of all the people she could lie with, you... You're disgusting!"

That again. "We haven't slept together," I tried to explain but was cut off by his angry, "Yet!"

I took a deep breath. After counting to three, I let it slip out through my nostrils.

"That's right. Not yet. And maybe—probably–not ever, but let's be honest. If I have that opportunity, if she actually wants to, you know, do all of that with me... I have to,

Tony. I have no choice in the matter. I mean, come on. You guys were a thing, and you've seen her naked. I'm betting she looks awesome naked, right? How could I ever say no?"

What I thought was a perfectly reasonable take on the whole situation apparently struck a different chord with the warlock. His eyes narrowed. His nostrils flared. Even in the waning moon's pale light, I could see his cheeks flush with anger. Always a little slow on the uptake, I was starting to realize that maybe I'd hopped from the frying pan into a fire of my own making. Fortunately, Canute had made it to the riverbank, and his enraged cry of, "Douchebag!" brought my little tiff with a jealous warlock to an end.

"If you touch her, if you look at her, if you even say her name," Tony threatened, "you're dead."

And with that, he turned and fled, fur vest flapping in the breeze as he sprinted into the night.

"What is her name?" I called after him, but it was no use. The warlock was gone.

Canute wasn't, though. Taking a page from Tony's playbook, I took off at a run and didn't look back until I'd made it to my bike. It was a short ride home, but I almost crashed three times, so convinced was I that either an angry troll or crazy warlock was about to pounce from a shadow. By the time I'd made it back to my apartment, I was a wreck. Weary, frazzled, and thoroughly dejected. All I could think was what an utter failure I was. Canute didn't have his goat, Clarissa didn't have her glass eye, and I had a mortal enemy named Tony.

Considering my life, it was par for the goddamned course.

The next morning, I found a phone book. Yeah, computers and the internets. I know they exist, and I even sort of know how to use them. Jay had also impressed on me how easy it is for certain ne'er-do-wells to manipulate them to their own nefarious bidding and find people that would prefer not to be found, so I avoid them as much as one can in this modern world. I wanted analog. I wanted paper and ink. I'd had my own phone book once upon a time, but then winter happened, and I hadn't been able to afford my gas bill, and clawfoot bathtubs make surprisingly good fire pits, so I didn't have a phone book anymore and had to go looking for someone else's.

And I found one.

That alone should've been cause for parades, a big ceremony full of important dignitaries, a key to the goddamned city, and the personal guarantee from the President of the

United States of America that I would never, ever have to use a telephone again. When the attendant at the local gas station agreed to let me leaf through their worn and battered copy, I could've kissed him and then kissed myself for being smart enough to ask the attendant at the local gas station if they had a phone book. I rifled through the pages, past all the Sandersons and the Smiths, and then suddenly I was in the Stiltons. I flipped back a page, forward again, and cursed.

Clarissa Steyer wasn't listed.

*Hop online*, a reasonable voice suggested from somewhere in my brain.

*Piss off. I'm not doing it*, I replied.

*She's probably on Facebook or Twitter. Maybe she even has her own website.*

*NO*, I pushed back, annoyed I was even considering using social media. I wasn't social. I was anti-social. The antithesis of social. The polar-flipping-opposite of social. So, no. It was my way or to hell with the whole thing.

I asked the gas station attendant if I could swap out the white pages for some yellow ones and flipped to the M's. The Metro Pages was listed, so I memorized the number and headed back to my office. After tossing my jacket across one of the safes, I dropped into my desk chair and picked up the phone. Three rings later, a too-chipper voice answered.

"Metro Pages! How can I be of service?"

"Geez, buddy," I exclaimed. "Maybe stop taking your once-a-day twice a day."

"Absolutely!" he agreed. "How can I help you today?"

I massaged the bridge of my nose. "Clarissa Steyer, please."

The guy dropped the fake enthusiasm and any pretense of being friendly at the same time. "Metro Pages is in no way, shape, or form responsible for what may or may not happen to individuals that read the "Ope! It's Your Horoscope!" section. Any allegations of harm or misfortune will be directed to our managing editor. I'll transfer you now..."

"Wait!" I tried, but was too slow. The receiver crackled with a scratchy instrumental version of a Nirvana song, and then another voice came on the line. Unlike the last one, this voice was tired and made no effort to be anything other than that.

"Metro Pages. Editorial Department. Shane speaking."

"Hey, Shane. Sorry, I got transferred to the wrong department. I was trying to reach Clarissa Steyer."

"Please know that Metro Pages is in no way, shape, or form..."

"I know, I know. I'm not calling to sue or whatever," I said, shoving the words in edge-wise. "Clarissa is a client of mine, but I don't have a direct number for her."

"A client? What for?"

Shane couldn't see my scowl, but I'm sure he heard it in my voice. "I'm in no way, shape, or form obligated to share that information with you."

"No, I mean, why would you want her as a client? Are you crazy?" he asked.

That wasn't exactly auspicious. "Uh, no. Maybe. The jury's still out on that one. Look. She needs something, and I can get it for her. Okay, that sounds bad, but it's not. She hired me but didn't tell me how to get a hold of her, so I'm trying to find her so I can... Crap. That sounds worse," I grumbled, exhaling in frustration. "I just need to get in touch with her, and this is the only angle I've got."

"... I could take a message," Shane hedged, "but she doesn't come to the office much. She doesn't live too far from here, but usually mails her stuff in. We're expecting the June horoscopes in the next day or so. Even if she does come in, I'm not going to give it to her. I'll pass it to Todd. Maybe he'll see her and can get her a message."

"Is Todd the energy drink addict?" I asked, and was rewarded with a dry laugh.

"Yeah, the energy drink addict. So, what's the message?"

"Hang on, I'm still trying to find a bottle," I complained. "Oh, what the hell. Let her know August Shade called. She'll know what it's about."

There was a soft gasp, then a loud laugh.

"The personal effects repo guy? You got my buddy Dylan's Oasis CD back."

An uncharacteristic warmth started somewhere in my chest and began to spread. I wasn't entirely sure, but it might've been pride.

"He said the case was cracked," Shane added, and that little sliver of pride shattered into a million grumpy shards.

"Cases are like ten cents," I growled. "And I don't suppose he told you about the window I got thrown through."

Shane had the good sense not to press the issue, and I asked again if there was any other way to get in touch with Clarissa.

"Man, I really don't think you want to do that," he advised. "Girl's weird. Freaks us all out. Even us PN's," he added.

My eyebrows raised. "You're paranormal?"

I knew it was a rude question, but my curiosity had always been stronger than my sense of propriety. An uncomfortable pause stretched until Shane admitted that no, he wasn't actually a PN himself.

"Well, no. Not yet, at least. I'm a familiar," he whispered.

That was interesting. There were vampires in Minnesota, but only a few were old and powerful enough to bother with a familiar. The younger ones were too woke to hold a mortal in thrall. It offended their delicate Millennial sensibilities.

"I'm all for being good at your job, but her?" Shane continued, pulling me from my musings. "Too good, and not in a good way, if you catch my drift."

"Yeah, drift caught," I agreed. Even talking about her was giving me shivers. "Well, if you could pass her the message anyway, I'd appreciate it."

I gave Shane my office number even though Clarissa already had it, then let him know my rates were reasonable–you know, just in case–and hung up the phone, more frustrated than before I'd called. There had to be some way to get in touch with Clarissa Steyer. Some way to reassert my control over the situation. The envelope she'd stuffed with cash was still on my desk–sans the cash–and there was that P.O. Box address neatly printed in the upper corner. Worth a shot.

I was too cheap to waste one of my own envelopes, so I scratched out my name and address on the front and put her name and P.O. Box above it. I scratched out her return address and simply wrote, 'Don't bother.' Envelope prepped, I rummaged through my desk until I found a spiral-bound notebook with a few blank pages left and tore one free.

*Ms. Steyer, we need to talk, but you haven't made that easy,* I started and then scribbled out the line.

*Ms. Steyer,* I began again. *I'd like to discuss the particulars of your situation. Particular #1: Telling people your name is much easier than not telling people your name and making them figure it out in weird ways. Particular #2: Getting someone's personal effects back is much easier if you provide some indication of where they are or who has them. Particular #3: Horoscopes aren't real, and you're stupid. Zing! Bet you didn't see that coming!*

I scratched out those lines as well, crumpled up the page in frustration, and tore out a clean sheet.

*Ms. Steyer, Please contact me at your earliest convenience so we can discuss your case. Sincerely, Mr. Shade.*

I folded the letter and slipped it into the envelope along with a business card. Before I could even think about finding a stamp in the landfill I used as a desk, the phone rang. I froze and let it ring a second time. After the third ring, I snatched up the receiver and barked, "Psychics aren't real!"

"Um.. sorry?" a confused voice said. "I was, I mean. Is this August Shade, the personal effects repossession specialist?"

"Oh, yeah. It's me. Sorry. I've... Never mind. Yeah. August Shade, post-relationship personal effects repossession specialist. Licensed, bonded, and insured" I lied, then added another whopper. "Completely professional. Can I ask who I'm speaking with?"

"My name's Bret. We met a couple of weeks back at Uncle Sid's. The hotdog place. I was there with my girlfriend, and you gave me your card."

Ah ha... I thought with a satisfied grin. Hipster-boy with the capybara chick. I knew it. I fucking knew it. God, I'm good.

"Hey, Bret. Yeah, I remember. Sorry things with you and..."

"Darcy."

"Right," I agreed, and made a quick note. "Sorry things with you and Darcy didn't work out. You've called the right guy, provided that you need something that is actually yours repossessed. I return property to its rightful owner. I don't just steal shit. Clear?"

When Bret responded to the affirmative, I asked what particular effects he was interested in getting back and reminded him that exotic pets cost extra.

"What? Oh, that. We never got a capybara. We tried, but the local pet stores only have dogs and cats and hamsters and stuff. Anyway, yeah. Me and Darcy. We... You know, she... She..."

Hipster-boy got a little choked up. I had something stuck in my teeth. Priorities firmly in line, I ignored his rambling tale of woe and tried to use my pinky fingernail to pick the remnants of an earlier meal free. When my perseverance finally paid off, I flicked the little gob of what was probably hotdog to the floor and cleared my throat.

"Sorry. Right, sorry," Bret apologized. "So, yeah. The thing is..."

I jotted down some notes about a craft brewery coupon book that got you a free pint at over twenty different microbrews around town. Bret swore he'd bought it and that his ex didn't even like beer all that much. The phrase 'cider snob' was used a few times. I didn't care what either of them liked to drink. I was just glad to have a regular job to distract me from the headache that was Clarissa Steyer. After I'd finished collecting the pertinent details, I let the hipster know I'd be in touch soon and ended the call. The note I'd written for Clarissa was staring up at me. With nothing better to do than get some dork's beer coupon, I picked up the envelope and headed out to find a mailbox. As I walked, I told myself over and over that I was doing it because I chose to do it. Me. Not the stars or planets or anything else. Me. And I almost believed it.

Barely two hours after I'd dropped my note to Clarissa Steyer in a nearby mailbox, she scared the shit out of me. Literally.

After getting the beer coupon book back and delivering it to an annoyingly ecstatic hipster, I'd grabbed my usual lunch: a hotdog, some chips, and a pop; food of the goddamned gods. Hunger satiated, I had headed back to the office to see if any other suddenly single PNs had called. None had, but–as often happens when one has a diet like mine–the restroom did. The old converted factory Jay had his studio in didn't have private bathrooms. Oh, no. That would've merited actual rent. Instead, there were shared bathrooms in the hallways, a couple per floor. They all offered the same aesthetic: bare concrete floors, cinderblock walls, too-bright fluorescent lights, and metal partitions between the commodes that might've been gunmetal gray before they were covered in layers of band stickers and graffiti. My bowel movement had timed itself well. No one else was in the bathroom, and thank Christ, too. My mostly digested meal had swerved and screeched its way through my intestines, but was refusing to exit the tunnel.

Anyway, there I was–ass on the throne, hands on my knees, toes gripping the concrete, heels up in the air, and every muscle in my body pushing like a defensive linebacker on the one-yard line–when Clarissa frickin' Steyer said, "Oh, hi. You were looking for me, Mr. Shade?"

And the first wave of all that heavily processed food came exploding out.

"What in the fucking hell, woman?" I screamed over the sound. "Men's room! It's the goddamned men's room!"

With the warmer weather, Clarissa had traded her snow boots for more seasonally appropriate galoshes. They squeaked on the concrete floor until I could see them under the stall's door. "You've got nothing to be embarrassed about. Everybody poops. I might suggest you rethink your diet, though. Uff da. It smells like bad choices in here."

"Opinions are like assholes. Speaking of, please get the hell out and let me crap in peace," I begged through teeth clenched tighter than my cheeks. "I'll be back in my office in a minute."

"Probably more like five," she answered with a wry smile in her voice.

In typical spooky-ooky Clarissa fashion, she was right. About five minutes later, I found her in Jay's studio. From the looks of it, the two were hitting it off famously. She was admiring his current project, a multi-media installment he called *Shining Light on the Fake Moon Landing*. An old Betamax was plugged into a 70's-era TV and was playing Stanley Kubrick's The Shining. Where he'd found the player or a Beta version of the film, I had no idea, but he'd been excited as all hell when he'd brought them back to the studio.

He'd painted the Betamax white and stenciled "Property of," and the NASA logo on it. The TV's casing was painted a light gray and traced with black geometric lines to make it look like the outside of a spaceship. A little plastic American flag flew from each of its rabbit-ear antennas.

"Oh, geez. That's something else," Clarissa was saying. "You really think the whole moon landing thing was fake? I had no idea there were so many clues in *The Shining*. Never saw it. Too scary."

The lady had no idea what she was getting herself into. I cleared my throat, more to make sure I could wrap up my business with her than to save her from a trip down the rabbit hole with my conspiracy-loving pal. When they looked up, Jay immediately started laughing.

"I hope everything came out all right in the end," he quipped with a giggle and then added, "Or at least out your end right."

"You know what? It did—thanks for asking—and I saved it so you can use it for your next project," I growled.

That earned me a hurt look from my friend, one I knew I'd have to deal with later, but I set that problem aside to focus on the more immediate one. I pointed and waited without speaking until Clarissa took the hint. After we'd relocated to my office, I took a seat behind my desk and leveled a stern look at the woman seated across from me.

"Okay. Let's try this again. Hello, Ms. Steyer."

A smile balanced precariously on her face. When I didn't return it, hers fell. "Oh, Clarissa's fine. And can I call you August?"

"No. So. Hello, Clarissa. Thank you for stopping by my office. You're right. I have been trying to get in touch. I left a message at your office that I really doubt you've heard, and I sent you a note that there is no way you could have received since it's still in a mailbox on Broadway. Yet somehow, you knew I wanted to talk to you, and here you are. Seems like you know everything, isn't that right? Except for how to give someone your name and, oh, I don't know, a phone number."

She glowered. "Cripes, I don't know everything. I thought you already knew me, is all. When you didn't call, it occurred to me that maybe you didn't know me yet."

I scoffed. "Gee, full of yourself much? Better hop off that pedestal before the altitude gives you a nosebleed."

"I didn't mean it like that," she snipped and then added in a softer tone, "I'm sorry. This whole thing is frustrating."

"Oh, I know frustrating. Like when someone shows up, freaks me out with this weird, 'I know the future,' act, tells me to get something, gives me a stack of cash and nothing–and I mean nothing–to go on, and then pops into the bathroom while I'm having some quality me-time and complains that I haven't been in touch. That's frustrating."

She had the good grace to look embarrassed. Without invitation, she lifted a pen from my desk and tore a corner from a loose sheet of paper. A moment later, she'd carefully penned her name and phone number.

"There. Now you can reach me. And I am sorry. Things are tangled around you, Aug- Mr. Shade. I'm not sure what has happened or what hasn't happened, or what I'm supposed to do. Surprising you in the bathroom could have been funny. Something we'd laugh about. Jay thought it was funny."

"Jay spends his days inhaling paint fumes." I took her number and dropped it unceremoniously into my desk's sliding drawer, knowing it would be harder to recover from its cluttered depths than a seashell from the bottom of the Mariana Trench. "And what do you mean, things are tangled around me?"

The deerskin jacket had been replaced with a worn cardigan, one that she pulled at nervously, more animated than she'd been our entire first meeting. The sweater looked second hand. I wasn't judging. As a cheap son of a bitch myself, I just knew thrift when I saw it. Another moment passed while she seemed to collect her thoughts and set them in order.

"Folks think I can see the future. That isn't quite true," she started. When I didn't say anything, she steeled herself with a breath and continued. "There isn't a future. There are lots of futures, and yes, I can see many of them. Bits of them. Glimpses, shifting and changing like shards of colored glass in a kaleidoscope. Some are likely. Others, less so. If I try, I can see the likely ones more clearly than the others, and while I'm looking at them, the rest sort of fade."

My face must've perfectly conveyed my confusion because her expression turned sympathetic.

"Oh heck, I'm not real good at explaining it," she admitted. "It's like... Well, have you ever seen those optical illusion pictures? The ones that look like a bunch of dots and patterns, but if you let your eyes shift out of focus, you can see an image? Like a boat or an eagle?"

I nodded, pretending to understand. "Yeah, I saw one that was all abstract purple but then you could see a portrait of Prince. Pretty cool. So... you space out, and then you see the future?"

"I suppose that's as good of a description as any other, except it's the opposite. Instead of not focusing, I have to focus. Very, very hard."

"So, it's like the optical illusion pictures, except it's not like that at all."

"Yep, you betcha," she agreed, smiling again.

A tiny, bright spark of pain fired up somewhere behind my left eyeball, so I squeezed my eyes shut and pinched the bridge of my nose. Three deep breaths later, I asked–as politely as I could–if she knew she drove people crazy.

"I do," she admitted, and suddenly I felt like a jerk.

"I didn't... I mean, I wasn't... Oh, forget it," I sighed. "But you still haven't explained what you meant about me."

The nervous fidgeting resumed. Clarissa scratched her nose, then pulled at a loose strand of hair, then plucked at her skirt. It was so different from our first encounter that I was having a hard time believing she was the same person.

"I can't see the future around you," she finally confessed. "Not really. Not like I usually do. Every time I try to see one for you, the others don't fade. They get brighter. So bright. It's like trying to see a firefly in a room full of light bulbs. So many possibilities that I get confused. Everything gets mixed up around you. I think maybe I get some things right. Other things, though... I don't get them right at all. Like the message I left you. The voicemail. It wasn't in order, or the conversation we might've had we didn't actually have because something else happened instead. I keep trying to see the right things, but it all gets so mixed up. When I look at you, I always get to a place where I have no idea–none at all–what will happen because everything could happen. Like I said earlier, it's frustrating."

Despite still being confused, I did feel a bit better. She found me as annoying as I found her. In my book, that was a win.

"I'm still waiting for you to make sense," I pressed.

Clarissa looked past me, and her eyes glided across the office's back wall. She chewed her lip and drummed fingers on her thighs. She took a breath, opened her mouth, and didn't say anything. A moment later, she did it again with the same result. It was like watching a really indecisive contestant on a TV game show trying to decide between door number one, two, or three.

"You have four safes," she proclaimed.

"I do," I agreed, grasping for the new thread of our conversation. "I collect a lot of stuff for a lot of people. So?"

"Have you ever put something in one safe and forgotten which one you put it in?"

"No," I lied. "I have a system." I pointed out each safe lining the back wall of my small office in turn. "Stupid stuff, sappy stuff, valuable stuff, and dangerous stuff."

She raised an eyebrow at that before continuing. "Well, heck. That sounds very well thought-out. Well, let's assume the impossible. Let's say that one day you accidentally put something stupid in the sappy safe, and let's say you did that on a Monday morning. You've seen the future. You know that the stupid thing's owner is going to come on Tuesday to collect it. When they arrive, you're going to open the stupid safe, and their stupid thing will be right there, ready and waiting. You also know you have an appointment with a sappy person on Monday afternoon. But that afternoon, the stupid person shows up unannounced. By weird coincidence, the stupid person and the sappy person look a lot alike. You're justifiably confused. You were expecting the sappy person at that time, so you open the sappy safe, but you've also got stupid on the brain, so you grab the stupid thing you put in the wrong safe and give it to the sappy person. A stupid thing to do, but also understandable."

I blinked, trying to decide if she actually thought she was helping. She must've because she was waiting expectantly for me to say something. The best I could muster was, "No, you're stupid."

Clarissa sighed. "Understanding any future is tough, Mr. Shade, but understanding yours is darn near impossible. When I realized you could maybe help me, I looked and looked. In one, we met, and you weren't sure if you could help. I gave you my number. You called me back and left a message saying you'd try to help after all. I called to say thanks and agreed to bring payment. That one seemed as likely as the others. So likely that I convinced myself it had actually happened, but we were strangers when I arrived at your office. Something had changed, shifted. So much seemed the same, and yet a whole different future had unfurled. By the time I realized that I'd goofed, I was so scared I'd make another mistake that I barely dared to breathe. That doesn't happen to me often. I hope you understand."

"Sure," I lied again.

A shy smile reappeared. "I'm glad. And I'm sorry it happened again. There was a future where I surprised you in the bathroom, but that came out wrong, too. The future, not your poop. Although it seems like that didn't come out all that great, either."

It took me a second before I realized she'd tried to make a joke. As if any of this could be considered funny.

"Well, I'm so terribly sorry I've made things difficult for you. I'd offer to do better, but I don't really care. All I need to know is who has the glass eye you need back, which is really gross, by the way. Sorry. I don't usually judge, but your eye? Really?" I shuddered. "Anyway, just tell me who has it and where they live. That's all I need, then you and I can be done."

"I need this glass eye back," she said, tapping a finger against the pupil of her left eye. "Urgently, but I don't know who has 'em. I've told you. Things are out of order around you. Everything is possible, and nothing is possible, and I always get to a place where I can't see anything at all. Just blinding light and terrifying darkness and..." she trailed off, worry creasing her forehead.

I palmed my face. "Clarissa, I'm a post-relationship personal effects repossession specialist. Let's unpack that. We'll start with the first part: Post-relationship. Post. That's French for 'after.'"

"Oh, for Pete's sake. That's not French, Mr. Shade."

"Knock it off and just call me August. Christ, you're a pain," I cursed. "Fine. Swahili. Klingon. It doesn't matter. The point is, I get stuff back after people break-up, not before. And the other really, really important part of my job description: Repossession. You possessed it before. I help you possess it again. The only way that works is if you had it before and then you don't have it," I mansplained as patronizingly as I could manage. "You. Still. Have. Your. Glass. Eye."

She rocked back in her chair, and her good eye went far away. A shiver ran down my back, but I did my best not to let it show. A few tense moments passed–her looking all trancy and me trying to look like it wasn't freaking me out–and then she shook her head.

"I think... Think, mind you. I'm not sure. I think that maybe I meet someone because of you and..." she trailed off. For a long moment, she looked down at her galoshes, then quietly finished with, "I guess they get my eye."

There was a lot stuffed into that pause. Life and laughter and love, followed by heartache and loss and sadness and anger. Then, and only then, would my services be required. For a split-second, I understood the curse of prescience. I could see Clarissa's future–clear as day–and it was a sad one. She was going to meet someone. She was going to care about them, and it was going to end. It was a tragically familiar story–even the bit about the eye. People in love gave each other all kinds of weird shit. I didn't care about that. I simply didn't want any part of it.

*But one-thousand dollars.*

"Guess I'm adding matchmaker to my list of services. So? What's your type? Besides people that think eyeballs are romantic gifts."

Clarissa blushed, red flowing up from her cardigan's neckline all the way to her forehead. "Oh gosh, I don't know if it needs to be that deliberate."

I threw my hands up. "Well, why the hell not? How else am I supposed to help you meet the person that's going to break your heart and keep your freaking eyeball?"

As I watched my words slam into her, I immediately regretted them. She pulled her cardigan tight across her chest as if the worn yarn could shield her from the harsh realities of the world. Her eyes clouded, and a single tear explored the contours of her cheek.

"Shit. Sorry," I mumbled. "I'm not very good at this, you know, people stuff. Maybe we should call this one a bust. I'll give you your money back. Well, most of it. I drank some."

Clarissa's shoulders slumped in defeat. A moment later, she squared them again and rose from her chair. "I'm sorry I bothered you. Please keep the money for your troubles. Consider it a birthday present."

"My birthday isn't until November," I protested. As protests went, it was a bit half-hearted, but hey, five-hundred bucks.

The woman regarded me sadly, shrugged, and said, "I know."

Her galoshes squeaked on the concrete as she walked from my office, out of Jay's studio, and into the hallway, a recriminating metronome that echoed in my mind long after she was gone.

# CHAPTER 3

THE WEATHER HAD TAKEN a turn for the better. A few late April showers had cleared most of the sand and crud from the roads, and a few sunny May days had turned winter's brown into a spreading blanket of green. I'd reconnected a few clients with whatever it was they couldn't survive without and figured it was as good of a time as any to call it a day. Us Minnesotans are a pragmatic bunch. You get a nice day, you use it.

I decided to take a toodle–that's Minnesotan for a pointless meander to nowhere in particular–around the Chain of Lakes. It was one of the city's finest features: A string of small urban lakes connected by parkways and bike paths and bordered with everything from parks and picnic grounds to residential homes and high rises to high-end restaurants and cafes. After zipping over to the Mississippi's western side and skirting downtown Minneapolis, I headed to the top of the chain: an overconfident puddle called Brownie Lake. From there, a parkway traced the shorelines of Cedar Lake, Lake of the Isles, Bde Maka Ska, and finally, Lake Harriet. Altogether, it was over fifteen miles of easy driving; perfect for an early evening toodle.

My bike's engine rumbled, and its tires hummed on the asphalt. The twining sounds filled the space between my ears while I tried desperately to push everything else out. It'd been a couple of weeks since I'd parted ways with Clarissa Steyer, but I couldn't get her out of my head. It wasn't because I'd kept the money. She'd said I could keep it and who was I to argue? It wasn't because she was apparently an oracle, although that was remarkable enough to wind anyone up for a while. I still wasn't convinced she was the real deal but also couldn't convince myself she wasn't. Even so, that indecision wasn't what kept her firmly rooted in my brain. It was more like when someone says don't think about a thing and then all you can do is think about that thing. The more you try not to, the more you do. I tried not to think about Clarissa, so naturally, she was all I could think about.

Suddenly, a leisurely cruise around the city lakes wasn't at all what I wanted. I gave the throttle a twist and passed a couple of geriatrics puttering along in an old Buick. A few blocks later, I found exactly what I needed; a dog park lacking both dogs and people. After parking the bike, I strolled through the entrance and across the fenced-in area as nonchalantly as I could manage. A quick look around confirmed I was alone, so I ducked behind a thick stand of leafy bushes in the park's back corner and pulled off my clothes. After one more glance to ensure I was still alone, I shifted into a scruffy coyote and gave my legs a good stretch.

Shifting into an animal is a funny thing. You can't become something else and still stay you. Sure, you're still in there, but all the stuff that makes you human is mashed up with a whole bunch of stuff that is most decidedly not human. You're still in control, but it's like playing a video game with a slippery joystick and sticky buttons. You can make yourself do humany stuff, but it's a lot easier to do what the animal you've become wants to do. Shift into a cat, and you'll want to find a warm patch of sun and nap for days, with the occasional break to knock crap off of countertops. Shift into a pigeon, and the path of least resistance is to spread your wings and shit everywhere. Staying true to my shift's nature also helped a bit when I shifted back. The more I tried to stay human while wearing a borrowed body and using a borrowed brain, the longer it took to recover from the inevitable headaches and nausea. The doctors that had poked and prodded me to the brink of death when I was a kid called it physio-cognitive dissonance. They said PCD was the consequence of two very different minds trying to share the same brain. I just called it annoying.

The coyote wanted to investigate the many smells and stick to the early evening's long shadows while doing it. Fine with me. I'd taken a risk with this particular shift. Folks wouldn't take too kindly to the four-legged scavenger hanging out in a neighborhood dog park, so keeping out of sight was not merely part of my borrowed nature; it was prudent. Head stretched out on a scruff-covered neck, belly low to the ground, tail waving gently behind me, I poked around the park's perimeter. My nose reveled in an olfactory cornucopia, my eyes tracked a myriad of tiny movements, my tongue tasted the evening air. Whatever humanness I'd had dwindled to a mere spark, just enough to appreciate how completely simple my life had become. I trotted around the park and stopped to sniff a shrub. I lifted a leg to let the rest of the park's visitors know I'd been there, ambled languidly to where I'd stashed my clothes, and was tackled from behind.

I had no idea how they'd snuck up on me and, in the moment, didn't care. Teeth bared, I whipped my head around to snap at my assailant but only succeeded in chomping mouthfuls of air.

"Easy. Easy, now. No need to get so worked up. My boss wants to see you, is all."

Whoever he was, he was big, strong, and had at least some experience wrestling a coyote to the ground. How one picks up that particular life skill, I had no idea, but he obviously had it. While one hand pressed my head into the grass, the other clamped around my two back feet and squeezed them together painfully. Exerting my human will over the animal's instincts, I forced myself to relax.

"Good boy. There's a good boy," the stranger crooned like I was some stupid Labrador that had fetched his slippers. "I'm going to let go so you can be human again. Run, and I'll catch you. The boss wants to talk, so I can't break your jaw, but the rest of you is fair game."

It was a threat delivered in the most intimidating way possible: with utter nonchalance. He wasn't even threatening me. He was just describing reality, easy as calling the grass green or saying the sun will set in the west. That alone was scary enough to keep me firmly in line. That and the facts that one, he knew I was a shifter, two, he had caught me unawares without breaking a sweat, and three, he had a boss. When a guy like that has a boss, you know that boss is not someone to mess with.

As promised, he released my feet and shifted his weight off my head. The salty thought, *Great. Naked in public again,* passed through my mind, and then I was human. I quickly curled into a ball and took my first look at the guy that had a boss that wanted to talk with me. I'll be honest. He looked pretty good for a dead guy.

How could I tell he was dead? Call it an educated guess. Not many folks can have a face so clearly mangled and reassembled as his and still be alive. Coarse stitches wrapped across his forehead and wound down his left cheek. His nose was crooked, not in a broken sort of way, but in a ripped-off-his-face-and-stuck-back-on-in-a-hurry sort of way. The skin where his right ear met the side of his head was full of dully gleaming staples. His throat had an angry scar that circled his neck like a puckered flesh torque. It looked like someone had rejoined separated flesh with a soldering iron. His eyes were a little cloudy, like someone had spilled a couple of drops of curdled milk in each iris, and the skin stretched around them was sallow. So yeah, I figured dead. And if you're as dead as he obviously was and still up and moving around, that meets my standard for looking pretty good for a dead guy.

My captor was sensibly dressed in running shoes, jeans, and a purple Minnesota Vikings hoodie, and his hair was cropped in a way that bespoke utilitarianism more than style. Despite being annoyed by the circumstances, I found myself approving of his choices. If I died and had to keep hanging around the living, I'd want to be comfy, too.

"You're dead?" I asked.

"Kinda," the guy said, his voice marred with a raspy burr and weary as Eeyore on downers. "I was. Now I'm not anymore. I'm a revenant. Uh, don't you want to put some clothes on?"

I reached behind the bush to retrieve my clothes and dressed while considering his words. Revenants were when a dead person's spirit reclaimed their body. It was weird to be chatting with a scary campfire story in a dog park, but the world was a crazy place. After I finished dressing–a challenging task when you're also furtively glancing in every direction at once–I stood with that awkward posture most commonly seen when someone really has to take a crap, but the only stall is occupied.

"Well, come on, then," the man said and started walking.

I followed, his plain-spoken threat still firmly jammed in my mind, and tried a little small talk to ease my jangled nerves.

"So, who's the boss?" I asked.

"Tony Danza."

I laughed despite myself. "Funny. Seriously, though. I know a few of the who's-who PNs around town, and none of them have revenants or zombies or Frankensteins or whatever on the payroll. No offense."

"None taken."

"So? Who is it, then? Who do you work for?"

"Vilde Tanck," he answered, looking back over his shoulder. My blank stare must've done a good job of conveying exactly how little that meant to me. "Lefse Queen of Minnesota? No? She's a baker. She won some big awards for her lefse. That's why she's the Lefse Queen."

I stopped, forcing the big corpse to stop as well.

"You stalked me and attacked me and are currently dragging me off against my will because some lady that bakes lefse wants to talk?" I complained. "I have an office, you know. It's got a phone and everything."

"I went to your office," he said, "and you were just leaving, so I followed you. I thought I'd talk to you when you got to wherever you were going, but it doesn't seem like you were really going anywhere."

I bridled at the accusation in his voice. "You've never gone for a toodle?"

The man crossed his arms across a broad chest and flexed biceps bigger than my thighs. "No. Now, come on. You don't want to keep Ms. Tanck waiting."

"Or what? I'll end up looking like you?" I scoffed. I'd thought it was a ridiculous statement. The man's unwavering regard made me quickly rethink that particular assumption. "Really? Geez, what did you do, anyway?"

He resumed walking, and I hurried to catch up.

"Ever have Mrs. Olson's Lefse?" he asked while holding the fence's gate open for me. "You can get it at the grocery store."

"Once or twice, I guess."

"Me, too. Unfortunately, Ms. Tanck caught me in the act. I'd been clearing some dead trees from the back of her house and tossing them in a woodchipper to mulch them up. Took a break to have lunch. She saw the lefse package and pushed me into the woodchipper."

My jaw dropped. "You're lying," I managed after pulling it back up.

"Wish I was," he sighed. "Ms. Tanck says I shouldn't complain, though. Folks take me a lot more seriously now than they did before. She says that's nice."

I didn't doubt people took him seriously. I'd never met a revenant before and wondered if they were all sneaky as ninjas, crazy strong, and drove BMW's. The car waited by the curb, its black glossy paint and shiny hubs looking like they'd just rolled off the lot. My abductor politely opened the back door, and I slid inside, butt squeaking on the leather seat. After sealing me inside, he opened the driver's door and climbed behind the wheel. The engine revved, and we rolled forward toward what I considered to be a very uncertain future.

*I wonder if Clarissa saw this coming,* I thought and then roundly cursed myself. The whole point of the evening's excursion was to not think about her, but it was a lost cause. If getting abducted by a zombie ninja wasn't enough to drive thoughts of Clarissa Steyer from my brain, nothing would.


The car circled Lake of the Isles, wove through Uptown's unbearable traffic, and headed toward the North Loop's Warehouse District. I tried to enjoy the experience of riding in something worth more than I'd make in the next decade, but knowing that the lady I was about to meet tossed people in woodchippers took the fun out of it. The sun had dipped below the horizon, and streetlights glinted off the surrounding cars. I considered rolling down my darkly tinted window and screaming for help, but I knew Minnesotans well enough to know that they'd firmly mind their own business.

"So this Vilde Tanck pushed you into a woodchipper and then had you stitched back together and brought back to life so you could keep working for her?" I asked, trying to sound calm.

"Yep."

"I hope you got Employee of the Month, er… What should I call you, anyway? Tanck-enstein?"

"Ms. Tanck might actually like that," he sighed sadly.

"Tanckenstein it is, then," I decided, pointedly ignoring the look I got in the rearview mirror. "Nice to meet you. I'm August."

"Yep."

"Sooo," I drawled, "now that we're old pals, whadaya say you just drop me off at the next corner?"

"Nope."

"Look. I'm sure your boss is great and all, but you really can just let me out here," I suggested when he stopped at a red light. "That'd be fine with me, and I can make it fine with you, too. Just, you know, name your price. As long as it's less than, one sec…" I pulled my wallet free and counted the bills inside. "Thirty-three dollars."

Slightly clouded eyes crinkled in the rearview in what could've been a smile before they drooped again. "I like you. You're funny."

I cursed myself for not choosing comedy as a profession. Near as I could tell, no one ever sent reincarnated henchmen after comedians. Too soon, we were rolling down a paved-over cobblestone street in the Warehouse District. It was an upscale part of town, where old buildings had been converted into luxury condos above trendy restaurants, indie cafes, and boutique retail stores. Tanckenstein parked and escorted me to one with an old-fashioned, hand-painted sign above the door that read, "Tanck's Tasty Treats."

The Lefse Queen's henchman pushed the door open and set a little bell hanging above it tinkling. I followed him inside, and the smell of baking bread and powdered sugar enveloped me. It was a tidy little shop. The walls were whitewashed panels festooned with an eclectic combination of Scandinavian-themed needlework, oil paintings of picturesque countrysides, and framed awards from what must've been every bakery contest under the sun. Tanck had even picked up a blue ribbon at the Minnesota State Fair, which left me wondering how you'd eat lefse-on-a-stick. A glass case held various confections, and sleek wooden tables displayed things I assumed the right person could use in the kitchen. I flipped the price tag on one, widened my eyes, and reaffirmed my vow to never, ever make my own food.

"Velkommen, Mr. Shade," a profoundly feminine voice said. "I trust your trip here was a pleasant one?"

The voice emanated from the empty space around me. As it filled my ears, I smiled. I didn't want to smile, but my face didn't much care what I wanted. With a surprising amount of effort, I was able to make the unwilling smile collapse back down into my more typical and more appropriate frown.

"The trip was fine. Your henchman here has a nice car and is an excellent driver. The before-the-trip stuff, not so much. You know. Stalked. Tackled. Abducted. Call me crazy, but that's not my definition of 'pleasant.'"

"Leonard," the voice scolded, "You really must be more polite."

The big man shrugged apologetically. "Ms. Tanck, you always say that caution is the eldest child of wisdom. I wasn't sure if he was dangerous. Or housebroken."

A soft laugh filled the room, and my face pulled itself into an unwilling smile again.

"My apologies," the disembodied voice offered. "Leonard's methods are sometimes overzealous, but he is so effective."

"Unless you need him to win a beauty pageant."

"Ah, Mr. Shade. If I had that particular need, I would simply do it myself."

And with that, Vilde Tanck made her appearance. Or appeared. Or whatever. Suffice it to say that she wasn't there, and then she was, right in goddamned front of me. I gasped in surprise and jumped back, earning peals of musical laughter from the woman. That odd impulse to smile pulled at my cheeks, but my indomitable crabbiness was winning out. Nothing–and I mean nothing in the whole damned universe–can keep me from being crabby for long.

"Haha. Nice one. You really got me," I growled, heart pounding.

It took a moment to recover from the scare. When I did, I got my first look at Vilde Tanck. And look, I did. And all I can say is... Damn.

I've met plenty of pretty people. I've even met some beautiful people. And the PNs? Forget about it. The ones that can look human can be unbelievably hot. I had a fairy client once that was so surreally gorgeous that I'd refused to stand up from behind my desk when she was in my office and had kept my hands strategically folded over my lap. But compared to Vilde Tanck... At that exact moment, I realized that beauty wasn't in the eye of the beholder. Beauty was Vilde Tanck; full stop, end of flippin' story. The rest of us weren't even living in her shadow. We were like a flashlight beam reflected off a garbage can while she was the sun. I knelt before the vision I'd been blessed with seeing, so grateful that my worthless life had allowed me this one moment, this one perfect moment...

*Wait a sec,* a stubborn corner of my brain suddenly declared.

I'm still not sure how, but I managed to close my eyes and bite down on the inside of my cheek. My fingers curled into fists, and my nails dug into the meat of my palms. I forced myself to count up in fours–one, five, nine, thirteen–and kept counting until I got to fifty-three. Getting to each number felt like I was dragging my brain through molasses, but after the thirteenth increment of four, my brain broke free of her spell. I relaxed my fingers, unclenched my jaw, and opened my eyes.

My little glamor-hack had worked. Vilde Tanck was still there, and Vilde Tanck was still quite striking: A thick braid of platinum hair draped one shoulder like a stole, and flawless skin wrapped her face from pointed ear to pointed ear. Blue-blue eyes regarded me from either side of an elegant nose, and a wide smile showed impossibly straight and unnaturally white teeth. She was taller than me, lithe as a stalk of summer wheat, and garbed in a traditional Norwegian bunad dress. With its high bodice, long sleeves, and flowing skirt that brushed the tops of her bare feet, it made her all the more sensual by letting the imagination reveal what the dress itself didn't. Yes, she was beautiful. Gorgeous. Regal...

But she wasn't like a goddess or anything. A moment before, she'd have been a three hundred on a scale of one to ten. After shaking her glamor or whatever it was, she was a twenty-seven, tops... with a cow tail. The tip of that bovine bonus was curled demurely around her left ankle. Not exactly a turn-on, even for a shifter like me.

"Fool me twice," I complained, regaining my feet and shaking my head. "You're a huldra?"

Vilde's eyes narrowed, and her tail slipped up under the dress's hem. "Ja, indeed. You know your elves, I see."

"In my line of work, you get to know a lot of things," I replied, after taking a steadying breath. Leonard's circumstances made a bit more sense. Elves, no matter what kind, weren't to be trifled with. In my experience, they were arrogant, temperamental, always acting better-than. It was like their fingers had been genetically engineered in one of Jay's secret government labs to push all of my buttons. If I was going to survive this encounter unscathed, I'd have to be very, very careful.

Or not.

"How about we stop with the games and cut to the chase," I suggested brusquely and then added with a disdainful sneer. "I'm sure you have some other super important stuff to do, like... I don't know... making cookies or whatever."

There was a moment, the tiniest of moments, when I saw my future, and it was bloody. Then her smile turned a bit less homicidal and a bit more pleasant.

"Ja. As you wish, Mr. Shade. Please join me in the bakehouse. Leonard, you will mind the shop."

The huldra turned and strode across the room, bare feet padding softly on the floor and her gown–and tail–swishing with each step. The whole walking thing might've been for show. The way she moved, she could've just as easily floated. I followed her through a swinging door and stepped into what she had so quaintly referred to as 'the bakehouse.'

I'd never been in a bakehouse before. When my brain heard the term, it conjured up images of a kitchen. I had a kitchen, so I was confident I knew what to expect. Sink. Stove. Fridge. A few cabinets under a countertop and a few cupboards above. Maybe even a microwave. As I pushed through the door, I quickly realized the error of my assumption. To call Vilde Tanck's bakehouse a kitchen would be like calling Lake Superior a pretty little pond. The space was surprisingly big. From the storefront, one would never guess how much square footage Tanck's Tasty Treats actually consumed. A butcher block slab dominated the room's center. One end held a stainless-steel sink. The other, a glass cooktop where a large pot simmered and sent up wisps of steam. A mixing bowl, flour-dusted rolling pin, ricer, and a large manilla envelope filled the space between. The rest of the enormous room was an orderly assembly of stainless-steel counters and shelves connected by steel roller conveyors. The cold effect of all that gleaming metal was made unexpectedly cozy by the warmth of large ovens, and the light spilling through expansive windows across the back wall showed an absolutely stunning view of...

"Is that a fjord?" I gasped.

It sure looked like a fjord. Not an alley or the back of the building behind hers or any other totally normal thing. What I saw was an actual, honest-to-god fjord, its indigo waters stretching away between high, craggy cliffs until it curved out of sight near a horizon lined with...

"Mountains. Because, of course, I can see mountains from your kitchen window."

On top of geology that simply had no business being in Minnesota, the light filling the bakehouse came from a midday sun. I knew full well that the sun had set. I'd watched it from the backseat of a BMW. To see it lighting up a bluer-than-blue sky outside of those windows bent my brain more than the distant mountains.

"Nice view," I remarked as I set a shaking hand on the butcher block countertop. "Not to brag, but I'm a bit of an expert on glass, and I can honestly say I've never seen glass like that. Windows are supposed to show you what's on the other side. Not... that."

"Ja. It is a silly indulgence. A window to my home, my true home. I am glad it pleases you."

"Uh-huh," I lied as my brain tried to reconcile what my eyes were seeing with what it knew to be true. "I need a drink. Are any of those whiskey?" I asked as I pointed to a shelf that held a variety of bottles.

"Nei," she replied as she took a simple apron from a hook, looped it over her neck, and neatly tied the straps around her waist, "but I think you will find the bottle on the end of the lowest shelf a worthy substitute. And please, do help yourself to some lefse."

I grunted and poured a finger into a convenient tumbler, then added a few more fingers and a thumb for good measure. The lefse was stacked on a nearby platter. Holding my drink in one hand, my other picked up a piece of flattened potato bread slathered with butter, sprinkled with sugar, and rolled into a convenient-to-eat little tube.

"You want something?" I asked.

"A glass of the Lignell & Piispanen Lakka would be delightful."

I carried my drink and Norwegian treat to the kitchen's island and tilted my head towards the bottles.

"Help yourself," I encouraged her amicably. "Try not to spill, though. Whatever you said sounds expensive. Be a shame to waste it. Oh, and you should try the lefse," I added, my words muffled a bit by a mouth recently stuffed with buttery, sugary bread. "It's not the best I've ever tried, but it ain't bad."

We locked eyes across the wide island as I tested my new theory. I'd decided that she needed me alive. Why? I still didn't know, but that was beside the point. Tanckenstein had made it pretty clear that if I needed to be dead, I'd be dead. I wasn't. That meant I had leverage, and if a lever says, 'Don't pull!' I just can't help but give it a tug.

"I'm beginning to suspect that you don't like me, Mr. Shade."

I shrugged in agreement, took a sip of the brown liquid, and suddenly liked her very much. I had no idea what I was drinking, but it was good. Really, really good. Suddenly, the whole ordeal seemed worth it, even if it meant it would be my last night above the dirt.

"Holy shit!" I exclaimed. "What is this?"

Tanck smiled. "Expensive. Please don't spill any. It'd be a shame to waste it." When I chuckled at the riposte, she continued. "Consider it a peace offering. I am sorry about the circumstances of our meeting. I trust that Leonard conveyed the urgency of my situation. Were I not in such need of your services, our meeting could have happened quite differently."

The amber liquid that wasn't whiskey but was so much better burned pleasantly as I took another sip, and the lefse really had been good. I found myself relaxing and reframing my perspective on the encounter. Had it really been so bad? Yeah, Tanckenstein had abducted me, but I got to ride in a Beemer, see a fjord and some mountains, spend time with a pretty lady, and drink whatever this stuff was...

Seeing my guard lower, Vilde smiled her appreciation and set to ricing potatoes. The pot had just come to a boil on the island's cooktop. The huldra twisted a dial, lifted the heavy pot easily, and drained it into the sink. After returning it to the cooktop, she took out rough cut chunks of potato, set them in her ricer, and squeezed them into a wide bowl. After about half of the pot's contents had been riced to her satisfaction, she gestured to the envelope. The invitation was clear, so I reluctantly set down my glass and picked it up. Inside was a glossy eight-by-ten photo of a book: leather-bound and–judging from its construction and the evidence of wear around the edges–quite old. Its cover was embossed with the Zodiac's twelve signs circling a stylized sun whose rays reached out from behind a crescent moon. In the center of the superimposed sun and moon was a skull with a snake twining through its empty sockets.

"What you are looking at is mine," she informed me as she resumed her ricing. "It is called *The Thirteenth Zodiac*. I was in a relationship with someone. I left it at their home. The relationship ended, and they have refused to return it. I believe that this is your area of expertise, no? Retrieve it for me, and you will be handsomely rewarded."

I took another sip and contemplated the woman. "You aren't asking, are you?"

"I am not," she agreed.

"Why me? Why not Leonard?"

Tanck set the ricer aside, and her large and luminous eyes narrowed. "Jeg beklager. My apologies. I thought that you were the post-relationship personal effects repossession specialist. I did not realize that Leonard possessed such skills. Did I perhaps push the wrong person into a woodchipper?"

The alcohol kept my blood from freezing in my veins, but I still felt very, very cold. After a moment, the storm clouds that had gathered in her eyes dispersed, and the huldra smiled.

"You see? To make lefse, one must rice the potatoes. Not peel. Not chop. Not mash. Specific jobs require specific tools, Mr. Shade."

I let being called a tool slide and raised a skeptical eyebrow. "And you realized this when, exactly?"

Tanck's eyes narrowed again. "Today," she finally admitted after a long pause. "This afternoon, to be exact, when I was reviewing my horoscope in light of some recent events. I always heed my horoscope, Mr. Shade, and in this case, it was perfectly clear that I needed your services, and I needed them immediately."

I laughed. She didn't, so I stopped but arranged my face to ensure every inch of it oozed skepticism. Apparently, the huldra didn't appreciate it when someone openly doubted her convictions. With a huff, she wiped her hands on her apron and glided to a section of counter holding a myriad of books between simple wooden block bookends. A slender arm reached out, and her long fingers slid a large, square book from its place. After returning to the bakehouse island, she set it on the counter between us and gestured for me to open it. Dubious, I pulled at the ornate cover and realized it was an old-fashioned scrapbook. The pages were made of stiff, coarse paper. Metal clips were affixed to each page and arranged to hold the corners of photos or clippings. In this case, the clips held the corners of carefully cut-out "Ope! It's Your Horoscope!" drivel that had been dreamt up by Clarissa thrice-damned Steyer and regurgitated in the *Metro Pages*. Each month's words had obviously been closely analyzed by Tanck. I saw red underlines and notations in the margins. All of the signs had some level of notation, but Virgo had received the most attention by far.

*Unbelievable,* I cursed inwardly as I flipped from January to the current month's page.

"I am a Virgo. Do you know what that means?" Vilde asked.

"You're almost as gullible as Libra and more gullible than Leo?"

Her eyes narrowed yet again. If it hadn't been for the alcohol, I might've wet myself. Thankfully, the booze gave me just enough liquid courage to return her glare with one of my own. When it came to glares, I was master class.

"Virgos are an earth sign," she said after deciding I'd be better off enlightened than eviscerated. Rounding the island, she positioned herself beside me so close I could feel her warm breath on my cheek. "Virgos are resourceful, hardworking, and practical."

"Horoscopes are Greek," I challenged. "And you're... not. Shouldn't you, I don't know, be listening to Odin or something?"

I saw the tip of her cow tail twitch from the corner of my eye. "Odin is a Leo," she hissed. "Now, perhaps you should talk less and listen more, nei?"

I sipped, nodded, and did my best to look contrite. It must've been a convincing act because Tanck continued in her lecturing tone.

"Virgos understand quite well the importance of detail and structure. They know that nothing should be left to chance and are driven to create perfection. Perfection, Mr. Shade."

Another sip, another nod, plus I widened my eyes a smidge. Seemed like the appropriate thing to do. When she continued to stare at me, I widened them further and let my lips part just a bit. I was about to add a very impressed, "Whoah," but caught myself. Her expression forced me to reassess my earlier conviction that I was a good actor.

Vilde sighed. "The book in that photograph is something I want dearly, something that was mine and must be mine again. I have wondered how I would reclaim it. Now..." she breathed, staring intently at me. "Please turn back to April."

I took another swig and did as I was instructed. My eyes found Virgo, but I didn't need to bother reading the words. Vilde recited them from memory, Clarissa's folksy words sounding surprisingly natural with the huldra's Norwegian accent.

"You've had to learn some things the hard way, haven't you, Virgo? Like love isn't always sunshine and rainbows. This is a heck of a good time to think about all you've learned the past few months. The new moon will be stirring up all sorts of energies and giving you a chance to take what you've learned and put it into action. Sure, love can be a real pain in the derriere, but only if you're sitting down. Get yourself up and start making those plans to get what your heart really desires."

I *hmph'd,* but my skepticism was met with calm certitude.

"May, please," Vilde instructed.

Obligingly, I turned the heavy page. My eyes found Virgo's corner of crazy in May's asylum, but again she spared me the trouble of reading it for myself. Hearing the huldra read *Ope! Its Your Horoscope!* would've been funny had she not so evidently been treating each hokey-dokey word as gospel.

"You know what season it is, Virgo? No, not deer season. No, not pheasant. For cripe's sake, no, not duck. Geez, are you even from around here? It's Gemini season, and for you, that's better than all of the above. It's time to close the book on those more intimate issues, the really emotional ones. A partnership will help you get what you need. Just know that partnership can take more shapes than a log at a chainsaw carving contest."

Tanck finished her recitation, took her scrapbook, and returned it to its place. Without turning her head, she reiterated what I suppose she thought were the salient bits.

"I have learned things the hard way, indeed. I am not from around here, as I am sure you know, so it is obvious this is speaking directly to me. It is time to close the book on intimate issues. Could it be any more clear? A partnership is needed. You asked, why you? Why not Leonard? It is obvious. He is the log that has felt the chainsaw while the partner I require can take many shapes."

Vilde turned to face me, her beauty almost impossible to bear. "You see, Mr. Shade? It is time to progress with my plans. As unlikely as a partnership with the likes of you may be, the clarity I feel is unmistakable." She pierced me with her radiant eyes. "I trust that now you understand?"

*I hate you, Clarissa Steyer,* I grumbled to myself.

"Fine. Sure. You've convinced me," I said in a hearty tone. "Neat stuff, those horoscopes. Super specific." I threw back another swig of the potent brew and said, "Speaking of specifics, let's get the important ones out of the way. Who has the book, where do they live, and you said, 'Handsomely rewarded.' Define 'handsomely,' because my definition might be a smidge bigger than yours."

What followed wasn't exactly a negotiation, but I still dragged it out long enough to have more lefse and another glass of that fantastic liquor. It was a damned good thing, too. After hearing all the details of the job, I really needed a buttery, sugary pastry and a stiff drink.

# CHAPTER 4



*Ope! It's your horoscope, Scorpio!*
*Always plan ahead, but remember: A plan is just a list of things that won't go as planned.*

---

"**I** THINK THAT'S ONE of your best."

Jay *hmph'd*. It'd been weeks since my crack about me saving my shit so he could make art with it, but he was still a little salty. I'd tried beer, a portobello mushroom sandwich from his favorite spot, even a tee-shirt with 'Conspiracy Realist' emblazoned on the front. but had yet to win my way back into his good graces. That last attempt had earned me a brief smile, but then he'd used the shirt to wipe paint off a brush while calmly pointing out that there were likely micro-tracking devices sewn into the seams.

"C'mon, man. I said I'm sorry. Clarissa rubbed me the wrong way. I was more pissed than usual, and I shouldn't have said what I said. How long are you going to be mad?"

Jay didn't look at me. Instead, he scrutinized his completed project.

"I'm not mad, August. I'm hurt."

"You. Don't. Make. Shit. You are an artist. You channel the very essence of creation. You take the improbable and make it real. You expand horizons. Challenge perceptions. Redefine the very fabric of the universe. You're a god," I gushed. "A great big, creative god."

That got a laugh.

"You're an asshole," Jay replied. "You really like it?"

I honestly did. Me and art weren't exactly compatible, but this particular creation managed to short-circuit my general aversion to the finer things in life. The old diner tabletop jukebox had been lovingly restored and simultaneously appealed to my appreciation for music and affinity for anything older than I was. Jay's efforts had focused mainly on the song catalog that would flip rigid page after page when you pressed the back-and-forth buttons. The little cards with song titles and artist names had been removed. In their place, the left-hand page had a musician's portrait skillfully painted by Jay, and the right-hand page had a single song by the musician at the top with a number to play it. Beneath the song info was a hand-typed note debunking the circumstances of that particular musician's death, real or faked. It was currently showing the King of Rock and Roll in his classic knock-kneed, swinging hips and flailing arm pose. The song "Suspicious Minds" was written across the top of the opposite page. Beneath it was a list of first-hand accounts of Elvis sightings after August 16th, 1977.

"It's insanely cool," I breathed. "Does it work?"

In response, he handed me a dime. I dropped it in the slot and pressed a button to cycle through the cards. Paul McCartney, replaced by a double. Jimi Hendrix, killed by the CIA. Tupac, alive and well in the South Pacific. When I got to Kurt Cobain, I hit play, and "About A Girl" jumped from the speakers.

"Unbelievably, superbly cool. Immersive and subversive, and the portraits are fantastic. Damn, Jay. You've outdone yourself."

Finally, my friend's face lit up with a genuine smile, the first he had offered since my shitty little shit comment. The relief I felt was surprising. I guess you don't know what you've got 'til it's gone, and Jay's friendship was something I never wanted to put at risk again.

"Well, what do you say we celebrate?" I asked. "It's beer o'clock, isn't it?"


We popped the tabs on a couple of cold ones and settled in, him in a rickety camping chair and me on a cracked bean bag. The open window filled the studio with warm light and a cool breeze, and the jukebox's music filled the space around us. Jay relaxed with the contentment only the happy end of a long endeavor can bring. I tried to match his mood, but the previous night's adventure was dragging me down.

"What would you do with five-thousand dollars?" I asked after a thoughtful swig.

"Lead shielding for the walls and ceiling, obviously. Finally stymie those snooping G-Men. Why? What would you do?"

I'd been wondering the same thing. Vilde Tanck had offered me five-thousand dollars. A five with three more zeros after it. For a book. It sounded insane until you heard the rest.

"Probably hire a bodyguard. If I did take this particular job, I think I'd need one."

I brought Jay up to speed on the previous night, starting with Tanckenstein getting the drop on me, recounting my meeting with Vilde Tanck, and finishing with a name.

"You're shitting me," he breathed. "She wants you to repo something from Dieter Saint James? He's big time, August. Like 'Forbes list of richest people' big."

"And a vampire," I added. "Old one, too. Maybe the oldest one in Minnesota."

My friend glanced around nervously. "If that's true, you wouldn't need a bodyguard. You would need to fake your death, get plastic surgery, and start a new life on Mars." Jay pushed a shaking hand through his hair. "How did you get caught up in this?"

That was the funny part. "A horoscope by Clarissa Steyer," I laughed.

Jay didn't laugh. In fact, he screamed.

"What? It's not that big of a deal," I reacted, startled. "I'll tell Vilde to shove it. I won't take the job. Horoscopes. Vampires. Cripes," I said with a laugh. "I'm dumb, not stupid."

Jay had stopped screaming, but his face was still stretched into a mask of stark terror. I realized he wasn't looking at me; he was looking past me toward his studio's door. Curious, I twisted in the bean bag–the motion producing a farty sound–and saw Tanckenstein standing inside the threshold.

"You should probably go wipe," the tall monstrosity offered in his sad-sack, raspy voice.

"That was the beanbag," I protested. "If it had been me, you'd be dead again. What are you doing here, anyway?"

Stein walked into the studio and proceeded to loom–actually *loom*–over me.

"You know why. You need to get Ms. Tanck's book."

I shook my head angrily. I don't like being threatened, intimidated, bullied, or told what to do by anyone or anything.

"The hell, I do," I growled. "Nope. Not worth it. I'm not going anywhere near Dieter Saint James."

Up until that moment, I hadn't realized that looming could have degrees.

"Yes, you are," he stated after making sure I'd taken full notice of his even more intimidating loom.

"No, I'm not."

A long, sad sigh slipped through the big cadaver's purple lips. "Ms. Tanck was right," he complained dejectedly and then squared his shoulders. "August, I like you. You're funny, but you won't be as funny without a tongue. Please say you'll take the job. Please," he repeated as I stared up from the beanbag in shock.

An icy dread settled heavily in my gut, but it didn't take long for the rising heat of my anger to thaw it.

"So, it's gonna be like that, is it?" I asked through gritted teeth.

When Stein nodded, I took a long breath in through my nostrils and let it slip out through my pursed lips. I counted slowly down from ten to one. I pictured kittens playing in a grassy field. After all of that, my blood pressure was still redlining. I muscled myself up from the beanbag and went toe to toe with the much larger man.

"I can shift into a gorilla."

Vilde's henchman didn't blink.

"An elephant."

Again, nothing.

"I said, an *elephant*. A great big one. Tusks and everything."

That, at least, got a reaction. Tanckenstein shrugged.

"Fuck," I cursed. "How strong are you, anyway?"

"Pretty strong," he admitted.

Danger is a funny thing. We tend to react more strongly to the imminent kind. Sure, breaking into Dieter's place and stealing a book would be dangerous, but in a yeah-but-that's-later sort of way. Having my tongue pulled out at that exact moment...

"Fine. Great. Sign me up. Glad to be part of Team Tanck," I said with forced nonchalance. "Jay, meet Tanckenstein. Me and him work for the same lady. Stein, this is Jay."

My friend's eyes were wide as saucers, and his mouth worked like it was full of peanut butter. When he was finally able to make words, the ones that came out were, "Dead. He's dead. You weren't kidding. The guy's dead."

"Kinda," the two-legged jigsaw puzzle agreed sadly. "And my name's actually Leonard."

The not-dead dead guy crossed the space and held out a hand wound with scars, staples, and stitches. Jay recoiled like it was a cobra and blubbered something that might've been, "Eek, no way," or maybe, "Yeep, old hay," or even, "Heek, no play." It really was anyone's guess. The little jukebox picked that moment to switch off, the sudden silence adding to the awkwardness. Leonard–a.k.a. Tanckenstein because it really was a much better name–raised an eyebrow and dropped his hand. Something that might've been hurt skittered across his expression but was gone before I could even be sure it had been there.

"Got another one of those," he asked me, pointing at my beer.

"You can drink beer? Huh. You struck me as more of a formaldehyde-on-the-rocks kind of guy." I hit up the fridge and grabbed a couple of cold cans. "Don't mind Jay. He hasn't met many zombies or whatever. Jay, don't be rude," I scolded while passing Leonard the beer, "or he'll eat your brains."

Tanckenstein took the beer. "I'm not a zombie. I'm a revenant," he clarified after taking a drink.

Jay had recovered enough from the shock to push himself to his feet and offer a tremulous apology. When Tanckenstein extended his hand again, Jay tentatively took its grasp. When he didn't explode, he gripped the offered hand more firmly and gave it a shake.

"I'm sorry. I really am sorry," he said. "That wasn't like me at all. I just. I haven't, you know. Met a formerly dead person before. I'm Jay."

Tanckenstein replied with a nod. "You're an artist?" he asked as he leaned in to admire the musician portraits in the jukebox. "Ms. Tanck says artists are the only ones who don't go through life looking at the back of their eyelids."

And just like that, any reservations Jay had about a dead guy threatening to rip his friend's tongue out vanished. While the artist blushed, Tanckenstein snapped a few picks of the jukebox with his phone, then found a chair and dragged it over. After plopping down, he turned his jaundiced eyes toward me and asked, "So, what's your plan?"

By 'plan,' he apparently meant a plan to get Vilde Tanck's book back from a vampire that was as old as sin, stinking rich, and–if rumors were true–impossibly mean. Like, kick puppies to break in a new pair of loafers mean. The more I thought about what I knew about Dieter Saint James, the more I thought Tanck was getting a bargain by only paying me five grand. Scenarios flashed through my mind in glaring Technicolor. I'd knock on Dieter's front door, ask for the book back... and he'd pull my kidneys out through my nostrils. I'd sneak in, grab the book, get caught, and he'd pull my kidneys out through my nostrils. I'd hire a homeless guy to climb down the chimney, and he'd catch that guy, pull his kidneys out through his nostrils, and then find me and–yep, you guessed it–pull my kidneys out through my nostrils. There wasn't a single scenario I could dredge up that didn't end with me dying a painful and kidney-free death. But, hey, at least I'd die with clear sinuses.

"I don't have one," I confessed. "Hell, five minutes ago, I wasn't doing the job. Now you expect me to have a plan? Christ, you're annoying. I'm way out of my league, Stein. Unless you think you can go toe-to-toe with a centuries-old vampire."

"Maybe," he said with a shrug. "Ms. Tanck says I shouldn't underestimate myself."

"Leonard," I started carefully, using his actual name to convey how important I felt my next question was. "How strong are you? Like, if you were a *Dungeons and Dragons* character, what would your stats be?"

His eyes widened a smidge. "I didn't peg you as a gamer, August. No offense, but you need friends for those types of games, and you don't strike me as much of a people-person."

I waved off his spot-on observation and Jay's delighted laughter and pressed the question. This job had 'suicide' written all over it. If I really did have a superhero in my back pocket, I wanted to know.

The reanimated man took a thoughtful sip of his beer. "My D&D character sheet? Never thought about it that way. I guess I'd be high strength and dexterity, high constitution, moderate wisdom. Pretty low charisma," he said, his puffy, purple eyelids sagging in self-recrimination, "but I'd definitely have a weapons bonus for things like clubs and crowbars."

Jay cleared his throat. "Sorry, um. I was kind of wondering how high 'high' is."

"I can lift the Beemer's tail off the ground," he said. "And Ms. Tanck has this idea that really big rocks look pretty in the backyard gardens. She calls them glacial artistry. I have to pick those up and move them around from time to time. They're pretty heavy." He tapped his chin thoughtfully. "One guy Ms. Tanck had me go after threw a knife at me. I caught it. Another guy shot me, and, well, that didn't really do much. Then I tossed him into a wall that was probably, oh... I don't know... maybe ten, fifteen feet away? Guy looked like a juiced orange after."

"Okay, okay. Geezus, man," I exclaimed. "Stop talking. Please, just stop."

While Tanckenstein had been detailing his exploits, Jay had shrunk into a ball in his camping chair. "Why? Why would you do that for her?" he asked, aghast.

Broad shoulders lifted and fell. "I owe her my life."

"But she only saved your life after she had you killed," Jay said slowly, each word heavy with incredulity.

"It's complicated," Tanckenstein agreed. "Anyway, how are you going to get that book, August?"

We were right back to where we started, except it was even harder to think of a plan when I knew that failure could end with me getting thrown... oh, I don't know... maybe ten or fifteen feet into a wall and pulped like a juiced orange.

"Beers?" I asked to buy myself time to think. When they both nodded, I grabbed a couple of more cans and tossed one to each. After popping the tab on a fresh one for myself, I settled back into my bean bag. "So, what do we actually know about Dieter Saint James?"

For the next half hour or so, we pooled our collective knowledge. From what we put together, there were actually three Dieter Saint James. The most public version was a successful but reclusive businessman that lived in Wayzata, a western suburb full of richie-rich rich people. That Dieter Saint James owned a staggering number of tanning salons throughout the Midwest. When Stein shared the source of the vampire's enormous wealth, I snorted hard enough to send beer out of my nose, and Jay did a full-on spit-take. The second Saint James was a little shadier. Rumors about money laundering, extortion rackets, and more were continually swirling, but nothing ever stuck. If there was an honest buck in this bank account, it was very, very lonely. The third Saint James was the one the PNs whispered about after checking over their shoulders. If the rumors were true–and Tanckenstein assured us they were–that Saint James was a necromancer.

"He brought me back," Tanckenstein confessed. "After Ms. Tanck tossed me in a woodchipper, she felt pretty bad, so she had Saint James stitch me back together and bring me back to life. Now I have to work for her for as long as Dieter's alive, which will be a long time."

"Wait. Vilde had Dieter Saint James make you a revenant, and now you have to serve her for, like, eternity? No offense, Stein, but I'm not sure who's worse: Dieter or your boss."

"You gotta love the poetic justice," Jay added thoughtfully. "She kills you, he brings you back to life and gives you back to her, she sends you to help August rip him off. It'd make a great daytime soap for the clinically insane."

Desperately seeking an off-ramp from the conversation we were on, I asked if Tanckenstein knew where the old vampire lived. He calmly informed that the Saint James estate was a castle on the shores of Lake Minnetonka.

"So, when you say 'castle,' you mean what, exactly?" I asked, a headache starting behind my left eyeball. I wasn't cut out for this. My job usually involved knocking on someone's door, informing them that they needed to hand something over, and then leaving with the thing. Sure, some of the jobs were a little on the sneakier side, and others got a bit rough, but most were straightforward enough. Storming castles wasn't exactly in my wheelhouse.

"I mean castle," Tanckenstein replied matter-of-factly. "Built with big stone blocks. Turrets. Narrow windows. Even a moat. Supposedly, it's a block-by-block replica of one in northern Romania that's been in his family for generations."

The burgeoning headache worked its way around the back of my skull, so I squeezed one eye shut and knuckled the flesh behind my ear. "Great. Just flippin' great. We'll pop over to Wayzata, swim across a moat, break into a castle, grab the book and be back in time for last call. Piece of cake."

"There's a drawbridge, so no need to swim, and we can take my car," Tanckenstein offered in what he must've thought was an optimistic tone.

As if how we'd get there was all I had to worry about.

After deciding to take the night off and reconvene in the morning, we'd gone our separate ways. Jay kicked us out of his studio so he could lock up. Tanckenstein said he could give him a ride home since he was already nowhere near Ms. Tanck's, and driving an extra few minutes couldn't make things any worse. To my surprise, Jay accepted. Despite knowing the guy for years, I was continually amazed by his ability to take literally anything in stride, even a lift from a walking dead guy. Vilde Tanck's henchman reminded me he'd be at my place promptly at ten the next morning. And me? I knew I had a busy few days ahead. I also knew that there was a good chance they'd be my last. Seemed like a waste to just go back to my dumpy apartment and count mouse poops until I fell asleep, so I opted for a few beers and a Hail Mary. What can I say? Death loomed, and I didn't want to shuffle off this mortal coil with any more regrets than absolutely necessary.

I popped home for a cleanish shirt and headed straight to the bar—yes, that bar—fingers and toes crossed that the succubus would be working. When I pulled open the heavy door and peered into the gloomy interior, she was the first and only thing my eyes saw. My feet moved the rest of me, and my belly hit the bar like a Higgins boat beaching on the Normandy coast. The bartender startled, then smiled.

"August!" she purred. "Been a while. I was starting to think you didn't like me. What do you need?"

"The answer to three questions," I blurted out. "Am I still on your list, what time do you get off work, and what's your name?"

The guy next to me guffawed. I ignored him and held my breath.

"You seriously don't remember my name?" she asked after a long pause.

No good excuses came to mind, so I shrugged.

"Well, if you can dredge it up, then yes and around two. Maybe earlier if it's slow. You need a beer to help your memory?"

Three beers later, I still couldn't remember her name. The clock was ticking, and desperation was setting in.

"Juniper," I called out when she crossed to the far end of the bar to refresh a woman's Cosmopolitan.

"No."

"Alice," I tried while she poured a round of shots for a group of obnoxious twenty-somethings that were celebrating one member of their ranks surviving another year.

"Nope."

"Rebecca?" I guessed when she came back from the basement with a pail of ice.

"Swing and a miss."

"Can I get a hint?"

She rolled her eyes and pulled her phone out of her back pocket. The succubus didn't call or text or selfie or anything one would normally do with a phone. She just held it up with an expectant look. The case had the pin-up girl I remembered from before.

"Phone," I puzzled. "Phone. Phone. Phonecia! No, that's dumb. Text. Call. Call... Colleen? Collette?"

Her lips pressed together, and her eyes flashed. The phone slid back into her jean pocket—no small feat given how big the phone was and how tight her pants were—and she turned her profile to me. Her knees locked, her back arched, and she leaned forward, hands sliding down the front of her thighs. Her tank top stretched dangerously tight across her breasts, her perfect lips puffed at the straight bangs brushing the top of her dark eyebrows, and her long eyelashes batted coquettishly. It was the exact pose of the girl on the phone's case. I stared, along with the four or five other people lining the bar. A lot of words ran through my brain, but none were names. She waggled her rear end and set other parts of her swaying as well.

"Jiggles?"

That got me a laugh and a middle finger, but didn't get me any closer to her actual name.

My fourth beer was half empty, and the clock on the wall was smugly informing me I only had about an hour to get it right. I wrangled my libido into submission and forced myself to think. It had been winter when she'd called. I couldn't remember much about the day, much less the month, but I knew my socks hadn't matched. My feet had been up on my desk, crossed at the ankles, when the phone rang. I'd reached for the receiver and cursed when I realized I was rocking a one black, one orange sock combo. I don't know why I'd been so annoyed. I don't pay a lot of attention when I get dressed. I have clothes. Some go on my upper half. Others go on my lower half. If I get that right, I call it a win. But that particular day, I'd been pretty ticked about my Halloween-themed ankles.

So. That was good. I knew it had been winter, and I'd been wearing mismatched socks. Progress. What else could I remember?

Her voice. I figured that I'd hear that voice in my dreams for the rest of my life. It was the kind of voice that seeped into you, into the parts of you that you forgot were there, and made them all warm and tingly. If a voice could give you a massage, promise you a winning lotto ticket, wrap you up in a fuzzy blanket, pour you a hot cup of brandy, and hit you with a thousand volts all at the same time, it still wouldn't compare to what it was like to hear her voice for the first time. Small wonder I'd missed part of our conversation, including the bit where she'd probably told me her name. By the time I was able to focus on what she'd been saying, she was already talking about Tony and the little satchel of herbs she wanted back. I'd taken down the warlock's address, promised to swing by his place later that week, and guaranteed that I'd have her herbs by Sunday afternoon.

"Super Bowl Sunday!" I proclaimed.

The guy next to me gave me a look and shifted a couple of inches further away. I didn't care. Details were coming back. Nothing overly helpful yet, but that was okay. If I could pry another few loose, maybe I'd find the key log and clear the jam.

It had been the week before the Super Bowl, so the last week of January. Winter had been kicking ass and taking names. I remembered waiting for the bus that would get me across town and freezing my ass off. It had been cold that week. Freezing. Single-digit highs and below-zero lows.

"And I was wondering if the bus driver would mind if a wolverine caught a ride," I recalled, earning another skeptical glance from my next-stool neighbor.

"What?" I asked. "It should tell you something that I'd rather talk to myself than you."

That remark earned me a testy "Asshole" before he moved a few stools further down the bar. I gave him a goofy grin and went back to dredging up anything else I could remember about that day.

Tony the Warlock lived on the city's south side in a brownstone almost as crummy as mine. The big difference was that his building's security door still worked. I'd found his name and apartment number and then buzzed every door except his. A moment later, an irresponsible neighbor let a stranger in. I loved irresponsible neighbors. They made my job so much easier. I'd already made it up the first flight of stairs when I heard the building's security door shut. Two more flights, and I was jogging down a dimly lit hallway's mildewed carpet, head swiveling as I looked for the door with his number. After finding it, I'd pressed my ear against the door and stilled my breath for as long as I could go without breathing. I didn't know how much noise warlocks typically made when they were home but figured there'd be something. The muttering of ancient curses. The bleating of soon-to-be-sacrificed goats. The bubbling of a cauldron full of snips and snails and demon-dog tails. I hadn't heard any of those things, nor the more common sounds of apartment living, so I'd picked the lock and stepped into Tony the Warlock's domain.

I took another sip of beer and let my mind fully explore the memory of that first experience with bat shit crazy. Tony's apartment had been incongruity incarnate. I remembered thinking that someone had taken the worst parts of a frat house, tattoo parlor, comic book convention, and magic shop, stuffed them in a blender, and poured the resulting sludge all over a one-bedroom apartment. I also remember thinking there was no way in hell I'd find a little satchel of herbs amidst all the insane crap he had piled on every flat surface.

"Hey!" I called out and waited for the bartender to turn her head. When she did, I asked, "Remember when I grabbed your little sack of herbs from Tony's? What did you say they smelled like?"

She raised an eyebrow and sidled closer, one hand idly wiping the bar with a towel along the way.

"Musk and honeysuckle," she replied with a confused smile, "even though they most definitely are more than that. I did tell you what they're for, didn't I?"

Had she? Hell if I could remember, so I shrugged.

"Well, let's just say if you swallowed them too slowly, you'd get a stiff neck. Think you'll need some for later?"

*Stiff neck?* I thought. *What did that... Oooh.*

I waved off her question and awkwardly assured her I was good to go. I brought my pint glass to my lips to hide my blushing face and turned inward again. Musk and honeysuckle. Another moment from that day found its way into my consciousness. I hadn't really known what either one smelled like, so I'd stopped by a little corner store on my block before heading to the bus stop. The lady that ran it loved incense and oils. It didn't take long to find a little vial labeled "Midnight Musk" and a pack of incense called "Heavenly Honeysuckle." I'd shoved each to my nose and taken good, long sniffs before I'd waved my thanks and headed back into the cold.

When I'd been in Tony's apartment, staring with awe at the staggering amount of crap one douchey human had fit into a few hundred square feet, I'd decided a quick shift would make life a lot easier. After shrugging off my winter coat and kicking off my boots, my legs and arms dwindled, my ears stretched and drooped, my nose and mouth lengthened, and a wiry tail sprouted from right above my ass-crack. A moment later, a bloodhound in a gray sweatshirt and boxers was casting its head about and sniffing the air. There were a million smells to wade through, but two, in particular, lit up like the filaments in a Tungsten bulb: the sweet, heady smell of musk and pungent, fruity smell of honeysuckle. I'd followed the twining scents into the bedroom. The trail had ended at a bedside table. Bingo.

All I would have had to do was shift back to my human form, quickly pull on my clothes, grab the herbs and get out. Easy peasy. I would've had the prize, and Tony the Warlock would've been none-the-wiser. But no. I had to be a jerk.

The wait for the bus had been long, the bus ride itself had been longer, and I'd had a lot of coffee when I'd started the day. I'd traipsed over to a pile of clothes on the floor, lifted a leg, and let a warm stream loose. Then I'd trotted back into the living room, found a pile of dusty leather-bound books on the floor, and had given them a good soaking as well. There had been a pair of boots by the front door–really over-the-top boots with three-inch-thick soles and as much shiny metal as black leather–that were practically begging to be filled with pee, so I obliged. I had just returned to the bedroom and hopped up onto the bed–my stubby legs requiring a few attempts before I'd made it–when I'd heard the apartment's front door open. Tony the Warlock had walked in, crossed through the living room, and stopped in the bedroom's doorway right as I'd started to piss on his pillows.

I chuckled at the memory and took another sip of beer. It really had been funny. He'd screamed a few obscenities and then leaped for the bed. I'd hopped to the floor and heard more cursing when he realized he'd landed face-first in a puddle of dog piss. I'd shifted back into my human form, yanked open the bedside table's drawer, and grabbed a little leather pouch that was resting amidst a few condoms, a tube of something I refused to think about, and some fuzzy handcuffs. I'd raced for the exit and slammed the bedroom door behind me right as Tony slammed into it with enough force to rattle the windows. The door opened into the bedroom, so I had grasped the handle with both hands, braced my feet, and pulled as hard as I could. Tony had pulled from the other side just as hard, maybe even harder.

We'll never know who would've won that impromptu tug of war because I had counted to three and then let go. The door had sailed open, and Tony had careened backward, cursing like a sailor after slamming up against the far wall. They were impressively angry words, words I'd never heard before. Despite a sudden interest in expanding my curse lexicon, I'd put the precious time to good use. I'd yanked on my clothes and high-tailed it out of there, laughing the entire way back to the bus stop. My client had stopped by my office later that week. I'd discovered that she looked every bit as good as she sounded on the phone, had drooled and babbled as we traded a little leather bag for a fistful of bills, and then we'd parted ways.

"It must've been there," I mused. "Guy was obsessed with her. There must've been something with her name on it."

I finished my beer and glanced at the clock. The hands told me more than the time. They told me it was time for some drastic measures. I spun on my stool and headed for the bathroom. Once inside, I pushed into the handicap-accessible stall without a moment of guilt, stripped, and prepared to shift into the only thing that could possibly help in my current situation. I just hoped the stall was big enough to hold an elephant.

A moment later, my ribs pressed against brick on one side and the metal partition on the other. I could feel the toilet against the backs of my gray and wrinkled legs, and my broad forehead rested against the other wall. I flapped my ears a bit and curled my trunk. The elephant was more than a little freaked out. The neighborhood dive bar's bathroom was not the wide-open savanna. I forced myself to relax as much as I could, thought back on when I'd been in Tony's apartment, and let details cascade across my awareness. I knew I had to be fast–someone discovering an elephant in the handicap-accessible stall was definitely going to raise eyebrows, especially because I didn't have a wheelchair–but I also knew I couldn't rush the experience. It's absolutely one-hundred and twelve percent true that elephants have excellent memories, but that doesn't mean it's like a Rolodex you can flip through until you find the right card. Their memories are more associative and rely heavily on smells. Lucky for me, the bathroom smelled quite a bit like Tony's apartment. I focused on the cornucopia of scents, layered in what I could recall from my brief foray into his bachelor pad, and let the memories swirl around me like leaves riding a strong breeze.

*Yes. THAT! What was that?*

I'd been remembering the bedroom in a totally next-level way. My human brain had some general recollections of the basics. It knew the room had a window. It knew the walls were a deep purple. It knew there'd been carpet and some furniture. That was about it, though. Let's be honest. Human brains generally suck when it comes to remembering shit. My elephant brain, though, knew quite a bit more. It had been two windows, not one, and they'd been double hung with gray, gauzy curtains tied back with lengths of thin silver chain. The walls hadn't just been purple; they'd had a matte finish and had been covered with heavy metal band posters. The bed was queen-sized with a black pleated leather headboard, black satin comforter, and matching pillows. The bedside table was a chintzy excuse for hand-welded industrial steel, rubbed and stained by some schlub in a distant factory to give it a smelted and sooty look. There'd been a pedestal in one corner that was carved from dark and smokey-smelling wood with a fake skull on top, and a three-tiered bookshelf made of unfinished lumber spanning stacked-up cinder blocks lined the wall opposite the windows.

All interesting details in their way, but none were overly helpful until my elephant brain noticed an open spiral-bound notebook on the bookshelf's top board. It sat between a tome titled *Eschatology: The Means to the End* and a copy of that month's *Metro Pages*. There, right there, were a few scrawled lines of what Tony probably thought was poetry. My human brain had completely forgotten that I'd stopped to glance at the page. My elephant brain didn't just remember; it had memorized the flippin' poem:

"Night's mistress, winged desire

Sweet release of passion's fire

On my lips, Betty's name

Consume me with your passionate flame

The seas will boil, the land will crack

The skies will fill with clouds of black

One caress will set us free

No one left but you and me..."

Suddenly, her little clues clicked. My ears flapped as I shook my head. I really did put the id in stupid. The case on her phone, the classic pin-up pose with her straight black hair and bangs. Gorgeous and gothy. Sex incarnate as only a succubus could be. And her name was...

"Betty, like Betty Page!" I hollered, triumphant. Of course, I didn't actually yell, "Betty," because elephants can't talk. They can trumpet, though, and the sudden and very loud blurting was about as close as an elephant can get to saying Betty or any other name for that matter.

"What the fuck?" a shocked voice exclaimed from the other side of the partition.

I melted back to my human form, flushed, and quickly pulled my clothes on while trying not to think of what my bare feet had been standing in. A moment later, I nonchalantly stepped out of the stall and saw the guy I'd sat next to at the bar earlier.

"I wouldn't go in there," I advised. He nodded, wide eyes following me warily as I skipped from the bathroom.

"Betty, Betty, bo-Betty!" I sang as I hurried back to the bar, grinning like a simpleton. "Banana-fanna-fo-fetty. Mee-mi-mo-metty. Betty! Sex, sex, bo-bex. Banana-fanna fo-fex…"

Last call had come and gone while I'd been away, and Betty was shooing the barflies out with all the usual lines:

"You don't have to go home, but you can't stay here."

"You have too had enough, Rodney. Your urine sample has an olive in it."

"Sure, you can stay if you want to pay rent."

I watched her all googly eyed while she rounded up the regulars and shuffled them out of her bar. Maybe it was the beer, or maybe it was the euphoria of knowing her name and knowing all the crazy, kinky stuff that was sure to follow, but I was stupefied. Every movement, every gesture, every expression on her gorgeous face was stunning.

"You, too," she said.

"Me too, what?" I asked, elbow resting on the bar and chin propped on my fist.

"Off you go. I've got to lock up."

I winked. "You bet. You got a pen back there? I'll write down my address."

Betty sighed. "Gee, hon. Guess I'm not feeling it. Maybe next time, huh?"

Next time? Next time? Her words rekindled thoughts of a vampire in a castle and my kidneys coming out through my nostrils. There wouldn't be a 'next time.'

"But… Your list. And me. I'm on it. And your name's Betty. I know that now." She raised an eyebrow, but I foolishly pressed on. "So that means that we're, you know. You and me and the naked stuff, right?"

She sighed again, crossed her arms, and glared. "You really are something, August Shade. A regular Cyrano. Look, hon. I'm honestly not that hungry, and–call me crazy–but I just don't find your childish entitlement to be all that sexy."

Ouch. That tossed my buzz and libido into a bucket of ice water. After the shock wore off, I wasn't mad. Frustrated, embarrassed, and plunging into my usual dark swirl of dark thoughts, but not mad. Hell, I couldn't fault her. I saw myself in a new light, one that revealed me to be nothing more than another half-drunk weirdo that hadn't given any thought to her or who she was or what she might want. I don't think I'll ever be known as Captain Chivalrous, but I'm also not a complete asshole. At least, I hadn't thought I was one until that exact moment.

"Yeah. Um, yeah. Well," I stammered while fumbling for my wallet and pulling out a couple of twenties. I just wanted to be gone–gone and alone–and the few moments spent trying to pay for my beers were excruciating. I finally got the money on the bar and turned for the door. A few steps later, she called my name.

"Yeah?" I asked, turning.

"Did you shift into an elephant in the bathroom?"

I hunched my shoulders and ducked my head. "Maybe."

"Why?"

"I really wanted to remember your name, and they have good memories."

Betty pursed her lips and *hmph'd*. "That's... sweet. Weird, but sweet. Have a good night, August the elephant." Her fingers flicked me toward the door like she was brushing crumbs from her lap.

"You, too, Betty the bartender."

Later, as I lay across my couch alone, a bottle of whiskey dangling from my listless fingers, I thought of all the things ordinary people did when they were into someone. The little ways I could've shown interest. The flirty stuff I could've said. The questions I should have asked. What kind of music did she like? Did she have a favorite restaurant? What about current events or politics? How long had she been tending bar? Which of her boobs did she like better?

My ineptitude pressed me deeper into my mattress. I'd never been much for dating, and the reasons why were on full display. I was an idiot. A selfish, grumpy idiot with the emotional intelligence of a sea cucumber. Even Tony had more game than me, a realization that almost sent me swan-diving from my window. Only the fact that I lived in the basement kept me on the couch. With a world-weary sigh full of petulant self-pity, I set the whiskey on the coffee table and stumbled to my bedroom. The room tilted and sent me falling past the mattress and onto the floor. Hell, I couldn't even get using a bed right.

# CHAPTER 5



A HEAVY POUNDING ON my door dragged me from my slumber, and I woke with a scream.

"End of the world!"

The pounding on my door stopped, but my heart was still hammering. Whatever nightmare I'd been drowning in had been a doozy. My shirt was damp with sweat, and my hands were shaking. Details were fading faster than sidewalk chalk under a garden hose, but I still gasped for breath while my wide eyes frantically tried to see every possible catastrophe lurking in every possible shadow. Only the fact that my mattress was on the floor kept me from scurrying beneath it.

"No," a familiar mopey voice said from the other side of my apartment door, "it's morning, but I get that some people might confuse the two."

I managed to find my feet and staggered across the dingy box I called home. When I pulled the door open, Leonard filled the resulting space.

"I brought breakfast," he informed me as he welcomed himself in. "Egg and cheese on English muffins. One with bacon. One with sausage. I didn't know what you liked, so I grabbed both. I hope you're not vegetarian. You're probably vegetarian. Ms. Tanck says I should be more considerate. I'm sorry. I didn't think that you might be a vegetarian."

I swiped the bag from his hand and pulled one at random from inside. "That's Jay," I reassured him. "He only eats plants. I only eat things that had a face. No coffee?"

The large man held a cup up in response, steam rising enticingly from the lid's sip-hole. I snatched it from his fingers and burned my mouth as I sucked down the scalding brew. Between gulps, I devoured both sandwiches while Tanckenstein watched with unmasked envy.

"I don't need to eat anymore," he lamented. "I can, and sometimes I do, but it all tastes like bath towels and comes out weird later."

I tried to push out the image he'd lobbed into my brain. While I scrunched up my face and shook my head, Tanckenstein considered the two pieces of furniture I owned. Leaving him to make his own decisions, I headed for my kitchen sink and pulled off my shirt. While I splashed lukewarm tap water into each armpit, Stein pulled out the month's *Metro Pages* from his hoodie's pouch, unfolded it, and flipped to the back.

"Ms. Tanck says you have to read your horoscope, and Jay says you're a Sagittarius," he explained. "Let's see... Um, looks like June could be a good month to move ahead in your career. You'll get a new opportunity, something big time. Lucky you. Of course, it doesn't mention that you could die a horrible death, but these things are always so upbeat. What else? Something, something, moon and Jupiter. Oh, you'll need more than hands to grab that prize. Not sure what that means. Maybe you should start carrying an oven mitt or some tongs. What else... It says someone will lend you strength." Tanckenstein scratched his chin. "Guess that's me. Spot on so far."

"Please stop," I growled while I hunted for a cleaner pair of socks than the pair I'd slept in. I was half-successful and decided that would have to do.

"Can't," Stein apologized. "Ms. Tanck swears by these things and said I have to read yours."

I found a stick of deodorant behind a half-empty box of cereal and rubbed it in my pits while Tanckenstein continued his torture.

"There's a bit about Neptune's difficult angle to the new moon. I guess that means that a job might look a little too good to be true. Says you should be careful and ask questions."

"Will you please shut up?"

"Probably not that kind of question. Hmm. Mercury will be in retrograde next month, so you're supposed to hurry up and finish big projects. Oh, and you might get relationship news." The large man raised a stitched-on eyebrow. "Do you have a girlfriend, August?"

"No. And if you say one more horoscopy word, I swear to Pete I'm gonna rent a woodchipper."

I leaned over my kitchen sink, splashed water onto my face, and scrubbed my stubbled cheeks. Hands still wet, I pulled and patted my hair until it felt like it was only going in a few different directions. After wiping my face with the paper napkins that had accompanied the breakfast sandwiches and pulling on a different—and hopefully cleaner—shirt than what I'd slept in, I pronounced myself ready to roll.

Tanckenstein gave me a long look. "Don't take this the wrong way, August, but I think I'm starting to understand why you don't have a girlfriend."

Memories from the prior night surfaced. I wasn't going to give Tanckenstein the satisfaction of realizing how right he was, so I didn't say anything as I followed him out to the car. I'd been expecting the BMW and walked right past the piece-of-shit on three wheels and a donut spare. It wasn't until I heard a scratchy throat being cleared that I stopped and looked back. Tanckenstein was standing next to the little rolling death-trap with an elbow resting on its roof.

"Where's the Beemer?" I asked suspiciously.

"Too nice," he replied. "Too new. We need this for the plan to work."

Watching Tanckenstein squish himself behind the little car's steering wheel was funny, but I was too confused to be distracted by the situational comedy for long.

"Plan?" I asked.

Stein put the beater in gear, and we lurched forward. A loud grinding signified the transmission's Herculean effort to get from first to second gear. Another grind heralded the jump from second to third. I was actually pretty impressed when he got it up to fourth gear but still double-checked my seatbelt, just in case.

"A potential plan," he placated. "You didn't have a plan, and Ms. Tanck says I should know when to not let perfect be the enemy of good, so I made a plan," he explained. When I glared, he added, "It doesn't have to be *the* plan."

Tanckenstein's explanation of the plan took less than two minutes. Then, for the next half hour or so, we argued and debated, negotiated and sparred around every facet of that plan and a host of others. It was exhausting, but at least thinking about my possible death at the fangs of Dieter was a nice distraction from the almost certain death the little car promised. It rattled down the freeway too slowly for the other cars around us, but still much too fast for my tastes. Finally, Stein took an exit. After winding through a series of residential neighborhoods, each less trafficked and closer to the lakeshore than the one before, he let the car roll to a stop. I released my seatbelt and leaned forward to take in the view.

High stone walls. Check. Narrow slits for windows. Check. Turrets cutting sharp silhouettes against a background of low-hanging clouds. Check. An actual drawbridge and moat. Goddamned motherfucking check. It was, in fact, a castle.

Despite Tanckenstein telling me that yes, Dieter Saint James lived in a castle, an honest-to-God castle, I'd stubbornly refused to believe it. Even as my eyes took in the hulking mass blocking half the sky, I still wanted to think it was a prank. I was sure that Tanckenstein was going to finally crack a gory smile and admit that, no, Dieter didn't live there. He lived in a little one-bedroom in a fourplex back in town, or a chic condo full of exposed brick and floor-to-ceiling windows, or an RV in the parking lot of the local big-box store. The car's engine muttered while I waited for the punchline, but Tanckenstein kept his silence. Finally, the little thread of denial I'd been clinging to snapped, and I cursed. A lot.

"Fuck. Goddamned son-of-a-bitch piece of shit vampire and his straight-from-Satan's-asshole castle. Fuck!"

Tanckenstein blinked at my sudden outburst and then returned his attention to the world beyond the windshield. I forced myself to do the same, and the Saint James estate again filled my vision. It was a sprawling expanse littered with low outbuildings hunkered between old trees and dominated by the medieval monstrosity. It looked big enough to house a small town, and I found myself wondering how the old vampire kept the place clean.

*Probably wipes the floor with the bodies of his victims,* I thought, *and then shoves a few under the doors to stop drafts in the winter.*

"Well, there it is," Tanckenstein observed, pulling me from my dark ponderings.

"Yep," I answered. I might've said more, but there really wasn't much else to say.

Our ride was glaringly out of place, and we were reluctant to draw attention by staying too long. We'd already decided that after a quick reconnoiter, we'd find a place to lie low for a while, so Tanckenstein convinced the car to make a U-turn and started back the way we'd come. The car's jerks and stutters and the road's bends and turns made it feel like a cheap carnival ride through a pretty swank neighborhood. Lake Minnetonka was more than a big lake. It was a sprawling body of water rife with inlets, coves, and bays. The modest homes lining its shores started in the upper six-digits, and the vampire's estate had to be worth millions. After weaving our way back to the slummier neighborhoods where the houses only cost four or five-hundred thousand apiece, we pulled into a strip mall that had a diner at one end. I poked my head in and then waved for Stein to follow. It was perfect. Despite its small size, it had an inexplicable number of dark corners. Seriously. I don't know how a place could have more corners than walls, but this place pulled it off, and they were all dark. It was practically begging for a shady shifter and a not-dead dead guy to plot and scheme over a steaming plate of tater tot hotdish and an ice-cold pop.

Tanckenstein sat in a creaking chair, shadows draping him like a worn blanket while I shoved the last bit of hotdish into my waiting mouth. I'd made it perfectly clear that I wouldn't be doing anything while eating except thoroughly enjoying my food. There was a strong likelihood that it would be the last thing I ever ate, and I didn't want to ruin it by talking about the plan.

"Now?" he asked as I licked my fingers and sighed.

"Fine. Wait, no. Not quite yet."

There was still a little pop left in my glass. I sucked on the straw until every sweet drop was gone, set the empty glass down reluctantly, and finally nodded.

"Okay. About the plan." I held up a finger to stop Tanckenstein from saying anything, took a deep breath, and stated, "It's a stupid plan. A terrible, idiotic plan that wouldn't even work in a bad made-for-T.V. movie. Vilde won't get her book back, and I'll be dead, which makes it a flat-out rotten plan."

The plan I had decried was the one Stein had proposed and the one we'd been arguing about since we'd left my apartment. The car didn't have a radio, so there had been little else to do besides ponder how we'd get into the veritable fortress, find Vilde Tanck's book, and get out alive. We'd actually considered lots of plans. All were impossible except for one: Tanckenstein's. That remaining plan ended up being *the* plan by default, but just because it was possible didn't make it good.

"August," Tanckenstein said, turning my name into an admonishment. "Ms. Tanck says..."

"I don't care what Ms. Tanck says. It's not going to work," I protested. "It can't work. No one can be that gullible."

He sighed, the sound reminding me of a fan ruffling loose papers on a desk. "Yes, they can. Stick to the script. You wanted to take a drive around the lake despite the storm. Your car started giving you some trouble. You need a place to stay for the night, and you'll get a tow truck in the morning. Dieter will agree. He's not just old. Ms. Tanck says he's old-fashioned. He won't turn someone away at night during a storm. It'd be rude. When everything is quiet, you sneak out of your room and find the book. Then you grab it, and we leave."

The storm he'd referred to was definitely brewing and looked ready to break. Before we'd stopped for dinner, the sky had been filling up with thick clouds. In the short time it had taken me to pack away my tater tot hotdish, a strong wind had pushed even more clouds across the lake and piled them up in the evening sky. The rain hadn't started yet, but a torrential downpour was a question of when, not if.

"I'm going to get caught."

"You aren't. Not if you're careful."

"There are going to be guards. Alarms. Cameras. Lasers."

"Lasers?" Tanckenstein asked.

"Lasers."

The big man sighed again. "You're a shapeshifter. Can't you shift? Be a field mouse, or housefly, or maybe a spider. If you're tiny, you won't have to worry about the lasers."

I scoffed. "A spider? Do you have an idea how long it would take a spider to crawl through an entire castle? Even if I had a spider in my repertoire–which I don't–that's the stupidest idea yet."

I was getting mad, and when I get mad, I get stubborn. My heels dug in hard enough to practically crack the diner's linoleum floor. Tanckenstein decided I was scared and making excuses. It was a stalemate. He wasn't going to relent, and I wasn't going to budge. After another glare-off, he finally yielded.

"Ms. Tanck says you're the one for the job, so you're the one for the job. I trust you, August."

I looked across the table suspiciously but didn't find a trace of sarcasm, just calm acceptance in his milky eyes.

"And I guess we'll go with your plan," I grumbled.

The storm chose that moment to break. Heavy torrents of rain suddenly fell from the sky and pounded the earth below. A long sigh escaped my lips. The plan was officially the plan, and it was time to set it in motion. I ran to where we'd parked but was still soaked through when I squeezed in behind the steering wheel. I reminded myself to count my blessings. At least I had a seat. Tanckenstein had folded himself into the little car's tiny trunk.

"All good back there?" I called out loudly.

"Not really," a muffled voice replied.

I retraced our earlier route, the car complaining about the many turns, me complaining about sitting in a puddle, and Tanckenstein complaining about the trunk's size. The curtains of rain sluicing down the windshield had rendered the headlights worthless and made it virtually impossible to see more than a few yards. I slowed to a crawl and willed the car to stay on the road. In what seemed like a lifetime later but was still too damned soon for my liking, I followed what I hoped was our earlier route until, miraculously, the wrought-iron gates of the Saint James estate materialized out of the rain.

"Execute Plan Dumb-as-a-Motherfucker, phase one," I whispered.

While the knuckles of one hand whitened on the steering wheel, my other hand pressed the horn. A few short bursts didn't accomplish anything, so I laid on it for a good half-minute. I was about to tell Tanckenstein that I'd told him so when the gates swung apart. I took my hand off the horn and waited. When nothing else happened, I put the car in first gear and alternately gave it too much gas and too little. The violent lurching made the half-digested hotdish in my stomach curse and threaten, but I clenched my jaw and stuck with the plan. Just because I couldn't see anyone didn't mean I wasn't being watched. I hoped my performance wasn't too over-the-top and worried briefly about poor Tanckenstein knocking around in the trunk. Then I remembered it had been his plan and subsequently stomped on the gas and then the brake again.

"Sorry," I called over my shoulder. "Car trouble, you know? Real pain in the ass."

His unexpected response was muffled, but I still understood him perfectly: "Ms. Tanck says it takes one to know one."

I barked a laugh and then forced my face back into its more natural grumpy frown. It wouldn't do to have someone catch me talking and laughing when I was supposed to be alone and pissed about my POS car. I idled up a long, crushed-stone driveway, the gray rocks virtually indistinguishable from the gray rain that enveloped me. The drive curved and brought me broadside to the front of the castle. I let the car lurch a couple more times and then put it in park without using the clutch, the gearbox giving a grinding curse in response. A twist of the key and the poor engine finally got a well-deserved break. I stared hard into the deluge and tried to see across the drawbridge. I couldn't see any lights winking from any windows, and the rain made it impossible to make out many details of the castle's front beyond a vague, dark rectangle that I assumed was the front door. Seconds stretched into minutes, but no one appeared. I tilted the rearview and gazed into my own worried eyes.

"Well, August... Time to do what you do."

I stepped out of the car and into the deluge. Crossing the handful of feet from the car to the lowered drawbridge's lip was more akin to swimming than walking. I figured I couldn't get any wetter if I jumped into the moat. A slightly deranged giggle slipped through my clenched teeth as I considered the idea, but my sanity prevailed. For all I knew, that moat was inhabited. Twenty paces brought me across the bridge and up to a pair of wooden doors so massive that the word 'door' barely applied. They were easily ten feet tall, wide enough to let a garbage truck through with room to spare, and solid as slabs of granite. What they lacked in artistic detail, they made up for in sheer imposing mass. The prospect of knocking seemed ridiculous–no one could possibly hear my puny rapping above the storm–but I didn't see any other options. I raised a fist, pulled it back by my ear… and the doors opened. Throwing caution to the strongly blowing wind, I quickly stepped through to escape the punishing rain. I wiped the water from my eyes and blinked them a few times before looking around.

When my eyes sent their signals back to my brain, my brain sputtered and stalled because it didn't have a point of reference for what I was seeing. Most of my clients lived in normal places: apartments, old houses, suburban McMansions, even the occasional fancy condo. Staring dumbstruck into the cavernous room I'd entered, I recalled stories of astronauts seeing the wide expanse of outer space for the first time and going into a sort of trance. My brain simply couldn't accept a structure as big as the Saint James castle as a place that someone lived. The sense of endless space was amplified by the near-lack of light. The only illumination came from a fireplace at the far end of the enormous room. Up close, it'd be taller than me and probably hotter than an industrial kiln, but from my current vantage point, it looked barely bigger than a campfire.

"Hello?" I called into the void. "Sorry to bother you. Um, car trouble, storm, yadda yadda, and I was thinking I could spend the night because why not, right?"

I cringed at my own stupid words. Whatever fantasies I'd harbored about being able to act my way out of this mess dropped like an off-Broadway flop's final curtain. I was screwed. Good and truly screwed. Only the fact that my entire life had been a series of debacles that I'd somehow survived kept my pulse steady.

"You survived the hospital," I reminded myself. "This ain't nothing. Just a big, spooky castle and a mean old vampire."

"Mean? Is that what they say?"

I screamed. Don't judge. I did point out that the whole experience was pretty damn scary. After clawing my heart back down from my throat, I stammered and sputtered and stumbled and stuttered for what felt like an hour before the voice recommended that I hush, and so I did.

"Better. Much better. Thank you," the man I could only assume was Dieter Saint James said.

He didn't look old. Hell, the guy barely looked a day over fifty, and he didn't look mean. Smarmy, sure, in a used car salesman kind of way, but not mean. The guy was wearing a performance turtleneck under a lightweight blazer, pleated khakis, and comfy-looking loafers. His hair was dark brown, parted on the side, and held in place by what had to be an enormous amount of gel. His face was that shade of orange only a spray tan can produce, an inviting smile wrinkled his cheeks, and the firelight's glow cast shadows on his–I shit you not–dimples. As if all of that wasn't disarming enough, his eyes twinkled. Fucking twinkled. I'm not talking about the shine of a nocturnal apex predator's eyes. The eyes of every vampire I'd ever met had a little preternatural light. That was there, to be sure, but what I saw was the twinkle of a well-humored soul, like the tell before a really corny dad joke. I saw that twinkle and instantly wanted out. Nothing–not the rumors, not the tall tales, not even the whispered horror stories I'd heard about Dieter Saint James–was as terrifying as the oh-so-genuine and guileless mirth in his eyes. Well, that and the spray tan. A vampire with a fake tan? If that ain't looking straight down the mouth of madness, I don't know what is.

"That's what some people say," I conceded, deciding honesty was the best policy. Well, not total honesty. If I'd been completely honest, I would've told him it's what everybody said.

Dieter sighed. "I imagine some people would feel that way. One's reputation takes on a life of its own after a point. Well, my soggy friend, you have me at a disadvantage. You obviously know me, or at least think you do. However, I know nothing about you. Nothing, except that you are obviously in an unfortunate situation."

I felt a sudden empathy for soldiers that stepped on landmines. You hear the faintest of clicks and know that your next step ends with a kaboom. That rush of empathy was followed by pure resentment. I did not like being trapped–not at all–and the only response I was capable of was a churlish one.

"Damn right I am," I growled. "I got turned around in the storm, and my car's not going to make it another ten feet, never mind home. I hate that car. I'd sell it, but only someone suicidal would buy it, and I don't want that on my conscience. Sorry, but you were the only port I could find in this storm. If I can hole up for the night, I'll get it towed in the morning."

Those eyes twinkled again above a sympathetic smile. "Ah, such misfortune. Of course, you can stay the night, Mr..."

"Johnson. Lenny Johnson," I offered while extending a dripping hand.

The vampire took my hand in his own and gripped it firmly. I couldn't suppress a momentary shudder, and his already wide smile got a smidge wider.

"Well, let's get you settled in, shall we?" he offered. "My staff is indisposed, but I think I remember where the guest rooms are."

The vampire turned, and I followed. I felt my future dwindle like the firelight behind us but kept my chin up and shoulders squared. No one lived forever, and at least my last meal had been a damned good hotdish with crispy tater tots on top. We climbed flights of stairs and finally stepped into a wide hallway lined with heavy, ornate doors. The space between the doors indicated that the rooms themselves were more likely suites.

"Big place," I commented. "Must cost a fortune to heat."

Dieter smiled. "I think we both know that looks can be deceiving, Mr. Johnson. This looks like a medieval castle because I took great pains to ensure every detail was authentic. Each stone was hand quarried. The mortar was hand mixed. The labor required to raise this castle was immense, I assure you. But woven into its archaic facade are all the modern amenities. Conduits for electricity. Ductwork to ensure air circulates freely. Can't have must or mold, now can we? And the floors? Radiant heat. You can stroll through the halls barefoot on a January night and never catch a chill. Marvelous, isn't it?"

"Very," I agreed, perhaps a tad too quickly. His words, 'I think we both know that looks can be deceiving,' had set every hair on my body on end. "So, do you have lots of barefoot guests strolling the halls?"

The vampire smiled that grandfatherly smile. "On occasion. I've been known to entertain from time to time, and sometimes guests stay a bit longer than they planned."

We'd reached the fourth door in the row, and Dieter offered a slight bow.

"Yes. Well, here we are," he said heartily. A gentle push sent the door swinging on silent hinges. "I hope this will do. You'll find clean towels in the bath. If you get hungry, there's a pantry at the bend in the hall. If you need entertainment, continue past the bend. The minor library has quite a selection. Nothing compared to the grand library, of course, but hopefully, its offerings will be sufficient."

I nodded my thanks and inched into the room. I immediately noticed a large mirror sitting atop a vanity and tried to position myself where I could catch Dieter's reflection. No easy task when you're trying to be sly, and I ultimately failed. Not that I needed proof. I knew the jolly visage was a convenient mask hiding the monster beneath. There's just something indescribably cool about seeing a floating, empty shirt in a mirror.

"Rest well, Mr. Johnson. I'm sorry about your car troubles, but at least they will be in the rearview mirror soon enough," he predicted with a sly glance toward the room's vanity and a chuckle at his own bad joke.

I put a hand on the doorknob and swung it gently shut while he stood there smiling. Long seconds after the door had been closed, I heard footsteps dwindle, each step softer than the one before. In my overactive imagination, it sounded like the dripping of blood from a torn-open neck. Finally, I convinced myself that Dieter was truly gone and that I was alone. Plan Dumb-as-a-Motherfucker was going exactly the way it was supposed to.

"And I still hate it. It's a terrible, no good, absolutely rotten plan," I muttered but shouldn't have bothered.

No one ever cared what I thought.

# CHAPTER 6

*Ope! It's your horoscope, Pisces!*
*Your romantic life will be hotter than the cheesy heart of a Juicy Lucy.*

T HE ABILITY TO WAIT. It's a skill, maybe even a virtue, that most people don't possess. Most people fidget. Their eyes roam. Their fingers tap. Their mind wanders to all the things they'd rather not think about, and they reflexively grasp for distractions. For people like that, waiting is a subtle torture. The slow drip of water on their forehead. The inexorable stretching of shackles on the rack. The endless looping of their least favorite song. It frays their nerves, breaks down their self-control, strips them down to the most basic fight-or-flight instinct. It drives them–in a word–bonkers.

I was squarely in the 'most people' category. I hated waiting. My job required a fair amount of it: waiting for someone to get home, waiting for someone to leave, waiting for sunset or sunrise, waiting to get paid. It was why I always carried a distraction. A crossword puzzle, a bent-up paperback full of pulp fiction, something I could consume with just enough of my brain to keep the stir crazy at bay. As I lay in the room's luxurious bed, I realized a glaring gap in the plan. I had nothing to distract me while I waited for an opportunity to snoop around. Suffice it to say that I damn near went bonkers.

After the vampire had deposited me in my room, I'd waited anxiously for the trap to spring. When no scythes swung down from the ceiling, no poisoned darts whistled past my ears, and the floor didn't fall out from beneath me, I waited another hour or so for the inevitable moment when shit would get real. Those couple of hours of waiting were exhausting. One might not think that staring with barely contained dread at a bedroom door would be all that hard, but it is. It really is. You strain every sense to its limits, afraid to blink, afraid to breathe. You curse your pounding heart because it's all you can hear when you need to be listening for the tap of footsteps, the creak of a turning doorknob, or the click of a secret panel about to open. Muscles you didn't know you had start to ache. Sweat breaks out in every uncomfortable place your body has to offer. It sucks. The only upside to that sort of waiting is that it's active. It consumes all of your attention. The downside is that it simply isn't sustainable. Eventually, your guard slips, your mind wanders, and–poof–you're bored.

I'd given up being vigilant and distracted myself by exploring my room. It didn't take long. The space was as big as my whole apartment, but sparsely appointed. A king-sized four-poster bed. A dark wooden wardrobe. The vanity with its oval mirror in a tiltable frame. An ornately carved chair with a thick quilted cushion. A private bathroom with modern plumbing, which I'll admit was a surprise until I remembered that the castle's owner would never tolerate guests using a chamber pot. A window that didn't open. The view it might have offered was stolen by the dark night and heavy rain. The floor was flagstone and a shade darker than the stone block walls. Despite the austerity, it was comfortable enough. Just boring. There was no trap door behind the bed, no secret passageways through the panels inside the wardrobe, no Wonderland through the looking glass. It was nothing more than a room.

"The hell with this," I muttered. "It's been hours. He's probably reclining in an open coffin, watching Bela Lugosi films, and drinking sherry. Sherry. Not blood. Sherry. The coast is clear, August. Get going."

I put my hand on the doorknob, my insides turned to ice, and I returned to the bed to wait anxiously for another hour.

Honestly, it was the boredom and its promise of driving me nuts–not bravery or any obligation to actually do the job I'd been hired to do–that finally pushed me from the room. When I ventured out, each step I took was careful as a cat in a room full of sleeping dogs. Our trek to the guest wing had been long and poorly lit. I'd been soaked with cold rainwater and scared out of my wits. Even so, I'd tried my best to keep my bearings. Since I'd turned right out of my room, I was likely making a clockwise circuit around the castle's center and heading toward the stairs. My plan was simple: climb to the top of the haystack and feel for the needle on my way down.

I say, 'feel,' because Vilde had given me little to go on besides a picture of the book and the guidance that I'd feel it when it was close. I'd pressed her for details, but she'd only smiled cryptically and told me words couldn't describe the feeling, but it would be unmistakable.

It wasn't much to go on, but I wasn't worried. I was good at my job. I had a knack for finding things that didn't want to be found. That, or maybe having my own share of carefully buried secrets made it easier for me to unearth someone else's. Whatever it was–gift or sympathy for the furtively inclined–it rarely took me long to find what I was looking for. You just had to know where to look. When I reached the stairway, I started to climb.

The castle was quiet. I hadn't seen any evidence of another person, human or otherwise. I hoped that the staff wasn't as nocturnal as their boss. I hoped the soft squeaking of my still-damp boots wouldn't carry. I hoped my ragged breaths after climbing all those damned stairs would be mistaken for the howling wind outside. Mostly, I hoped the book wasn't on Dieter's nightstand.

"He's a braggart," Vilde had told me. "A gloater. A pompous ass. He knows how rare the book is, so it won't be somewhere private. It will be somewhere on display. Protected, yes, but visible. He'll make sure that any guest sees it so they know he possesses it."

She had practically spat the words, her beautiful face so contorted it was almost unattractive. Almost.

"Protected how?" I'd asked, doing my best to sound professional. I don't think I succeeded. By that point in the conversation, I'd had a fair amount of the really expensive booze.

Vilde had put a thoughtful finger to her lips. "Dieter wouldn't want anything to mar the view of the book, so I doubt it will be in a case. And while the old bat certainly loves what modern technology can offer, he's also a bit of a traditionalist. I would assume some protective charm or spell. I did mention that he dabbles in the dark arts, didn't I? Will that be a problem?"

"Nope," I'd lied, the booze in my belly and dollar signs in my brain giving me a level of confidence that exceeded my common sense.

Now, standing in a vampire's castle in the middle of the night, that easy confidence seemed oceans away and impossible to reclaim.

"Think, August. Think," I whispered as my feet carried me as far as the stairs would go. "What would the scary old vampire do?"

The top of the stairs opened up to a narrow hallway. It dawned on me that there were very few ways out of the castle, a realization that sent my stomach plummeting. With a hard swallow and muttered curse, I forced my feet to move step by careful step. All of my senses were as open as I could get them to be. Eyes wide, nostrils flaring, ears practically quivering from the strain of listening for anything and everything. Even my tongue was trying to help. It protruded slightly from my parted lips as if it could taste impending disaster. Barely ten agonizing steps later, I stopped.

"What am I doing?" I wondered out loud. "C'mon, August. You aren't stupid."

I silently debated that point with myself. I had plenty of reasons to believe I was, in fact, quite stupid. Top of the list? I was intentionally looking for Vilde's book in the part of the castle it was least likely to be. She'd made it very clear that the book would be someplace prominently displayed, like a trophy. Someplace guests would have to see it and appreciate its significance. Creeping around the upper reaches of the castle, tiptoeing down a hallway that led to nothing but spare—and most likely empty—rooms, smacked of stupidity.

*Or fear,* I realized.

And there it was: the truth of things. I was terrified of finding that damned book. I knew where it was, where it had to be. Dieter had mentioned a grand library. Looking anywhere else was nothing but dumb.

*Unless you're scared of going there,* I admitted to myself.

"Fine. Fine! I'm scared, all right? Geezus. Let it go, already."

I took a deep breath, held it, and exhaled through my nostrils. I'd been afraid before. I'd been about as scared as a person can get and had somehow survived. This was nothing, *nothing,* compared to the abject terror that had defined my reality for years.

"But it's still scary," I objected and then retorted with, "Yeah, but seriously, dude. Stop being an asshole. Go downstairs. Find the book. Now."

My feet didn't move.

"I. Said. Now."

Reluctantly, I reversed my trek and padded quietly down flight after flight of stairs until I finally emerged into the foyer. The fire still burned as brightly as when I'd arrived, which left me convinced it was probably enchanted. It would take a small army continually carting in entire trees to keep a blaze that big alight. I crossed the open space warily, eyes darting to plumb the depths of the ever-shifting shadows. A swinging door a few yards to the side of the massive fireplace beckoned. I pressed a hand against it and was rewarded for my perseverance. The room I entered was, without a doubt, the grand library.

My breath caught in my chest as I took in the magnificent space. The immense fireplace opened on both sides. In the foyer, its light pushed harshly against a vast emptiness. In the library, though, the orange and yellow glow washed over darkly lacquered wooden shelves stuffed with countless spines, long tables adorned with hooded desk lamps, and comfy overstuffed chairs. The intelligent blend of functional and artful seating arrangements didn't cause me to catch my breath, though. Rather, it was two specific details that stilled my lungs and set my heart pounding.

The first was a wooden lectern opposite the room from the fireplace. No bookshelves or other furniture crowded it. Instead, they seemed to keep an almost reverent distance from the lectern's contents: a single book bound in dark leather. Suddenly, I understood what Vilde had tried to explain. I could feel it. I could actually feel it. The odd sensation hadn't registered in my conscious mind. It was only when I was looking directly at the book that I became aware of the heaviness in my stomach, the stuffy plugging of my ears, the subtle ache in my joints and molars.

The other detail that froze me in my tracks was reclining easily in an armchair a short distance from the pedestal. Dieter Saint James sat with an open newspaper spanning the space between his hands, its bottom edge resting gently on top of his crossed legs.

"Hello," he remarked politely, peeking over the newspaper's top. "I see you've found the grand library. Plenty of good stuff in here, but I seem to recall recommending the lesser library near your room."

I swallowed. "Oops. Must've taken a wrong turn."

Dieter folded his paper and set it aside while regarding me thoughtfully. "It's so easy to do that, isn't it? Turn left when you meant to go right. Stop when you should have gone ahead. Charged blindly forward when a simple moment of thoughtful consideration would've paid dividends. Entire lives can be changed forever because of a simple wrong turn."

He waited, which led me to assume he wanted me to say something, which resulted in my lips pressing even more tightly together. After an awkwardly long silence, the older man sighed.

"Yes, well. I'm prone to waxing philosophic. Always happens when I read my horoscope."

I couldn't stop my eyes away from shifting to the paper he'd been reading. The *Metro Pages* rested innocently on the table beside his chair. Because of course.

"Anything good?" I asked.

"I suppose that depends on how you interpret them, don't you agree?" he replied amicably and lifted the paper again.

I cursed myself for being a complete idiot while doing my best to keep a blandly interested expression on my face as the old vampire shared his horoscope.

"Let's see. Events around the Full Moon, that's tonight, by the way," he interjected before continuing, "are cooking up trouble. On a more personal level, sparks are set to fly... in all the right ways! Ahhh," he sighed. "See? Could mean any number of things."

My face squelched despite my best efforts. "If you say so."

"I do," Saint James agreed. "For example, I suspect that you, Lenny Johnson, are the one that's cooking up trouble."

I saw his eyes lift and look over my shoulder, and then one muscular arm wrapped around my neck from behind while a hand grabbed my wrist and pulled back hard. I felt my shoulder strain and back arch uncomfortably. The rough hands spun and shoved me into one of the reading chairs. With a snarl, I gripped the arms and started to stand, but a hand pressed me back down to the cushions.

I looked up and saw a couple of dead Oompa Loompas. How could I tell they were dead? Well, he had a face with dimples, a cleft chin, and what had to be three bullet holes, and she had the sunken and withered look of someone that had already seen the bottom of a grave. So, yeah. Dead. The more I considered them, though, the more I vacillated on that Oompa Loompa comparison. They were too tall, and neither had the outlandish hair or lederhosen or goofy shoes. He was wearing a sturdy blue and black flannel, jeans, and cowboy boots. She was wearing subdued tan slacks and a matching blazer over a dark grey blouse. Their faces, though... Both were the same spray-tanned orange as Dieter's. So, yeah. Oompa Loompas.

I giggled. It must not have been what the pair were expecting. The guy looked at the woman, and the woman hauled off and slapped me.

"Ow," I complained. "Why?"

As if in answer, all hell broke loose.

A heavy wooden end table crashed through from the other side of the fireplace and sent chunks of still-burning logs and curtains of flame into the library. Dieter screamed in surprise, and his henchmen—Henchpeople? That seemed a little more PC—dove in opposite directions. The man rolled to a knee, pistol drawn. Three sharp cracks split the air, followed by a calm question.

"Do you see anyone?"

The henchwoman responded with a negative. I twisted my head and saw her sprint in an arc around the room's perimeter and toward the fireplace. The scattered logs had set a few of the chairs closest to the fireplace aflame, and the nearby tables were smoking. Ignoring the impending disaster, she headed toward the door that connected the library to the foyer on the other side of the wall. It was designed to swing both ways. Right as her hand touched its surface, something on the other side pushed violently. I heard what had to be the sound of bones breaking as she cried out in surprise. The door recoiled and swung the other direction as more shots rang out. A tightly grouped collection of splintered holes appears in the wood as if by magic.

"Forget him!" Dieter roared. "Put out the fire! Put it out!"

"With what?" the injured woman shouted. "Should I piss on it?"

Dieter's face had taken on a new and terrifying aspect. Gone were the oily smile and twinkly eyes. In their place, an expression of twisted rage contorted his features.

"I'll rip your head from your neck and use your body like a blood-filled Super Soaker," he spat, "if you don't extinguish that fire now."

The vampire's vitriol seemed a bit excessive, but to be fair, the aforementioned fire was spreading. Slowly still–the heavy woolen rugs resisted the flame–but if the flames licked even one book on a shelf, the library and quite likely the entire castle would be lost.

"Sooo…" I drawled, foolishly drawing attention to myself but unable to contain my nature, "the modern amenities in the archaic facade don't include sprinklers?"

One second, Dieter was a half-dozen yards away. The next, he had me by the neck. I stretched my toes down in a frantic effort to find the floor while my fingers scraped ineffectually at his hands.

"This library is priceless!" he screamed. A bit of a lisp stretched the esses due to the suddenly lengthened incisors protruding whitely from his mouth.

"That sthertainly sthucks," I croaked back.

I should've known better. It isn't polite to mock someone's speech impediment. The vampire heaved, and I sailed across the library. I had just enough time to bemoan how many times I'd been thrown–more than seemed necessary by any count–before I collided with a bookshelf. As I crumpled to the floor, I realized how much more getting thrown into bookshelves hurts compared to speakers and windows. One shelf had caught my shoulder blade, another my ribs, a third my hip, and a fourth my knee. It felt like getting hit with four baseball bats at the same time, and I involuntarily curled up against the waves of pain.

"Get the book, August!" I heard someone roar.

I clawed my way up from the pain and opened my eyes. Tanckenstein was ballroom dancing with the Oompa Loompa guy, each hand's fingers intertwined with his partner's. His jaw clenched, and the cords of his neck strained as they moved in a slow box step. Tanckenstein had claimed he was strong, really strong. The simple fact that the other guy was clearly his match made my blood run cold. Rather than follow his very straightforward instructions, I sat transfixed by the awesome contest. Vilde's henchman took a heavy step forward and pressed Dieter's man toward the smoldering rug. Another step and both of the guy's feet were in the burgeoning flames. Tanckenstein was driving the other man back slowly and inexorably, but he might as well have been pushing a semi with its emergency brake on up a steep hill.

"The book, August! The book!"

I jolted and then pushed my way up from the library's floor. Unfortunately, Stein's loud reminder of my very specific task also clued in Dieter to our sneaky goal. I saw him turn to the pedestal and then impale me with his eyes.

"Shit," I muttered. My entire side hurt, and I couldn't think of a single shift that would even my odds against a centuries-old vampire. The only card I had left in my deck was wile. Craft and cunning and cleverness had gotten me out of a few pinches in my day. No reason they wouldn't get me out of this mess, too.

I nodded to Tanckenstein, but he didn't notice. He was still grappling with the other man while the woman awkwardly spread clouds of white chemicals from a fire extinguisher. Despite everything, I felt a bit bad for the lady. Using a fire extinguisher when only one of your arms works had to be tough. So yeah, Tanckenstein didn't see my self-assured nod. Dieter did, though. With a smug grin, he positioned himself directly between me and the pedestal holding Vilde's book, incisors gleaming in the wild firelight.

I squinted, crouched, and took a feinting half-step, pleased to see Dieter twitch in that direction. I feinted again and was rewarded with another twitch from the angry vampire. Then I pivoted and ran in the other direction. As I passed one of the many bookcases lining the walls, I shot out a hand, grabbed a random book, and sprinted straight for a window near the corner.

*See ya, suckers,* I thought, triumphantly.

Not to brag, but I'm a bit of an expert on glass. I've gone through enough windows, bounced off of enough windshields, been hit over the head by enough vases, and broken enough mirrors to know a thing or two. Which is why, I realized belatedly as I rebounded from the clear pane with a surprised curse and fresh burst of pain in my shoulder, I should've known that the windows in Dieter's prized library in his damned castle would be impossible to shatter.

"August?" I heard Tanckenstein exclaim. "What happened?"

"I got the book," I croaked, raising a hand to display my prize. "Well, a book, at least. Wily escape plan didn't go so well, though."

I heard him say something uncharacteristically unkind and then heard a pained roar. Stein had managed to pivot, twist, and toss the other man Judo-style into the gigantic fireplace and was now running toward me, long legs pumping. He was a few feet away when the vampire collided with him like a battering ram. In a way, it was funny; the diminutive Saint James sending the relative giant lurching to the side. Stein recovered his feet, only to have Dieter slam into him again and shove hard with both arms. This time, it was Tanckenstein that was airborne. He collided with a bookshelf, and I winced sympathetically.

"You!" the vampire cried. "I should have known. You tell that treacherous elf it's mine!" Dieter howled. "She might've found the inscription that revealed its location, but I was the one that brought it up from the infernal depths."

"No, you didn't," an unexpected voice butted in.

The woman had managed the dual feats of first pulling her companion from the flames and then hosing him down with the fire extinguisher, all with only one working arm. The guy was a nightmare in the flesh, a ghoulish hulk of mottled, bubbling skin and smoldering rags dusted in white like a powdered donut from hell. He wobbled on his feet as sickly smelling smoke rose up from every inch of his broad frame. Between the two of them, though, she was scarier. Much, much scarier. The anger emanating from her was so intense it made the massive fire feel like a space heater.

"We got it, you pompous ass," she snarled. "Now Luke looks like a hotdog that got dropped in the campfire, I can't use my arm, and all we want–the only thing we want–is a little fucking credit, you piece of shit."

"You dare..." Dieter breathed. "You insolent, ungrateful maggot. What would you be without me? Dead, that's what. A lifeless husk full of tumors and embalming fluid rotting in the ground. And you," he continued, turning his tirade on the still-smoking man, "wouldn't be any better."

Tanckenstein had regained his feet and was gingerly massaging his shoulder. "He brought you guys back, too? I figured there were more of me. Nice to meet you. I'm Leonard. My boss pushed me into a woodchipper and then paid this one to piece me back together."

"Mona," the woman said curtly. "I died of cancer. This is Luke. He was shot in a drive-by."

The charred corpse waved and tried to say hello, but the word came out as a raspy cough.

The acrid taste of smoke in my mouth made me realize my jaw was hanging open. I closed it, worked my tongue around a bit, spat to the side, and smacked my lips a few times. It didn't help. The very air of the grand library tasted like smokey ass.

"Sounds like you two could use a new boss," I mentioned after spitting again in vain, "and Vilde Tanck seems okay. A little intense, sure, but if you're going to be henchmen... Er, henchpeople? Whatever. Anyway, if you're going to be hired muscle, wouldn't it be nice to do that for a less shitty person?"

I think Luke nodded. Hard to be sure since he was still wobbling. It had to be hard to stand up when your legs had been swapped out with a couple of deep-fried turkey drummies. Mona, though, had obviously warmed to my suggestion. She took a menacing step, but it was toward Dieter, not me or Stein. Luke bent over and placed his hands on his blistered knees and coughed out a few gouts of black smoke, then rose back up and started closing on the vampire as well.

Dieter's face writhed and contorted with a maelstrom of emotion, and then settled on a smug little smile.

"I see. Come on, then. Take your swing. Rebel against your lord and savior. Topple your god."

Mona tilted her head. "You want to do this?" she asked Luke quietly.

"Fuck it," he coughed. "This day can't get any worse."

Before the two could press any sort of attack, Tanckenstein stepped between them and the vampire. "Sorry, but I can't let you do that. Quit, sure. But hurt Dieter? Nope."

Mona gaped, incredulous. "Why?"

"Ms. Tanck still has a soft spot for this one," he admitted. "I don't think she'd like me letting him get roughed up, even if he deserved it. Which you do," he added, looking over his shoulder. "Sorry for the language, but Ms. Tanck says you're an asshole. She does still have feelings for you, though."

That icky taste let me know my jaw was hanging open again.

"Um, Stein," I whispered loudly. "Shouldn't we just, you know, let them work things out themselves and et-gay the ook-bay?"

"She said that?" Dieter breathed, ignoring me completely while a wholly unexpected expression transformed his face. The smarmy salesman-turned-terrifying vampire had suddenly become a lovesick little puppy with wide, hopeful eyes.

"Not in so many words," Tanckenstein admitted, "but it's obvious."

"She won't talk to me. We were going to rule the world together, and now she won't even return my calls."

With a start, I realized I was in my element. How many times had I had this exact conversation? I dealt with broken hearts. People–or other things–that had found and lost love. Holding hands one day, sharing a toothbrush the next. Someone that laughed at your jokes and actually cared when you cried. That feeling that your puzzle piece had finally found its match. Losing that was tough. Double-tough. Sure, it was hard to imagine people like Vilde Tanck and Dieter Saint James sharing a toothbrush, but truth is stranger than fiction.

"He's right," I groaned as I pulled myself to my feet. "You can hear it in her voice. Sure, the words she uses are pretty nasty: Vile, conceited, narcissistic, orange. It's not the words, though. It's how she says them. Tanckenstein here is absolutely right. Vilde still loves you, and you obviously still love her." Then inspiration truly struck. I waved a hand at the mostly smothered blaze. "It was in your horoscope, remember? Flying sparks."

Mona laughed an ugly laugh. "What is wrong with you people?"

"Is it so hard to believe?" I asked quietly. "So impossible that people like Vilde Tanck or old Dieter here could love someone as much as you love Luke?"

She gasped, and Luke turned his poached-egg eyes to look at her. "What does he mean?" the overdone hotdog rasped.

"Nothing. I don't know. They're crazy. They're all crazy."

"You love me?" Luke pressed.

Mona vehemently shook her head. "Of course not. No. We're partners. That's all."

The smoldering corpse took a halting step toward her. "Is that all?" he asked, smoke slipping from between his lips.

Her eyes narrowed. Her lips pressed into a thin line. The fist on her good arm clenched. She shook her head.

"I love you, too," Luke coughed quietly. A final step closed the distance, and he wrapped her in a crispy embrace, careful not to jostle her broken arm. Lips that looked like little bacon rolls parted in a smile. He leaned in, those nasty little bacon-lips searching for hers and finding them in what had to be the most disturbing kiss I'd ever seen. Mona resisted at first, then reached up with her good hand and curled her fingers into the remaining clumps of hair on his pink and oozing scalp.

"Maybe there's hope for you yet," I mentioned as I crossed to Tanckenstein and rolled my eyes toward the gruesome pair. "Looks obviously aren't everything."

He tried to hide his surprised smile and failed. Even Dieter was grinning at the tableau. I decided to ride the moment and mentioned that we'd just take Vilde's book and be on our way.

"Oh, no. That isn't possible," Dieter said. "Please do give Vilde my regrets, but the book is mine. If that means we'll never be together, so be it. I'll rule the world alone."

"Again with the ruling the world," I muttered. "What is that book, anyway?"

"She didn't tell you?" Dieter asked. "No. Of course, she wouldn't. Well, I think we're done here. I have to reprimand these two and then call the insurance company. You've made quite a mess of my library," he admonished.

Mona and Luke had ended their Hollywood-length kiss and now stood hand-in-hand. "We're going with them," she stated. "We're done here. Let's call it a day and not make things any worse. Deal?"

Dieter rolled his eyes to the heavens and sighed. "Ah, the folly. This emotional interlude has been amusing, but it doesn't change anything. You two work for me. You aren't going anywhere."

"We quit," Luke rasped, his smokey voice plainly exasperated. "That literally means we don't work for you anymore."

The vampire moved so fast I actually heard the air whoosh. One second, he was standing near the book's pedestal. The next, he was nose to nose with his overcooked minion, arm buried up to its elbow in the man's chest. I heard a wet thwap as Dieter released the heart he'd grabbed, and it fell to the floor behind Luke's back.

"Stein…" I warned.

"Yep," he agreed and ran for the book. Three steps later, he reached out a hand for the leather-bound tome and went sailing backward. His trajectory sent him straight at Dieter, and he slammed into the vampire's back like a bowling ball hitting the headpin.

I didn't think. Thinking would only get me killed, and I very much wanted to live. So without thinking, I shifted, only realizing after I'd become the coyote that I wasn't human anymore. I stretched my four legs, leaped, and grabbed the book in my open jaws. It tasted like spoiled meat. Tossing that gross thought aside, I ran for the doorway. The vampire plunged down from above and landed superhero-style in front of me, so I skittered off to the side. Cut off from my escape, I made for the long tables that stretched across the room. I'd just found shelter beneath one when its far end was obliterated by Dieter's fury. The little human part of my brain coolly wondered how he planned to explain a bunch of smashed tables to his insurance. Meanwhile, the coyote was fully freaking out and running for its damned life.

An insane game of whack-a-mole ensued, with me as the mole and a really pissed vampire trying to whack me. Dieter leaped and descended, leaving veritable craters in his wake. Only the coyote's quick reflexes kept me from ending up as a furry pancake on the library floor. I didn't know how long I could keep up the game. The book was heavy in my jaws–heavier than something its size had any right to be–and coyotes don't have a ton of stamina. Eventually, I'd be a split-second too slow, and that would be it. So long, August Shade.

I made for the door again, my haphazard flight sending me toward Mona and Luke. The woman had collapsed to her knees and was cradling the dead-again man's head in her lap. In the moment it took to pass them, I saw her hand move from caressing his burned brow to retrieving her pistol from her shoulder holster. A heavy thud and curse sounded behind me–Dieter missing by scant inches yet again–and then gunshots filled the air. I have no clue how many bullets a typical gun holds, but Mona's apparently had a lot, and she seemed determined to use them all. I skittered to a halt and looked back in time to see Dieter jerk repeatedly, spin and fall. Mona stood up, face contorted with fury and gun still spitting lead into the vampire's chest.

"Come on!" I heard Tanckenstein yell. He'd made it to the swinging doorway and was holding it open. "Run!"

I stretched my four legs and moved as fast as I possibly could. I'd cleared the threshold to the foyer when the gunfire briefly stopped. There was a metallic clatter and loud click, then more gunshots, and finally, a heart-wrenching scream.

"Go, go, go!" Tanckenstein commanded, and I did.

Dumb luck was on my side. Tanckenstein had left the front door ajar, the drawbridge was down, and the car was right where I'd left it, the only difference being that its trunk was up. I skittered to a stop beside the little beater and let the heavy book fall from my jaws.

"What are you waiting for?" Tanckenstein had caught up and was standing anxiously next to the car's door.

I tilted my muzzle up. My ears folded back, and my tail curled under my furry little behind. I'd have to shift back to my human form to admit that the keys were clipped with a carabiner to a belt loop on my pants... and my pants were back in the library. Losing keys is easy. Losing pants is harder–not impossible, just harder–but I'd still managed to pull it off. A pathetic whine slipped through the coyote's lips.

"You don't have the keys, do you?" Tanckenstein concluded.

I ducked my head, unable to meet his eyes. He collapsed against the car's side with a depressed sigh and slid down to sit on the gravel drive. I sat beside him, tail curled around my feet. We both looked at nothing for a moment, each lost in our own thoughts, and then looked up in unison when Dieter Saint James stepped from the castle's massive front door and into the night.

"Crap," Tanckenstein cursed as he pushed himself upright, cracked his knuckles, and settled into a classic boxing pose.

I would've seconded that assessment, but coyote mouths weren't made for swearing. With an inward sigh at the irreparable damage I was about to inflict on the shirt and boxers I'd managed to keep on after shifting into a coyote, I went badass gorilla. I used a rear leg to kick the book under the car, thumped my chest with my fists, roared into the night sky, and readied myself for a fight I really didn't think we'd win.

# CHAPTER 7



*Ope! It's your horoscope, Aquarius!*
*You might be the Gray Duck, but you should still let the other Ducks go.*

THE ONLY CELL I had to compare my current one to was the hospital room I'd been confined to as a kid. It killed me to say it, but that room had been nicer. It had a bed with a mattress, was clean, and even had a window, albeit with shatterproof glass. The cell Dieter had dumped me in after easily handing my gorilla-sized ass to me on a platter offered none of those things. What it did have was a disturbing amount of rat poop, dank water trickling down its stone walls, and a smell that made the inside of a hodag's ass smell like perfume. I had to give him credit, though. He wanted an authentic castle, and its dungeon was about as dungeony as you can get.

Time had passed, but I had no idea how much. Maybe an hour, maybe two. I'd tried to gauge the passing of time by counting how many times I'd said, "I hate you, Clarissa Steyer," but had lost count after a hundred or so. I really did blame her, too. My life had been completely fine–maybe not great, but good enough–before she'd walked through my door. If she hadn't so successfully rattled my cage, I wouldn't have been out for a drive to clear my head, wouldn't have shifted into a coyote to take a little evening stroll, and Tanckenstein wouldn't have nabbed me and dragged me back to Vilde Tanck and catapulted me into this steaming pile of shit.

*Tanckenstein would've found you anyway,* a stubborn corner of my brain pointed out.

*But Vilde decided I was the guy for the job because of Clarissa's stupid horoscopes,* the other stubborn part of my brain retorted.

*Good point,* the first stubborn part of my brain conceded, and I laughed haughtily.

"What's so funny?" Tanckenstein asked from the cell across from mine.

His question brought my spontaneous laughter to an abrupt end. There really wasn't anything funny about our situation. We were locked in cages in a dungeon. An actual dungeon. The fact that Dieter's castle had gone so far as to include that particular detail was impressive, but definitely not humorous. I gained my feet, careful to keep the threadbare blanket I'd been afforded pulled tightly around me. Clutching it with one hand, I wrapped the fingers of my other hand around a bar and tried to give it a shake. In the movies, there was always a bar where the mortar was loose. Unfortunately, the vampire hadn't seen those movies. These bars didn't budge. Even Stein's unnatural strength had failed to move a bar even a fraction of an inch.

"Are you sure you can't fit?" he asked. "That fat cat is the smallest you can get?"

A sigh escaped my lips. It was. It seemed like everyone thought shifters could just shift into whatever they wanted. That'd be swell, but the reality was it just didn't work that way. The list of things I could change into was eclectic, but not exhaustive. I'd tried my gorilla first and had as much luck bending the bars as Stein. I'd tried the elephant and had banged at the bars with my head. All I got was a headache. The cat was as small as I could get, and it was my usual rotten luck it was a chunky Maine Coon.

The energy it had taken to shift multiple times had soaked my mood in a bucket of black depression and left my muscles quivering.

"Even if I could turn into a mouse or a weasel or something, slip between these bars, and find a way outside, we'd still be stuck," I pointed out. "Maybe you forgot that someone smashed our get-away car after throwing it at a vampire. And missing, I might add."

The larger man's already sad face sagged even further. Despite everything, it made me feel even worse.

"Don't be like that," I scolded. "I lost the car keys. It wasn't your fault." Guilt at my own stupidity further soured my already rank mood, so I doubled down on one of my core tenants: When something's your fault, find another thing to complain about.

"I still don't get how you can be strong enough to shot-put a Japanese hatchback but can't break these stupid bars," I grumbled.

Tanckenstein wrapped his hands around the bars of his cell and tried again to bend them. As with his previous attempts, exactly nothing happened. "Magic, I guess," he replied with a forlorn sigh. "Who'd have thought the guy would have a dungeon with magic cells?"

"Obviously not us. Look. If it's all the same to you, I'm going to go sit in a corner and sulk until I catch pneumonia and die.'"

More time passed as I sat on the damp floor and tried to ignore my freezing ass. I was naked beneath the blanket. Between the coyote and gorilla shifts, I'd managed to lose or flat-out destroy all of my clothes. At least I hadn't worn my jacket. If I had lost that, I wouldn't have even bothered trying to escape. I would've just tilted my head back and pointed at my neck to make sure Dieter knew exactly where to bite.

A rusty screech sounded from the far end of the hallway. Footsteps were accompanied by a rough dragging sound, and then Dieter appeared, pulling a straight-backed wooden chair behind him. When he reached the space between the bars of my cell and Tanckenstein's, he lifted the chair with both hands and slammed it down onto the flagstone. I jerked back in response, the harsh sound forcing the involuntary reaction. The vampire sat in the chair with a deep, steadying breath and swiveled his orange face from me to Stein and back.

"My library is an awful mess. Those rugs were imported, and the tables were hand-made."

"Send the bill to my office," I suggested. "I'll make sure to wipe my ass with it before I send it back."

The vampire chuckled a happy old man chuckle. "Oh, you are a prize. Such a prize. I can see why Vilde likes you. She's always had a soft spot for the scrappy ones."

"That's true," Tanckenstein agreed. "When she told me to fetch him, I thought, 'But why that guy?' Then I met him and thought, 'Ms. Tanck's is definitely going to like him.'"

While Dieter and Tanckenstein shared a commiserating laugh, I glowered at the suddenly chatty guy that was supposed to be on my side. I wasn't sure what angle he was playing, but didn't appreciate it being at the expense of what little dignity I had left.

"I'll confess," Dieter said to Tanckenstein thoughtfully, "I don't understand why she'd send him to get the book, though. Even with your not inconsiderable help, and I mean that. You bested Luke and Mona. When I had you brought back, I knew you would be tough, but that certainly was impressive. As I was saying, though, even with your help, Vilde surely must've known it was a fool's errand. Him, getting the book from me? I'd be insulted, except I'm sure she had a deeper reason."

Tanckenstein nodded. "I think she was flirting with you." When Dieter arched an eyebrow, Vilde's henchman added emphatically, "It was in her horoscope. 'The longing for more intimacy in a relationship is on the rise, and opportunities that appear as challenges are likely to present themselves.' How long has it been since someone challenged you? I'll bet it's been forever. I'll bet you've been really bored, and then we show up. I mean, that was a pretty good fight. I threw a car at you. When was the last time someone threw a car at you?"

I couldn't help but add, "And missed," but I was thoroughly ignored.

A smile tugged at the corners of Dieter's mouth. "It was a good fight, wasn't it?"

Tanckenstein nodded. "See? And Ms. Tanck, I'll bet she's waiting to hear how it all turned out... from you."

The vampire's eyes went far away. "I do believe you may be right. The stars certainly do reveal the most unexpected surprises, don't they?"

I couldn't help the involuntary gag. This time, Dieter did notice me. He looked at me for a long moment. Well, not 'me,' exactly. More like my neck, specifically the part with the big vein full of blood.

"Yes, well. This was very... insightful," he mused and then suppressed a yawn. "Now, if you don't mind, I have a few calls to plan for, including one to our mutual acquaintance."

As Vilde's ex dragged his chair back down the hallway, I could hear him musing about where he and Vilde might go to get reacquainted, what he should wear, if he should reserve an entire establishment or have the pleasant din of others around them. It sounded like a lot of work and validated my own lack of a love life. Dating was exhausting.

"We really need to get out of here," Tanckenstein stated after the vampire was gone.

I looked across the hall and shrugged my exasperation. "How? We've got no options, Stein. We're stuck."

He was about to retort. For a perpetually mopey guy that had been pushed into a woodchipper, stitched back together, sold into bondage, beat like a drum, and tossed in a dungeon, he was suddenly and annoyingly perseverant. I watched his shoulders square with purpose, the lines of his face firm with resolution. His lips parted, and his lungs drew breath, no doubt readying the, 'Ms. Tanck says...' equivalent of a halftime speech for the losing team. Before the first we're-down-but-not-out-so-let's-go-get-'em syllable could be uttered, a new and unnoticed arrival pointedly cleared his throat.

"You," the man said, his attempt to sound authoritative undermined by his cracking voice. I couldn't really blame him, what with scary Stein on one side and mostly-naked me on the other. If I had been him, I'd have been a little on edge, too.

"You," he said again after swallowing hard and pointing at me. "Master said I need to find out your blood type. He prefers B-positive for breakfast but likes a nice AB-negative when he's relaxing after dinner. So?" he asked.

Something about the guy's voice struck a chord. I was certain that I'd never seen him before–and I hadn't–but I'd heard him. When he asked me again if I was B or maybe AB, it hit me.

"Shane from Editorial?" I blurted. "From the flippin' *Metro Pages*? You're Dieter Saint James' familiar?"

He squinted. "Yeah, so? Who are you?"

I grabbed the bars, completely forgetting that I'd needed at least one hand to hold my tattered blanket up. When the dungeon's damp cold pressed in on my bare skin, I decided I should probably just join a nudist colony and be done with it, given how much time I'd spent naked in the recent past.

"It's August. August Shade. The post-relationship personal effects repossession specialist. I got your friend's Oasis CD back."

"Holy shit," he replied with wide eyes. "What are you doing here? You're not the one that messed up Master's library, are you?"

A guilty shrug is all I could manage. "It wasn't on purpose. I'm on a job. Trying to get something back for Dieter's ex. That's all. This whole thing got blown way out of proportion. Look, you gotta let us out of here."

Shane shook his head. "No way. Can't do it."

"Can't or won't?" I pressed. "If it's 'can't,' we'll understand. But if it's 'won't,' well..."

An elephant's massive forehead slammed hard against the bars. Dieter's familiar squealed in shock and tripped backward until his back pressed against the bars of Stein's cell. The revenant's long arm reached out and wrapped around the familiar's throat.

"Keys," Tanckenstein stated in his sad, raspy voice, "or I snap your neck."

"No! Please, no. He'd kill me or worse."

Stein squeezed a little more, leaving Shane to suck air through a constricted throat. The *Metro Pages* editorial department pulled frantically at his collar, his ready-to-vomit expression turning panicky. Tanckenstein eased up a smidge, and the other man sucked in a gasp. Not a half-second later, he vomited all over the front of his expensive Western shirt. The colors blended really well.

After giving Dieter's familiar a few moments to catch his breath, Stein flexed his bicep again. "Keys," the revenant advised.

The poor guy quivered with indecision, tears in his eyes and vomit dripping from his shirt. With a mean nonchalance I hadn't thought myself capable of, I asked Tanckenstein if he liked volleyball.

"I'll bet that Shane from Editorial's head would work pretty well as the ball. I'll shift into a gorilla... What? Don't give me that look. You're crazy strong. I'm just trying to even the odds. Anyway, I'll shift, and then you serve..."

Shane shoved a hand deep into his pocket and pulled free a key ring with a coffin fob. "Here! Here!" he gasped. "Take them!"

The keys arced toward me and landed at my feet. After I'd set a big iron key to my cell's lock and heard a satisfying *thunk* when I twisted it, I swung the door open and freed my companion. Only after his door was open did Stein finally relax his hold on Shane's neck. The familiar crumpled to the floor, and the tears he'd been struggling to hold in burst free.

"We're good, right?" Shane begged. "I let you out, so we're good?"

Tanckenstein nodded. "Pretty much. We just need one more thing..." He reached out a large, scarred hand, grasped Shane's forehead, and then bounced the back of his skull off the cell's bars. The sound echoed down the dungeon's flagstone hallway, and my stomach did a somersault. "Sorry, but we need your clothes," he said as the vampire's familiar crumpled unconscious to the floor.

I squelched down my disgust at what I was about to do and stripped Shane down to his silk boxers. None of his clothes fit well, but as a second-hand store aficionado, that didn't bother me too much. The vomit soaked into the front of his shirt, though? Yuck. Major yuck.

"Okay, let's bolt," I said and started down the dungeon's hallway in the direction Shane had come from. I looked over a shoulder when I didn't hear footsteps behind me and saw Tanckenstein standing where I'd left him.

"We've still got a job to do," he informed me.

"Are you shitting me?" I exclaimed. "We're getting out of here." I shrugged off Stein's recriminating look and took a deliberate step toward freedom.

"August, we have a job to do. You have a job to do. If you don't, Ms. Tanck's going to be very unhappy. I get it. Dieter is scary. But I promise you, so is Ms. Tanck." He chewed his lip for a minute and looked to the side. "I have to do what she tells me, August. She told me to make sure you get her book, no matter what."

Indecision warred within me, a feeling not unlike the indigestion Uncle Sid's frequently inflicted on my bowels. I considered my options. He was right. Even if I could get away from Dieter, I'd be fleeing back to an elf that tossed people into woodchippers for eating someone else's lefse.

"We'll need a better plan than the last one," I grumbled.

In response, Tanckenstein's mangled face scrunched up in thought. "You saw Dieter yawn. It's daytime, so he's asleep. His henchmen and familiar are all out of the picture. Ms. Tanck says opportunity knocks but once. We could just go get the book and leave."

I glowered. "And then we what? Walk home?"

Tanckenstein leaned over and pulled Shane's keys from the cell's lock. I'd only noticed the stupid coffin fob and large iron key. I hadn't noticed the key with a Toyota insignia on it.

"I'll hang onto these," he said seriously. "Ms. Tanck says it's important to learn from our mistakes."

"Do those mistakes include agreeing to work for Ms. Tanck?"

I actually got a grin for that one.

Stein headed back the way Shane had come from. I was fine with him going first. If one of us had to die to give the other a sporting chance at getting away, he'd at least had more practice. When it came to dying, I was still an amateur and had no intention of going pro.


The dungeon hallway led to a winding stone stairway that went up and up and up. At the top, a heavy wooden door creaked on its hinges. After stepping carefully from the stairwell, we saw the entrance to the garage. Quick steps carried Tanckenstein across what could only be described as a medieval mudroom and through the door. A tense moment later, he returned.

"I found Shane's car. Let's get the book."

Moving like he actually knew where he was going, Tanckenstein headed further into the castle. After a short minute, I realized he did know where he was going. The smell of burnt wood and smoldering wool was strong and growing stronger. We literally followed Stein's reattached nose back to the library.

"There it is. Go ahead," he urged me, waving a hand at the book that had been returned to its pedestal.

"Paper-rock-scissors?" I asked, readying my hands for a lightning round.

Tanckenstein shook his head. "Something is protecting it. Not sure why, but it has to be you."

I maneuvered through the rubble and detritus that used to be furniture, each step ratcheting up the uncomfortable feeling that permeated my insides. It felt like I was a balloon being filled up with rank, fetid pond water. Swallowing the vomit that wanted to shove its way up my gullet, I made it to the pedestal and reached out for the book. A second later, I landed in a heap about fifteen feet back with a pained, "Oof!"

"Ms. Tanck says the definition of insanity is doing the same thing and expecting different results," Tanckenstein chided, as he helped me to my feet. "Whatever that spell is, it obviously doesn't like people. Maybe shift like you did last night and try again?"

I shook the collection of marbles that used to be my brain and heard them clatter around inside my skull. After telling Tanckenstein to close his eyes, I stripped out of the poorly fitting clothes I'd stolen from Shane. While far from ideal, they were the only clothes I had, and I didn't want to ruin them. Stein's eyelids squeezed shut. A moment later, I was naked. A moment after that, a scruffy coyote gripped the book in its jaws. The same rotten taste filled my mouth, so I swung my head and set the book sliding across the floor. After quickly shifting back and pulling on the too-short trousers and too-tight Western shirt, I told Tanckenstein he could open his eyes again. We approached the heavy book and stood on either side of it. After a staring contest made it clear that Stein wasn't going to touch the cursed thing, I leaned over and stretched a hand slowly toward the book. Every hair on my arm stood on end, and my molars set to grinding. I let my index finger lightly touch the cover and quickly recoiled.

"You okay?" Tanckenstein asked, voice tight with concern.

I was, and I wasn't. Nothing had happened when I touched the book. At least, nothing obvious. I hadn't flown backward, so that was obviously the protection spell guarding the book's pedestal rather than something weird about the book itself. My finger was still attached to my hand. It hadn't melted or shriveled or fallen off. I still had all my hair. I hadn't suddenly gone blind. Literally nothing physical had happened to me. It was what happened inside of me that had caused me to yank my hand back. In the split second that my finger touched the cover, my mind had exploded with horrible images of fire and smoke and screams of agony. It was like an IMAX of misery had flipped on inside my skull and soaked the back of my eyeballs with every horror known to man, plus a few that mankind still hadn't discovered. It had been downright awful.

"I'm not touching that thing again."

The flat refusal in my voice reached him. With a sympathetic nod, Tanckenstein jogged from the library. It was probably just a couple of minutes, but it felt like forever had passed before he returned with a thick towel.

"I found a linen closet," he explained. "Think this will work?"

He spread the towel on the floor, and I flipped the edge of the book with a toe. Bret's too-large shoes must've offered some level of insulation from the book's evil, because all I felt was a quick wave of queasiness that passed in an instant. The book went up and onto the towel. Tanckenstein pulled the towel's corners together to fashion an impromptu sack and hefted it curiously.

"Heavy," he observed. "C'mon. Let's go."

Thankfully, I heard the scraping. Without thinking, I masked. It wasn't a real shift. I couldn't actually become someone else, but I could borrow their face for a minute or two and wear it like a cheap mask. When a woman pushed through the library's swinging door, Shane—or at least a very rough facsimile of him—was standing in his stained Western shirt next to a large not-dead dead guy.

"Oh, hi Shane." The new arrival offered while setting down her bucket and mop. She was dressed in a light-blue smock. Yellow rubber gloves covered her hands, and a hairnet covered most of her hair. "What a mess, right?"

I quickly scribbled a smile across my borrowed face. Tanckenstein glanced at me, and I saw his tacked-on eyebrows furrow. A moment passed, then another. I grinned like an idiot, and Tanckenstein stared anxiously. Yeah, I knew I was supposed to say something. Anything. Never mind that I knew my voice wouldn't sound like Shane's. The real reason for my frozen vocal cords was simple terror. I'd thought that a woman had walked through the door. That wasn't exactly true. Or maybe it was, but I needed to expand my definition of 'woman' a bit and reconsider the verb 'walked.'

Some parts were there: The shape of her smock clearly indicated breasts beneath. Her waist tapered, then swelled into rounded hips. So sure, womanly enough, but the arms that showed past the edges of the woman's gloves were covered in mottled gray scales, the lips that parted when she spoke were thin and black, and the teeth that showed between them were pointed and yellow. And she certainly hadn't walked. Two legs didn't extend from the smock's hem. Instead, a snakelike tail as thick as my waist bent at ninety degrees where it met the floor and trailed a ways behind her. And that hairnet? It wasn't holding back hair. Beneath it, a nest of asps wriggled and squirmed.

Leave it to Dieter Saint James to have a fucking Gorgon for a maid.

"He's great," Tanckenstein finally said in a perfectly relaxed tone. "I'm new, and Shane was showing me around. Dieter asked us to get a few things out of here so you could clean up."

I noticed he kept his eyes down and told myself I should do the same, but I simply couldn't. I was too busy imagining Medusa sprucing up the place before Jason and his Argonauts popped by her statuary.

"Welcome," she replied with a slight lisp, while a forked tongue darted quickly between the tips of her teeth. Politely keeping her own eyes downcast, she asked, "I wonder what happened here last night. And poor Luke. I saw George toss him in the furnace this morning."

Tanckenstein nodded sympathetically. "Yeah, poor Luke. George, too. I've heard that guy gets the worst jobs. Well, Shane? What do you think? We should probably get this book out of here and let... What was your name again?"

"Hsthena,"

"Hsthena. That's a nice name. It was nice to meet you. We'll be going now."

The Gorgon turned to face us while we studiously avoided her studying eyes. "If you're supposed to help me, taking one book away won't do much."

The situation was starting to spiral. Dry scales scraped on the bare floor between the rugs as the Gorgon slithered closer. I kept my eyes firmly on the tips of Shane's shoes and fervently hoped Stein was doing the same.

"And that isn't the book from the pedestal, is it?" Hsthena hissed. "That book isn't supposed to go anywhere. Ever."

Another slow scrape. The Gorgon was close enough for me to hear the truly unsettling hisses of her aspy locks. A bead of sweat broke out on my forehead and made its way down the contours of Shane's borrowed face, and a nervous little squeak slipped through my lips.

"And George likes putting things in the furnace," she continued, each syllable dipped in suspicion and softened by her forked tongue. "I don't think you know George. I don't think Mr. Saint James told you to move that book. And I don't think you're Shane."

The maid's body twisted so that her torso swerved close to the floor and then swung up again; the move intended to get my downcast eyes to meet with hers.

*Don't look, don't look, don't look,* I pleaded with myself. *If only I was blind. Blind as a bat. Blind as a...*

"Wolverine," I breathed. A moment later, my favorite shift was furiously trying to free itself from a human-sized Western print shirt and skinny slacks while a shocked Gorgon reared back and hissed.

My head whipped around, the wolverine's terrible eyesight revealing vague shapes and shadows without much detail. I hadn't intended to look at the Gorgon. That was the wolverine instinctively wanting to challenge its adversary, stupid little shit that it was. Lucky for me, whatever power lurked in Hsthena's eyes didn't work on my blurry-eyed little friend. That luck didn't extend to Stein, though. Even with my lousy eyesight, I knew a guy turning to stone when I saw it. He'd tried to tackle the maid in that split-second of distraction, but all it took was a glance, and Tanckenstein was Tanckenstone.

I wanted to run. I really did. Every last bit of my human brain was screaming to flee, to get the hell out of there and never look back. Unfortunately, most of my brain and all of my senses belonged to a fierce predator. My eyesight might've sucked, but my sense of smell was off the charts compared to my human nose. I smelled Hsthena and registered a mix of musk and spoiling meat, stomach-churning for a human but a clanging dinner bell for the wolverine. Suddenly, any control I had over my shifted nature was gone. I bared my teeth, growled, and leaped. Hsthena clearly wasn't expecting that. A tiny part of the wolverine's brain—a part that might've been August Shade—felt a twinge of sympathy. The poor lady was only trying to do her job and clean up a hell of a mess in the library. Now she was being attacked by fifty pounds of furious hunger bristling with teeth and claws. Talk about a bad day at the office.

I went for her neck. Only her height and unnatural, snakelike flexibility saved her from a quick end to our contest. My teeth found her shoulder instead and latched down while the asps that weren't trapped under the hairnet frantically struck and recoiled. I didn't care. Wolverines have a pelt plenty thick enough to foil all but the longest of teeth. Jaws designed to crush elk bones to bone meal worked on the poor maid's joint while she writhed in pain. Her giant snake tail sent us careening around the library, adding a fresh layer of disaster to the already-ruined space. A violent lurch shook me free and sent me tumbling across the floor. I found my feet and readied myself for round two, but all that remained of the Gorgon were the fading echoes of her panicked screams.

*Shit,* I thought as my blood cooled. *If she keeps that up, she's going to wake the dead. Undead. Whatever.*

I shifted back into my human form and instantly crouched, head swiveling for any hint of danger. When none appeared, I hurriedly snatched up Shane's clothes and dressed as quickly as possible, managing to get the pants on backward and not giving a single shit. Stein towered over me while I dressed, petrified mid-lurch with arms outstretched. Only his flesh had turned to stone. His no-nonsense jeans and purple hoodie still draped his frame like he was the world's ugliest mannequin.

"I'm sorry, Stein," I said, the words almost a sob. "I'm sorry."

My hand found the corners of the towel holding *The Thirteenth Zodiac,* and my trembling arm took the weight as I lifted. Moving as quickly as I could, I backtracked to the garage, found what had to be Shane's car, and reached for a set of keys that were hooked by a carabiner to a belt loop... Except they weren't.

Tanckenstein had the keys.

I sprinted for the library, too freaked out to care if my headlong charge might've sent me into a Gorgon's waiting arms or worse. I shoved open the swinging door beside the now-dark fireplace and ran for Stein's unmoving form.

"Keys, keys, keys," I muttered as I tentatively patted his hips. Even knowing the guy was literally stone dead, I still didn't want to pat his ass or grab his rock-hard junk if I didn't absolutely have to.

"ont. ocket."

I froze and slid my eyes to look askew at the human-shaped block of stone beside me.

"ont. ocket."

I looked directly up at Stein's face and stared. And stared. And then saw his eyes blink.

"Oh. My. Fucking. God." Each word came out as a disbelieving whisper. "Tanckenstein? Leonard? Was that you? It can't be. You're dead."

"inda," he agreed through lips that couldn't move, then said again, "ont. ocket."

"Ontocket?" I asked. "What does that... Oh!"

I shoved a hand into his jeans pocket and–sure enough–found the ring with its plastic coffin fob and the key for Shane's ride.

"C'mon," I encouraged and made it all of three steps before my feet stopped and my hand palmed my face. "Wait, that's stupid. You aren't going anywhere. Shit."

I needed to get him back to the car since there was no way I could bring the car to him.

"I'll be right back," I promised. "I'm going to see if I can find something to carry you. Don't move. Fuck, sorry. Just, you know. Hang on."

The path from the library to the garage was seared into my brain. When I burst into the garage, I immediately started looking for something, anything, that I could use to haul a six-foot-tall block of rock. There were six stalls, all occupied. One had Shane's compact sedan. There was no way I'd be able to fit Stein into that. The other five cars convinced me that Dieter Saint James was definitely compensating for something.

A classic silver Mercedes. Cushy ride, sure, but Tanckenstein would have to stick up through the sunroof. A shiny red Corvette that I immediately ruled out. A white Range Rover had potential, much more than the sexy little two-seater convertible whose make and model I hadn't a clue. It was the last one, though, that finally sparked a glimmer of hope: A black-as-night 1960's-era hearse.

"That one," I decided. "Definitely that one."

A row of hooks by the side door conveniently held five sets of keys. I quickly skipped the ones emblazoned with logos for Mercedes, Chevy, Range Rover. The remaining two revealed that the sexy little two-seater was a Jaguar. That meant that the classic hearse had to be the Cadillac.

"Because, of course, it is," I grumbled. If Dieter had to travel long distances, being comfy and secure from the sun wouldn't be enough. He'd want to make a statement.

*Rich people,* I grumbled.

The book went in the passenger seat, and then I swung open the rear double-doors. Plenty of space for a Stein statue once the coffin was removed, because of course, there was a coffin. A black, heavily lacquered coffin with gold trim to match the hearse itself. My spirits sank. The damned thing had to be two-hundred pounds. The thought of moving it–then getting back to Stein, somehow getting him into it, and then getting him into the hearse, all while a freaked-out Gorgon was slithering around the castle and screaming bloody murder about a shape-shifting Shane turning into a wolverine and trying to bite her snake-covered head off–was giving me one hell of a headache. I needed a plan, and I needed one fast.

"Think. Think think think. There has to be something."

And then I saw it, and that plan I so desperately needed appeared. My human strength was enough to get the casket gurney up to the hearse's bumper and to roll the heavy casket out of the back. My human strength was enough to hastily push it back to the library and through the swinging door to my petrified companion. But my human strength would never be able to get Stein into the coffin. Eyes frantically searching every corner and ears straining for the sound of trouble, I stripped and shifted into my gorilla. The poor thing was more scared than I'd been a second before. There was nothing jungly about a smashed and half-burned library in a fake Medieval castle. I forced myself to think calming thoughts–promises of bananas and termites and whatever else I could think of that would help settle my jangled simian nerves–and lifted the coffin lid. Next, I lowered a shoulder to Tanckenstein's midsection while one large, dark gray hand gripped an ankle and the other arm wrapped up around his back. A shift of my weight and Stein was horizontal across my shoulders in a fireman's carry. A short pivot, and I readied myself to deposit him in the waiting box.

"Orry, uddy," I chuffed through my gorilla mouth and let the big statue fall.

The sound was about what you'd expect if you were expecting the sound of a two-hundred and fifty-pound block of granite falling into a casket. I was just glad I'd managed to get Stein on his back. Unfortunately, his awkwardly extended leg and arms made closing the lid impossible. With no other options, I grabbed my discarded clothes, tossed them on top of my friend, and grabbed the gurney.

At that moment, Hsthena burst into the library, followed by none other than Mona. She looked pretty rough. Her clothes were the same as from the night before, with the addition of a sling for her arm. Blood and soot covered her face, and her hair was a ragged mess. Compared to her late partner, she looked phenomenal, but that was a pretty low bar.

"There! There! It's them," the maid hissed angrily, her forked tongue giving her a worse lisp than when Dieter had been yelling at me with his inches-long fangs. "Careful. It looked like Shane before it turned into a wolverine and bit me. Who knows what else it can do?"

I kept my eyes locked on the revenant and adamantly refused to let the gorilla flick its eyes to look at the Gorgon. The wolverine had been a fluke. I didn't want to test her power on other wildlife.

Mona stared back with a thoughtful expression. "Who knows, indeed?" she mused. "You go," she instructed Hsthena. "I'll deal with this."

"But," the Gorgon started, but ducked her head subserviently when Mona snapped, "Go!"

Snake-lady wriggled backward and only turned when she finally had to push through the door. A moment later, an undead dead lady stared across a castle's library at a gorilla with a human statue in a casket on a stainless-steel gurney.

*Nothing weird about this,* I thought. *Nothing at all.*

"You two have caused my boss a lot of trouble."

I pursed my lips, puffed my cheeks, and then bared my teeth, the gorilla equivalent of a middle finger. Then, because I couldn't be sure how much Mona knew about insulting gestures favored by giant apes, I raised a hand, slowly closed it into a fist, and then extended its middle digit.

The revenant laughed mirthlessly. "Yeah, I guess I deserve that." She stepped aside and swept her good arm toward the door.

"Well, what are you waiting for?" she asked when I didn't move a muscle. "For Luke," she explained.

Opportunity knocks but once. I leaned on the gurney's bar and heard its wheels squeak in protest of the weight it was being forced to carry. My gorilla feet slapped heavily on the floor as I tromped past her. Why the distance to the garage suddenly felt twice as long, I didn't know, but every step seemed an endless journey until suddenly, the journey ended. After positioning the gurney at the hearse's bumper, I gave the coffin a hopeful nudge and exhaled in relief when the open lid and Stein's outstretched arms cleared the opening. I melted back to my human form and rested a moment until the vertigo passed. Shaking hands pulled on the only clothes I had, and a deranged chortle slipped out when I got the pants on right. I slid behind the Caddy's wheel, pressed the garage door opener, and floored it.

While speeding down the highway, I counted our blessings. The sun was bright in a cloudless sky, the drawbridge was down, the wrought-iron gate swung open when I found the right remote, and soon the castle had dwindled to a dark and distant memory behind me. I knew I should've felt elated, or at least relieved. Against all odds, I'd managed to get the book and not die in the process. Soon, Vilde would have the book—whatever the fuck it was—and I'd have enough cash to drink as much shitty beer as my liver could handle. I was a winner. A damned winner. Even so, the mood in the car was dark. Tanckenstein might not have been a friend, but he'd been getting closer to being one with each passing day. Now he was an undead statue in the trunk of a hearse, and I had no idea what to do with him. A very powerful vampire was going to wake up when the sun set and be treated to a very unpleasant surprise, and that get-out-of-jail-free card Mona had thrown me had definitely been a onetime deal. Hard to stay upbeat when you knew the meanest vampire this side of Canada and his undead henchperson would be coming for you soon.

That, and the car stank. I cracked a window, but even the wind rushing in while I sped down the highway did little to change the oddly rank ambiance that filled the space. It was going to be a long drive home. With only the wind, the stench, and my own dark thoughts for company, I pointed the hearse toward Minneapolis and drove.

About a half-hour later, I maneuvered the hearse to the curb in front of Vilde Tanck's bakery. A shaky sigh escaped my lips as I made my way to the door and pushed inside, the little bell above the door brightly announcing my arrival. The huldra was in the process of balancing the till and looked up in surprise when I entered.

"Velkommen, Mr. Shade!" she exclaimed. "You have my book?"

It was still in the car. When I said as much, a hint of avarice marred her otherwise flawless features. The huldra was practically vibrating with anticipation. I didn't want to break the other news to her but figured it'd be best to rip the bandage off. I only hoped that if she killed the messenger, she'd let me stay dead.

"Stein, I mean Leonard, too," I said, voice hitching. "He's... He's..."

The huldra waved a hand dismissively. "I am sure he is fine. The book, Mr. Shade."

Her callous dismissal made a mockery of all we'd endured on her behalf. My fists clenched, and it was all I could do not to launch one at her perfect face.

"He is not fine!" I yelled and watched her eyes go wide at my outburst. "There was a fight, and we got thrown in a dungeon and had to break out, and then your ex-boyfriend's Gorgon maid turned him into a block of granite. Who has a Gorgon for a maid? Why would anyone have a Gorgon for a maid?"

Vilde stepped around the counter, cow's tail flicking from below the hem of her dress and eyes narrowing.

"Hsthena? Ah, you are right. She is a terrible maid. Not so bad in the summer, perhaps, but impossibly slow when the weather is cold. Why Dieter is so fond of her, I simply do not know. And now Leonard has her curse?"

I offered a stiff nod, and she laughed, actually laughed.

"I will deal with him later. Getting turned to stone. Uakseptabelt. Simply not acceptable," she translated for my benefit. "Dieter will pay, of course, but Leonard also must be taught a lesson. Perhaps I will keep him in my garden and let the birds poop on him. Perhaps then he will learn not to be so foolish. Now, I would greatly like to have my book, Mr. Shade."

It was too much. "After everything he's gone through for you... All you care about is some stupid book."

Vilde clucked her tongue at me like I was a problematic child about to be scolded.

"Yes, I care very deeply about my book. Leonard will be tended to but first, my book."

I glared. It was hard to comprehend something so surreally beautiful being so unbelievably cruel. Only her promise that Stein could somehow, someway be okay again cooled the heat of my burning indignation. My feet retraced their steps, and I retrieved the swaddled book while studiously refusing to look at what was in the back of the hearse. The book seemed to be as heavy as a bowling ball, and my strength was at its end. When I made it back inside, I let it fall from my fingers and land heavily on the floor.

"I am impressed," the woman crooned as she folded the thick towel back to reveal its contents. "Horoscope aside, I did not think that you would succeed."

I *hmph'd* in response. "Almost didn't. Your old flame is a real asshole."

A corner of Vilde's full lips crooked up. "Ja, he most certainly is. How did he look, by the way?"

"Orange." I took a deep breath and let it slip out through my nostrils. "So, you gonna do something with that book or what?"

I shouldn't have encouraged her. She reached down and grasped it. The expression on her face changed instantly, but it wasn't the look of unsettled revulsion I was expecting. It was a look of radiant joy. Pure, unadulterated bliss. I doubted I'd ever get to see Vilde Tanck orgasm but suddenly felt like what I was seeing was a close second. Then it occurred to me that her reaction was way beyond something as simple and primal as that. Her reaction to lifting that book in her perfect fingers was nothing short of rapture.

"What is that book, anyway?" I asked.

"Power, Mr. Shade. Destiny. The culmination of a long journey."

"Like Stephen King's Dark Tower?" I didn't read a lot, but that particular series had been fun.

She frowned at that, enough to crease the skin between her eyebrows and draw the corners of her mouth down. "*The Thirteenth Zodiac* cannot be read."

"Oh, so it's more like poetry." I hated poetry.

Vilde managed to end her lascivious regard of the book and look up at me. Her eyes were not kind. "Perhaps it is, Mr. Shade. Perhaps it is. Now it is time for you to go."

Her tail twitched, and I noticed a leather satchel by her bare feet.

"Do you want to count it?" she asked, a challenge sharpening the edges of her words.

I didn't and said as much. Hell, I didn't even want the money. It was pragmatism, nothing more, that made me lift the satchel before turning my back on Vilde Tanck and walking out of her bakery. What I wanted was to never see or even think of her, her ex, or that damned book again.

# CHAPTER 8



B ACK AT JAY'S STUDIO, the bag of cash tucked away in my 'stupid' safe, I settled into the beanbag and let its promise of safety and security and total normalcy envelop me. Jay grabbed a couple of cold pilsners from the fridge and passed one my way. Our hands simultaneously pulled the tabs, our throats swallowed in unison, and our lungs sighed in synchronized appreciation. After a bit of prompting from my friend, I unfurled the tale of storming Dieter Saint James' castle, pausing only to drink or when Jay exclaimed at one exciting moment or another. Telling it made it feel like the whole ordeal had happened ages ago to someone else entirely, rather than to me during the past twenty-four hours. Did I really fight with a centuries-old vampire and live to talk about it? Had I actually been locked in a dungeon? Was Tanckenstein truly a talking statue now? Could there seriously be a bag stuffed with thousands of dollars in my office? It all seemed impossible, and Jay agreed.

"Not to be a jerk, but I didn't think you'd pull it off," he admitted.

"I've been getting that a lot lately," I muttered.

Jay grimaced and fiddled with the tip of a thick dreadlock. "Sorry. You think Leonard will be all right?"

I wasn't sure how to answer. The Gorgon's curse didn't seem like something you could just walk off, but Vilde hadn't been too concerned about bringing back her servant. To be fair, some PNs can be pretty resilient and stubbornly hard to kill. Sure, Tanckenstein was pushing the envelope on how much one person could take, but, as a reanimated formerly dead person, I imagined he'd be even harder to bump off the board than most.

"I guess," I finally offered with a shrug. "I hope he has good insurance, though. I can only imagine what the medical bills will be."

We raised a toast to our kinda-dead friend and drank, Jay in quiet contemplation and me intent on obliterating every last memory of my Saint James adventure. I took a last swallow of beer, squeezed my eyes shut, and took slow, steady breaths.

"Sorry. Long couple of days," I muttered. "And I lost my keys. I'm gonna crash here for the night and get a locksmith in the morning."

When I opened my eyes, I found my friend staring at me worriedly.

"Go on. Go home. I'm fine."

Jay shrugged his acceptance. On his way out, he killed the large sodium lamps illuminating the studio and left me in the dim glow of the streetlights pushing through the dusty windows. I took a deep breath and closed my eyes again, but the hoped-for sleep didn't come. Something was nagging at me, an unscratchable itch that spread until my whole brain felt like it had rolled in a patch of poison ivy.

First was the five grand in my safe. I'd stubbornly refused to consider the staggering sum. It was a fair price for the job, I told myself, but could only keep up the delusion for so long. The weird vibes that the book put out were definitely something I couldn't explain away, nor was Vilde's orgasmic babbling about power and the culmination of a long journey, or Dieter's mean delight when he'd realized Vilde hadn't told me what the book was. I felt like a pebble had shifted on a steep, rocky slope, and an avalanche was about to follow. I felt like I'd been the one to kick that particular pebble. And, despite all reason, I felt like there was someone who had known that I would be the one to do it.

Opening my eyes again, I muscled my way up from the beanbag and headed to my office. A flick of my wrist turned the light on, and I rounded my desk. After dropping heavily into my chair, I pulled out a drawer and shifted its cluttered contents from side to side.

"C'mon. It's gotta be in here... Ah!"

Flourishing the small scrap of paper with Clarissa Steyer's number on it, I picked up the phone and dialed. A couple of rings later, a manic voice answered with, "I have no idea who this is," followed by a deranged giggle.

"... Clarissa?" I asked. "It's August Shade."

Another brittle laugh filled my ear. "Cripes. Of course, it is! Why wouldn't it be you? You're in all of them. Every damn one. It used to only be some of them. Now you're in all of them."

I looked at the number in my hand, then at the phone on my desk. I had used them both correctly, but the outcome wasn't at all what I'd expected. "Clarissa, are you drunk?"

"Uff da, no. Not in this one. Or maybe." Again, the slightly unhinged laugh. "Sure. Why not? Let's get drunk. That's why you brought the wine, right? Grapes and raisins and dust…"

An uncharacteristic worry made my eye twitch. "Clarissa, I didn't bring you wine. I'm not there. You're at home, and I'm at my office. We're talking on the phone," I explained in the soothing, rational voice I used whenever Jay had put away a few too many. With Jay, it usually lulled him into agreeable compliance. With Clarissa, it made her snort and laugh harder.

"Ope, sorry. Wrong one! Yes. We drink at a bar. Don't need to be psychic to know people get drunk at bars. I'm glad you asked. Oh, but maybe not. Maybe it's that one. He jabs with his right and is stronger than he looks. Aries and Sagittarius. Shit," she swore, the curse so unexpected I nearly dropped the phone. "If this is that one, I don't think my June worked. Oh, that could be bad. Or maybe not. Or maybe. Fuck it. I'll be at the bar in fifteen."

A loud *clack* signaled the end of the call, and the words, "What bar?" died on my lips. I considered redialing and then decided against it. I wasn't up for playing nursemaid to a drunk oracle, but the exchange did make me realize that I wanted another drink. I made my way to the studio's fridge, pulled on the handle, and borrowed one of Clarissa's recent curses. The round with Jay had used up the last of the beer.

About ten minutes later, I took a sip from a frosty pint glass and slid a hundred-dollar bill across the bar to an astonished Betty.

"You win the lottery?" she asked.

"Something like that. It's good to see you, by the way. Really good, if you know what I mean."

Betty pouted. "I do. If you'd stopped in last night, who knows? We might've had some fun. But me and Tony are back together now. I hate diets, but I'm trying the whole monogamy thing," she finished nobly.

*Last night?* I grumbled. *Instead of getting the shit kicked out of me and rotting in a dungeon, I could've been… Ahhhh, crap.*

It pained me to know how different my life could've been, but I still forced a smile. "He's a lucky warlock. What changed your mind?"

The bartender blushed prettily. "Someone left a copy of the *Metro Pages* here, and I was flipping through it when I saw the horoscopes." She looked off into some romantic distance. "Let's just say it helped me look at things a little differently, and then me and Tony... tried some different things." Her hands slid down her stomach and along her thighs while her lips parted in a soft sigh. After an uncomfortable moment–well, for me anyway–she remembered I was there. "So, I want to make sure we're clear: I'm strictly the one succubus, one warlock type now. No hard feelings, right?"

*There were hard feelings. That was the whole point,* I complained to myself while saying out loud, "None. I'm, um. Really happy for you. That's just... great." The words left a bitter taste in my mouth. In a sudden and juvenile attempt to turn the tables, I blurted out, "Actually, you know what? I'm seeing someone, too."

"Really? You?"

That hit below the belt. "Yeah, me. Why not?"

Betty shrugged. "You just don't seem like much of a dater. Oh, is this her?"

I turned with a confused look to see who she was talking about, and an oracle walked into the bar. Betty took in the slumpy stockings and drab skirt and oversized cardigan and gave me a look. I gave her a scowl. Clarissa gave us both a loud hurrah.

"We're in this one! And you," she accused the baffled bartender, "must be the Aries."

Betty's eyes narrowed. "... Yeah. And?"

"August is a Sagittarius. Usually, that's a good fit–really good–but you have a very clumsy sexual encounter in most of them. Weird, right?"

The succubus bridled. "I'm not capable of a clumsy sexual encounter," she snapped. "You've obviously never met a succubus."

"You're a succubus?" Clarissa asked as her eyes drifted out of focus. "Cripes. How the heck did I miss that? I've never met an Aries succubus, but yeah. Makes sense. Fire sign. Confident, passionate. Also impatient, short-tempered, aggressive."

"Only when someone tries my patience, upsets me, and makes me aggressive. Now, are you drinking? Because if you're not, there are plenty of not-bars you can go to."

I sat, jaw hanging down, completely befuddled by the exchange. Clarissa was weird, sure, and maybe wound a bit tight, but she'd always been nice enough. I'd never in a million years have thought she'd be capable of getting into it with anybody, much less a complete stranger. But now? Yeesh. Just went to show that 'Minnesota Nice' was as fickle as the weather. While I tried to process the change, she announced that she wanted a Sea

Breeze, then slapped a hand on the bar. "Now we're in that one. Sea Breeze. See breeze," she repeated, overemphasizing the first word while giving her eyeball a disconcerting tap, then added in a more serious tone, "Oh, shoot. I don't like this one."

"Your date's a real piece of work," Betty said with a raised eyebrow and then turned to splash rail vodka, cranberry, and grapefruit juice and a twist of lime into a rocks glass.

"She's not my date," I protested, but my words were drowned out by Clarissa's proclamation that this must be the one where we go on a date. When I turned wide eyes to the woman next to me, she smiled a huge, toothy smile.

"Sagittarius and Libra can have great sexual chemistry, but they've gotta be really relaxed with each other," she whispered loudly. "We eat pizza. You spill sauce on your shirt, and we both laugh."

Betty set Clarissa's drink down hard enough to send the glass's contents splashing over its rim. I'd given her one of the hundred-dollar bills from Vilde's satchel when I'd ordered my beer, but no change materialized. I raised a hand and readied a complaint about the eighty-some dollars I should've gotten back when Clarissa swatted my hand down.

"We're not in that one anymore," she chastised, and then drank half her drink in a series of gulps. "Drinks are expensive in this one." The woman pondered her already half-empty glass. "In one, you do something really dangerous and get a lot of money. Did you know that?"

All I could do was look at her in stunned silence. I'd called Clarissa because I was sure she must know something about the weird events of the past few weeks. Now, I wasn't sure she was sober enough to know what direction up was.

"I know about entropy and negentropy," she said abruptly. "Do you?"

My blank stare must've conveyed pretty much everything I knew because she giggled, finished her drink, and loudly ordered a glass of red wine. After Betty delivered the drink, Clarissa lifted the glass by its stem and peered at me over its rim.

"All right. Let's start at the beginning. Entropy is the gradual, inevitable decline into disorder. You ever do the gunny sack slide at the State Fair?"

I shook my head mutely.

"Oh, you should. You sit on a sack and go down this wavy slide. So fun. Anyway, sometimes they let too many people go at once, and folks get all jumbled up at the bottom. It's like that. The grapes used to make this wine, for example. There are forces that hold all of the molecules in a very specific alignment. Together, properly aligned, they make a grape: a living, growing thing. Pick the grape from the vine and set it in the sun. Eventually, those forces that pull all of those molecules into that very specific alignment weaken. The grape dries out, wrinkles, becomes a raisin. Let more time pass, and that poor excuse for a grape declines further, breaks down, and eventually becomes nothing more than a pile of unassembled molecules. There is nothing left that says 'grape.' It's just chaos. Raw material without order or structure. It's just stuff."

She paused. I stared. She drank. I did the same. After another awkward moment or two, she burped and then continued.

"Negentropy is the opposite. It is the intentional ordering of chaos. It's the force that made that grape in the first place. After that grape decomposes in the sun, all those little chaotic bits are gobbled up by insects, and negentropy turns that stuff into energy that helps those hungry little buggers grow in an ordered and expected way. Eventually, that insect will die, and entropy resumes its slow, steady march. Energy and matter are built up into things by negentropy. Energy and matter are pulled apart and rendered meaningless by entropy."

"If you're my date, you're the worst date ever," I muttered.

"I never chose to be like this," Clarissa snapped and then drank more wine. "You think I want this? It's horrible. Every moment of it is horrible. I wish I could have a normal life. Be a normal woman with a normal job and do normal things, like go on dates. Even bad ones."

"So why don't you?" I challenged. "What's stopping you?"

She stared at me like I was the world's biggest idiot. "Not much fun dating someone if you already know how it's going to work out. Kind of kills the mystery, don'cha think?"

I rocked back on my barstool, stunned by the new and unexpected perspective she'd offered. Maybe she really could see the future. And if that was true, she would know what was going to happen. Sure, she'd explained it to me. Not very well, maybe–or maybe I just wasn't the brightest star in the Sagittarius constellation–but I hadn't really considered all the implications. To never be surprised by a gift. To foresee the unavoidable argument. To already know if the make-up sex will be any good before you even undo the first button of your shirt. The more I thought about it–really looked at all the angles–the more my head spun. Worse, the more my heart broke for the woman sitting beside me.

"Have you always been, you know, the way you are?"

Clarissa shrugged, suddenly deflated. "No, not always," she admitted. "Not until I got this."

The oracle tapped her eye, a gesture I decided I would simply never, ever get used to.

"How?" I asked.

The woman rocked her wineglass and sent the red liquid gently sloshing from side to side. It was almost hypnotic. The red liquid climbed one side of the glass, then the other. As it receded from each side, it left no trace on the smooth surface.

"The usual way, I guess. Dad took me fishing when I was a kid. He told me to stand beside him whenever he was casting, but I was a kid, and kids are terrible at doing what they should. I saw a butterfly cocoon on a milkweed. The butterfly was just starting to crawl out. It was a Canadian Tiger Swallowtail. Ever seen one?"

I shook my head mutely.

"Oh, you should. They're beautiful. Yellow and black. Little bits of blue down by their little butterfly butts. So pretty. Anyway, I turned to tell my dad to come look right as he brought his pole back to cast. The fishhook snagged in my eye."

An involuntary gag almost sent my beer back up. It was a few moments before I was able to speak. When I was, all I could say was, "Yikes."

Clarissa nodded. "Yep. Yikes, indeed. Dad was furious. All the way back to town, he kept yelling at me. Telling me I should've known better. I should've known what would happen. And you know what? I believed him. I was eight years old. When you're a kid and your dad tells you something, you believe him, right? The whole way to the hospital, I was shaking. Crying. Kicking and writhing in my seat. Yeah, I was scared, and my eye was on fire, but that wasn't why I was such a mess. The horrible thought that it was my fault, that I should have seen what would happen, was screaming inside my skull."

She paused and took a drink. I didn't know what to say, so I hid behind my pint glass and drank as well. After another moment or so, she continued with her tale.

"We got to the hospital, and they rushed me right into surgery. I woke up full of drugs and short an eye. Mom cried a lot. Dad didn't say much. The hospital made a prosthetic eye, but I didn't like it very much. It wasn't mine. Years later, when I was in high school, I was at a little curio shop. You know the type. Mostly junk, but people would buy it because it was old and weird junk. Anyway, there was a small wooden box on a shelf. It caught my only eye, so I opened it up. Inside, looking up at me from a tiny red velvet cushion, was my eye. Mine. Its iris was a perfect match for the one I'd lost, but that isn't what I mean. It's hard to explain, but I looked at that little glass ball on its velvet cushion and thought, 'Oh! There it is.' I asked the woman at the counter how much it cost. She looked at me for a long time, then told me I should try it. She helped me clean it in the bathroom sink."

I held up a hand. "Wait. You washed it in a junk store's bathroom sink?"

"Don't be such a wuss," she replied. "Yes. I washed it in a junk store's bathroom, then I took out my prosthetic and put in this one. The woman asked me what I saw."

Silence settled between us again, and not just between us but all around us as well. It was like the world had taken a breath and held it. I perched on the edge of my barstool and waited. And waited. And then she spoke.

"I looked at her reflection in the bathroom mirror and then... I saw her. I saw the woman, but not beside me in the bathroom. I saw her counting the till. Tucking bills into a money bag. I saw her look up at a sound. I saw the flash, and I saw her grab her stomach and fall. I saw the blood, and a boot step in the growing puddle. I saw the man grab the bag of cash and leave. And then I saw her die. It was horrible, August. I tried to scream but couldn't. When the woman grabbed my shoulders, I flailed and fought but eventually she made me be still. 'Look again,' she said, so I did. I saw her at the til, but with a customer. I heard her tell the customer to have a good night. The customer bumped something on the way out and it fell from a shelf. The woman went to pick it up and then locked the front door. She went back to the til, counted the money into the cash bag, turned off the lights, and left out the back. And that was it. That was all."

The oracle turned to face me. A single tear had welled up in the lower lid of her good eye, and she absently wiped it away.

"That was my first vision. My first experience with seeing the what-ifs. I told her both visions. She smiled and thanked me. Three days later, my dad was watching the news and there was a report of a robbery. A woman was killed. Shot."

I tried to think of something to say—anything to push through the huge, uncomfortable tension that had swelled between us—but came up short. While I sat dumbfounded, Clarissa waved for Betty to bring another round. After the bartender reluctantly replenished our drinks, the oracle contemplated her glass of wine.

"It drove me nuts, August. Those two very different futures: One where she lived, and one where she died. One where the store's door was locked, and one where it wasn't. One where a clumsy customer had accidentally knocked something off a shelf, and one where that didn't happen. Why didn't that one actually happen? Why didn't that person go into the shop that day? If they had, the shop owner would've locked the door and lived. The more I thought about it, the more I thought about the possibilities, the more I started to see. I learned how to look through all those possibilities and find the more likely ones. Been doing it ever since."

She puffed out a frustrated breath; the exhalation lifting a loose strand of hair that had slipped down over her face.

"I see the futures after each possible future and all the futures after those. An endless web. Countless possibilities. A million million branching paths. It's awful, exhausting, but I can't not do it. So, in my own little way, I've been trying to use it for good. I try to guide the world toward the futures that lead to even better ones. The universe slides down its wavy slide toward entropy. I try to resist. I try to be negentropy."

I frowned, confused. "How? It's not like you could ever control all the possible events. People do what they're going to do, and there's no changing them. Trust me, I've tried. There's no way you could ever convince someone to... Oh."

When the stars aligned, it was all I could do not to slap myself on the forehead.

"Horoscopes. You use horoscopes."

Clarissa nodded with renewed vigor. "I'm not the first and sure hope I'm not the last. Turns out that people like me have used our talents to try and keep the world spinning for millennia. Of course, we haven't all been saints. There have been a few that have done their damndest to send it all to hell. They try to kick the world toward entropy. Lucky for the world, others resist."

I shook my head, trying to keep up. "And you're all Zodiac wonks?"

The woman drained half her glass, put a fist to her chest and belched, then finished her wine in another series of industrious swallows.

"Of course not. From what I've been able to learn, we've been all sorts of things. Did you know that we would've lost World War II if a certain community theater director in Montana had quit after the dress rehearsal instead of toughing it out and whipping everyone into shape before opening night?"

Not much to say to that, so I opted to say nothing, which in its own way was saying something.

"Astrology was a good fit for me," she continued. "I like it. The Zodiac is pretty neat when you really dig into it. I know most people don't take my horoscopes seriously, but I try to write them for the ones that do. The ones whose actions might have some significance. It's hard, August. So hard. And with each passing day, it's getting harder. Imagine trying to steer an ocean liner away from the iceberg's tip, but you can't turn the rudder yourself. You have to whisper in someone's ear and hope they'll whisper in someone else's ear and hope that person is the one steering the ship. And the whole time, there's you shoving more and more icebergs up toward the surface."

I bridled. "What in the hell do I have to do with any of this?"

Betty chose that moment to check in on us. I don't think I can take any credit for her sudden decision to dial up the sexual tension. It was more likely that a person just can't change who they are. Clarissa was prone to long, confusing diatribes. I was more often than not an unpleasant little prick. Betty was always horny. She rested her elbows on the bar, laced her fingers, and leaned forward. Luminous eyes looked up through long lashes, full lips curved into a suggestive smile, and cleavage promised that there was so much more to explore.

"Is she bothering you, babe?" she purred.

One succubus, one warlock, was apparently so twenty minutes ago. I stared into those eyes, thought of everything I knew about succubi, and considered how I had survived a pretty awful week and how, if anyone deserved a roll in the hay, it was definitely me. Yes, I was about to be a massive jerk, a grade-A asshole, but lightning doesn't strike twice.

"Oh. Well, I think. Um. I think we were pretty much done, aren't we?" I asked the oracle.

Clarissa's eyes—eye?—went far away. When she finally looked at me again, her expression was unreadable. "Did I drink a Sea Breeze?"

I shared a glance with the bartender, and we both nodded.

"Crap. I think we're back in that one," she said with deep apprehension. "Sea Breeze. Jabs with his right. Shit. I should've just had wine."


The next few moments felt awfully strange, almost like I wasn't actually living them myself but was watching from the outside, a confused spectator at some weird performance art thing.

First, I heard a familiar voice demand, "What's he doing here?"

Next, my head swiveled toward the voice. At the same moment that my eyes found Tony's face, his right fist socked me smack between the eyes. It hurt, but that first dose of pain was just the tip of one of those icebergs Clarissa had been babbling about. The real hurt came a second later when his left fist swung around and caught the side of my jaw. I took a wild swing in panicked self-defense and connected, but it was Clarissa who screamed, not Tony. A loud curse followed, and then she was off her stool and scurrying along the bar. One hand covered half her face, and the other grasped frantically for the little glass ball that was rolling away.

I lurched toward her, mortified at what I'd done, but before I could see if she was okay, an elbow came down hard on my back. The force bounced my forehead off the edge of the bar and rendered me momentarily blind. I had just enough time to wonder if maybe Tony had knocked my eyes out before I tumbled backward. I'd just found my feet and had locked eyes with the warlock when a strong gust lifted me. As I sailed past the row of barstools, arms extended helplessly and heels gliding above the bar's sticky floor, I wondered in a passing sort of way why I'd been spending so much time flying through the air. Then I crashed through the bar's door and tumbled ass over teakettle across the pavement until friction finally trumped inertia.

As I looked up at a streetlight and the stars dotting the dark sky beyond, one last coherent thought emerged from the wreckage of my battered brain.

"Heh. See breeze. Good one, Clarissa."

I blinked once, twice. A third attempt was only partially successful. My eyes stayed closed, and consciousness slipped away.

I woke up in a bed. A ceiling fan spun lazily above, and soft light from some corner of the room or other painted the walls a buttery yellow. The mattress beneath me was an immediate indication that things were far from normal. Usually, after a bender, I'd wake up on the couch if I was lucky. More often, it was on my apartment's floor. There'd even been a time or three when I'd regained consciousness in my office chair. Those were rough because my chair was a terrible place to sleep. My eyes closed, and I savored the soft pillow, warm blanket, and sense of relief that I hadn't slept in my office chair. My eyes snapped open when it occurred to me that my apartment didn't have a ceiling fan in the bedroom. Or soft pillows. Or a comfortable mattress. Or a–I squinted–floral print comforter.

"What?" I managed and instantly regretted it. Even that little sound sent a bolt of jagged lightning splintering through my skull.

"Shhh," a voice whispered. "Don't talk for a few minutes. I think you have a concussion."

"Winner, winner, chicken dinner," I muttered. Another lightning bolt arced behind my eyes. Only after its white-hot iridescence had faded was I able to ask, "What happened? How did I get here?"

Betty crossed into my peripheral vision and sat on the edge of the bed. The succubus had clearly just come from the shower. Her dark tresses were hidden beneath a red towel expertly wrapped around her head, and a matching terry cloth bathrobe hung loosely from her shoulders. A sash around her waist held it closed while still sharing a tantalizing hint of what was beneath. I felt myself stir before the pain in my skull squashed my libido. Her dark eyes watched my discomfort, and her full lips turned down.

"Sorry," she apologized quietly. Long fingers tugged the edges of the robe together, and then she laughed softly as disappointment washed across my face. "Maybe later if you're feeling better? I could use a little snack. Speaking of which, you should probably eat something. You like your eggs scrambled like your brain?"

"Fried like my nerves," I answered.

Betty stood with a nod and revealed exactly how short the bathrobe was. I squeezed my eyes shut in response and exhaled through my nose.

"Oh, sorry again. Let me get dressed. I might have something modest hiding in the back. I'm not really used to not turning guys on, but I'll try."

I nodded my thanks. When she emerged from her closet wearing loose sweatpants and a too-big sweatshirt, I asked again how I'd ended up in her bed.

"And did we, you know. Do... anything?"

Betty bristled at that. "If we had, you'd remember." Her icy tone thawed a bit when she added, "You weren't in any shape to do anything. I was going to bring you to the emergency room, but you kept saying, 'No doctor, no doctors,' like a skipping record, so here you are."

I muttered a soft thanks and kept my eyes closed while I gingerly explored the sides of my head with tentative fingers. Near as I could tell, my skull was still whole rather than a mismatched collection of shards. A relieved sigh escaped my lips, after which I stayed very still and tried not to stir any of my body's various aches and pains from their uneasy slumbers. I heard Betty leave the room. A moment later, I heard noises from what had to be her kitchen. Cupboards opening and closing. Dishes clinking. The sound of a gas burner and the sizzle of a hot pan. The metronome clicks of a toaster oven's mechanical timer. Smells found their way to my nose. Heavenly smells. I hadn't realized how hungry I was until my nostrils filled with the scents of fried butter and fresh-brewed coffee.

When Betty returned with a plate of eggs and buttery toast, I sat up in bed and snatched it eagerly from her fingers. The plate was clean before she'd even had time to set a steaming mug on the bedside table. Eggs and toast devoured, I raised the cup like a holy relic and said a silent prayer before bringing it to my lips. When Betty started to say something, I held up a finger to silence her. Only after about two-thirds of the steaming brown liquid had burned my tongue and settled comfortably in my gut did I lower my finger and allow the conversation to resume.

"That is really, really good coffee," I praised. "Didn't want to spoil it with talking."

The succubus took the cup from my hands. "So you're saying you like things nice and hot?"

I blinked. "I, ah. Yes. Yes, I suppose I do. I just..." I trailed off to stop myself from cursing out loud. Something was happening–something amazing–and it was happening at the worst possible time.

I'd fantasized plenty of times about getting together with Betty the bartender. In all of them, I was awesome. A total rockstar. A god. Humor me. When all you've got are fantasies, you gotta make the most of them. Now, though... On a scale of one to total-sex-guru, I doubted I'd even rate a negative four. Every part of me hurt. The energy I'd expended to sit up and eat had exhausted me. Staying conscious was a struggle. At the exact moment that I could've been doing all the things I'd wanted to do with her for so long, I wasn't even sure I could say the word 'sex', much less do it.

My tortured conundrum must've been plain to see. Her lips folded into a sultry pout, and she told me to lie back and close my eyes. I did what I was told and heard soft footsteps recede. A faucet ran and stopped, and then footsteps drew near. The mattress beside me compressed, and then a cool, damp cloth covered my forehead. It was glorious.

"Sorry about last night," Betty whispered. "Tony got a little carried away."

I succumbed to her ministrations but couldn't help responding, "As I recall, I was the one that got carried away. By his spell. Which slammed me through a door, dumped me on the street, and left me with a traumatic brain injury."

"Poor darling," she purred as she lifted the cool cloth, folded it over, and gently returned it to my forehead.

"It's okay. He's just stronger than he looks," I said, and then grimaced. "And he's left-handed and jabs with his right. Fuck. I hate her. I hate her so much."

Betty's fingers slid through my hair. "Who? Your date?"

"She wasn't a date," I snapped, churlishly defensive. "She was a client."

Again, her fingers worked their way through my hair, but this time, each fingertip pressed gently into my scalp. It felt wonderful.

"Tony is going to be so upset," she mused. "To go to all that trouble, and she wasn't even your date."

I cracked an eye open. "What trouble?"

"All of it. Getting into a fight with you. Arguing with me. Leaving with your not-date. You should've seen him. Fussing over her like she was some injured little bird that he had to nurse back to health. Well, two can play at that game." A fingertip traced my ear as she leaned in and placed a soft kiss on my forehead. "He's so melodramatic. You, too, you know. So angsty and mopey and prickly," she pouted playfully. "I'm August Shade. I'm crabby. I don't like anyone." Another kiss, this one on my cheek. "But you like me, don't you? You like me more than he does. You like me more than anyone, don't you?"

I did. I really, really did. My pulse quickened, every beat a distant thunderclap of pain in my head, but I didn't care. I reached up and pulled her toward my mouth. Our lips met in a long kiss. Her hand slid across my chest, down my stomach. Our mouths never parting, she shifted and twisted, one knee compressing the mattress beside me while her other leg swung over me and came down on the other side. Her hips pressed into mine as my hands explored the wonderful shape of her. The thunderstorm in my skull was raging louder and louder, but I didn't care. Couldn't care. There was a dream that was about to come true. An impossible dream. A wonderful dream. I could feel it. Smell it. Taste it.

It tasted a bit sour, which was weird. Like coffee. Like eggs.

Betty's hips thrust harder, a loud peal of thunder rocked the space between my ears, and that breakfast she'd made for me violently came out the way it had gone in.

The upside was that she'd been kissing my neck, so I didn't throw up in her mouth. The downside—one of a great many in that completely horrendous moment—was the staggering amount of my just-eaten breakfast that went down the loose collar of her sweatshirt. She screamed and thrust herself back so violently that she fell off the foot of the bed and landed hard on the bedroom floor. A torrent of swear words poured from her mouth while the last sticky bits of eggs and toast drooled from mine. Both ended at about the same time, and then there was a terrible, crushing silence.

"I'll clean this up," I started, but stopped when her head popped up over the bed's footboard. There was murder in her eyes. A barely contained rage.

"Get. Out." She stood, her back hunched in a vain attempt to keep the soiled inside of the hoodie from touching her skin beneath. "Now. While I'm still capable of patience. While I'm still capable of remembering that you had a really bad night. If you're still here when I get out of the shower, you're dead."

I didn't need to be warned twice. The second the bathroom door closed, I heaved myself from the bed, shoved myself into my clothes, and ran for the door. As luck would have it, Betty didn't live too far from a bus line. A few bucks, a transfer, and a hefty number of disgusted glares from morning commuters later, I was home.

I brushed my teeth twice but couldn't rid my mouth of the taste. I was about to scrub them a third time and instead threw my toothbrush hard at the bathroom mirror. It ricocheted off the dirty glass, bounced off a wall, and plunked into my toilet. I wanted to scream but was afraid that doing so would leave me unconscious on the floor. Instead,

I gripped the sides of the sink and forced myself to take long, slow breaths. In through my mouth, out through my nose. After ten or so, I'd regained enough control to pop a couple of painkillers. I knew from experience that they'd eventually dampen the angry signals every nerve was sending to my brain. I also knew it'd take something a lot stronger to quell the toxic mix of shame and self-recrimination that had moved into my recently vacated stomach. My worn and lumpy couch reluctantly took my weight, and I reached for the whiskey on my coffee table. An overflowing glass—never mind the early morning hour—soon set my mind afloat on a troubled sea, and I tried to let it all go. All of it. Clarissa. Betty. Tony. Vilde. Dieter. I wanted nothing to do with any of them ever again and told myself that was my choice to make.

# CHAPTER 9



*Ope! It's your horoscope, Leo!*
*No one knows how roundabouts really work. No one but you, that is.*

---

JAY HAD PROMISED TO buy all my drinks, and I hoped for his sake that he had a full wallet. It was going to take a lot of beer to get me through the day. One Jay, I can handle. A cut-rate hotel event center full of Jays? Uff da.

Why I'd agreed to join him at Minnesota's largest gathering of conspiracy theorists, nonconformists, anarchists, spiritualists, pagans, alchemists, paranormal fetishists, and more was a bigger mystery than who had built Stonehenge. What can I say? People make bad choices when they're bored. My tumultuous spring had given way to a relaxed summer in the weeks following my Dungeons and Dieters adventure. July's weather was warm but not hot. The humidity was surprisingly bearable. The mosquitos were out and about, but not overly homicidal. All in all, it was damn near perfect weather, and requests for my services had slowed to a trickle. Fun fact: Breakups spike during heat waves and cold snaps. When there's a spell of good weather, couples seem to make it work. Anyway, I'd been bored stupid, so agreeing to tag along to The Third Wall-Eye convention had seemed like a good idea at the time. Now hindsight was proving me wrong.

I was waiting for Jay to finish up with a couple of guys selling shiny skullcaps that were guaranteed to keep your thoughts to yourself. The three were in the middle of a heated debate about whether 5G was designed to amplify the mind-numbing effects of fluoridated water or to activate sleeper cells of CIA cyborgs to rise up and destroy the suburbs.

"No, no, no," a short, round guy behind the table was saying while tugging at his own skull cap. "When the 5G hits the fluoride molecules, blood loses its coagulative properties and can't supply enough oxygen to the brain. The 5G amplifies the fluoride effect by, like, seventeen percent. Makes us dumb as doornails."

Jay scoffed. "They don't need to amplify the effects of fluoride. It's obviously been hugely successful. Just look at SUV sales and how popular reality TV is."

The guy held his hands out. "I know, I know. I'm just saying that 5G's got nothing to do with the cyborgs, and they aren't going to destroy the suburbs, anyway. They want suburbia. They want McMansions full of electromagnetic fields and giant lawns soaked in endocrine disruptors. The cyborgs are going to keep hiding in plain sight. They're that super-nice neighbor that convinces you to try that new fertilizer, try that new rash cream, try that new easy-rinse shampoo. Besides, everyone knows the cyborgs communicate with their handlers via the UV spectrum. My cousin's girlfriend in the Philippines has aphakia. That's where your eye doesn't have a lens, and you can see UV light. She's seen the messages. That's why she's down there. Hiding from the Man."

"Your cousin's girlfriend *is* the Man," the taller, rounder guy behind the table practically yelled. "Why is he still talking with her? She's obviously a CIA plant."

I tugged on Jay's sleeve. "Um, shouldn't we, you know…" I suggested with a tilt of my head.

Jay gave me a sympathetic smile, took a pamphlet with the skull cap features and specs, and promised to circle back later. Protect Your Privates Pavilion was just one section of an expansive vendor hall. We'd started there because Jay wanted to find some window treatments that would block electronic surveillance but still allow plenty of natural light into his studio, check out the latest in VPN tech, and catch a tutorial on cryptocurrency. The skull caps 'guaranteed to keep your thoughts to yourself' had been an unexpected bonus.

When we crossed over into Area 52, Jay got a personal early warning system for the imminent alien invasion cleverly disguised as an old Casio wristwatch. We admired models of the spaceship that had crashed near Roswell, and I almost bought a tube of cream guaranteed to soothe chapped skin and make you taste terrible to reptilians. While I doubted its efficacy, I did have the occasional scaly customer and figured it couldn't hurt.

During our stroll through End Energy Suppression Alley, I learned you can build your own perpetual-motion engine in your basement with ordinary household stuff. Jay wanted to get a picture with a cardboard cutout of Nikola Tesla between two large Tesla coils. He was so excited that I couldn't say no.

The Paranormal Abyss was full of ghost hunters and people that had seen Bigfoot. It also had the most cosplayers. Everyone was dressed up as vampires, werewolves, mermaids, elves, gnomes, and more. Ironically, I didn't see an actual PN. Figured that I was the only one stupid enough to be there. Jay suggested that I should shift and pose for selfies. I said sure, I'd shift into a naked Jay and do just that. Jay stopped making suggestions.

"You're holding up surprisingly well," my friend observed. We'd crossed into the Ethereal Empire, and Jay had stopped to admire a set of chakra cleansing crystals.

"A condition that can only be guaranteed if you keep the beers flowing. Ready for another?"

Jay returned the bag of colored gemstones to the table and nodded. "Yeah, but I'd better get some food in me. You hungry?"

When I nodded, he steered me away from the table. "Let's hit the food hall. We have to move it, though. The Vortex Virtuoso is giving a talk in twenty minutes. The guy's awesome. He has the best podcast, hands down. Really knows his shit. After that? The Illumi-Naughties are doing burlesque. You're gonna love them."

Lunch was a tough decision: the Flat Earth Flat Bread with pepperoni and sausage or the bacon-double-Bilderburger with cheese. I'd settled on the burger that was 'so good it could rule the world' and had just finished my last bite when Jay impatiently dragged me from my chair, down a hallway, and into the convention's main event room. The chairs were mostly taken, forcing us to apologize and excuse our way to a couple of open seats in the middle. I'd just uttered a final, "Ope, sorry. Just need to squeeze by," when a projector screen on a dais at the front of the room lit up with the words, "End of the World: Gods versus Governments." A woman in a bent witch's hat, black miniskirt and a *How 'bout these magic orbs?* tee-shirt stepped out from behind the screen and up to a podium near its corner and raised her hands for attention.

"Hello, everyone. Hello. Okay, then. Let's quiet down a bit. Thank you." When the room's chatter had subsided, she continued. "I'm Sally Dupree, part of the great team that made this convention possible. Thank you for coming to Minnesota's seventeenth annual Third Wall-Eye convention. Some folks think the truth is out there. We know the truth is up north!"

Laughter, applause, and a few enthusiastic hollers followed that line. The woman let it go for a minute and then held up her hands again.

"Okay, okay. Geez, you guys. Settle down. It wasn't that funny. Anyway, welcome to our presentation on the End of the World. I double-checked the Mayan Calendar and am pleased to report that it won't be today. The end of the world, that is. Our presentation will continue as scheduled."

The crowd around me chuckled.

"Thanks. I'm here all week. Well, even though the end of the world may not be imminent, I think we can all agree that it doesn't feel too far off. The good news? We've been feeling like the world is going to end for a very long time. Our speaker today is an expert on eschatology. That's the study of the end of times. I know, right?" she added as the room filled with *oohs* and *aahs*. "Anyway, he will be exploring predictions of the apocalypse from major mythologies and religions, and sharing insights on what they–yes, *they*–are doing to hurry us down that dead-end street. I don't think he needs an introduction, but let's do one anyway. Our guest today has studied the storm and fathomed the fire, wrestled the waves and grappled the very ground itself. A true expert on the elements, his podcast has a 4.6 out of 5-star rating and a prestigious Webby Award. Let's hear it for the Vortex Virtuoso!"

I peered through the room's gloom to the table in front of the projector screen, suddenly curious to see what mage or wizard the convention had managed to line up for the main event. I hadn't been expecting anything other than conspiracy crackpots. The prospect of seeing a bona fide spell-caster was an unexpected surprise. That eager curiosity crumbled into dismay as none other than Tony the Douchebag Warlock stepped into the track light's glow and basked in the crowd's adoration.

"Thank you, thank you," Tony said regally as he tugged at the lapels of his fur vest and smoothed a hand over his dark mane. He took the woman's hand, bowed, and kissed her knuckles. "It is truly my honor to be here."

While the MC blushed and batted her eyelids, I stared at the warlock. My insides were reeling from the sudden pileup of unpleasant facts. Fact one, he was there. Fact two, I was there. Fact three, he had a room full of fans–actual fans–and fact four, I didn't. I've never been one for popularity contests, but still... Ouch. I inundated him with my surliest, saltiest glare and willed his bowels to have an unexpected and explosive movement, but no such luck. The douchebag released the woman's hand, and she promptly pressed it above her magic orbs while he stepped up to the podium and lifted a clicker from its top. Exuding a self-assurance that someone living in his apartment had no right having, he pressed a button, and the slide changed. The word 'eschatology' was emblazoned across the screen in large typewriter font. Beneath it, a dictionary definition explained that it was a noun and was the part of theology concerned with death, judgment, and the soul's final destiny.

"Humanity has been obsessed with the end of the world for as long as there have been people living on it," Tony began. "For just as long, humanity has tried to predict both the time and manner of the world's end. Since ending our entire existence is a pretty big task for a mere human to pull off, we've assumed it would be some god or other. That just makes sense, right? If some god or gods created the world, it stands to reason that only they could truly end it."

With a series of clicks of the projector's clicker, he flipped through a montage of a tsunami-wrecked village, a sun-parched desert, a flooded subway tunnel, a street of people leaning against a gale-force wind, icicles stretching from a house's roof to the ground, a fiery volcano mid-eruption. The slides resonated since they depicted exactly how I was feeling inside, especially the volcano.

"That's Tony," I finally managed. "That's him. Tony. The douchebag."

Jay looked at me with genuine surprise. "Him? The Vortex Virtuoso? That's Tony?"

It was one-hundred percent Tony. *Of all the gin joints in all the world...* I thought, deflating into my seat.

"Yeah. It's him. I can't sit through this, Jay."

"Shhh," the guy next to me said.

"Shhh, yourself."

"Shhhh!" some lady behind me said.

"What? Trust me. That guy's a one-trick pony that couldn't book a gig doing birthday parties at crack houses in Reno."

Jay put a hand on my knee and squeezed as more people angrily shushed me. My outburst had even managed to get the MC's attention. She stepped up alongside the podium and swung the mic to her face.

"Quiet, please," she snapped. "This is a safe space to discuss the things we can't talk about out there," she reprimanded with an expansive wave of her arms at everywhere outside the hotel's event room. "You either respect that, or you leave."

I glowered, crossed my arms, and pressed my lips firmly together. My eyes slid left and right and caught more than a few ornery glares, and I clearly heard someone say, "Watch that one. I'll bet he's an agitator."

"Real nice, August," Jay muttered. "Now I'm the guy that came with *that* guy. Thanks."

Something that might've been guilt lodged in my throat and prevented me from saying anything more. I stewed in my own unsavory juices while the douchebag looked at the crowd and tried to pinpoint the source of unacceptable disrespect that had disrupted his oh-so-important presentation.

"That's all right," the warlock finally said, his expression making it clear that it wasn't, in fact, all right. "Where would we be without skeptics? In fact, this very event wouldn't exist. The world's religions and governments have one thing in common: they don't like skeptics. I, however, find them refreshing as a summer breeze."

A quick burst of air whistled through the room and sent the front row attendees' programs skittering up in wild circles toward the ceiling. The room gasped in awe and then broke out in rapturous applause while Tony bowed deeply at the waist. The MC's eyelids were batting so intensely that for a moment, I wondered if they'd been the source of the wind.

"As I was saying," Tony continued when the applause subsided, "people have been expecting the gods to end the world for as long as we've been living on it."

A new slide appeared. It depicted a blue-skinned woman with black hair, a golden crown, and a long necklace of skulls. Her many arms held swords and torches and scepters and scythes. One held a severed head.

"Kali, the Hindu goddess of death."

Tony clicked, and the image changed to a golden chalice full of flames.

"Zoroastrianism's Frashokereti."

The slide changed again and showed a serpent eating its own tail amidst a backdrop of huge white-capped waves.

"Jörmungandr emerging from the sea."

Another slide, this one showing a rendition of the planet engulfed in raging flames.

"The Buddhist's Seventh Sun."

The next image was of a host of angels descending on a horde of demons.

"Christianity's *Book of Revelations*. In every major religion, there is a story, a myth that basically predicts an epic battle between good and evil. That battle will reshape the world, wipe away the evil, and only the good will remain. There are signs, timelines, triggers that vary from tale to tale, but they all arrive at the same place: the end of the world."

The room had gone deathly quiet. I glanced around and saw dozens of wide eyes and slack jaws.

"I have studied all of these and more. Eschatology, the study of the end of times, and mastery of the elements are as close as kin. One cannot harness the storm's power, the sea's might, the fire's rage, the awesome strength of the very ground we stand on without courting the final days. One cannot wield such power as I and not recognize its formidable and terrible potential, even–and this is neither bluster nor bravado but simple fact–the potential to end the world. It requires the utmost care to preserve the balance of nature when harnessing the elements. Tip the scales too far, and the world itself could slide into ruin."

A collective sigh filled the room, my own included but for different reasons. I just wished Tony could've seen me so he'd know how far I'd rolled my eyes.

"That is why what the governments of the world are doing is so concerning. Their clumsy attempts to seed clouds and control the weather. Their ill-considered seismic disruptors on the International Space Station to weaponize tsunamis. Their burrowing and fracking. Their controlled burns," he continued with air quotes, "that somehow always seem to get out of control. Those government fools have sought to control the very forces of nature with their devices and chemicals and ill-conceived schemes. Better to try and shackle Kali. Put Jörmungandr in a fish tank. Extinguish the Seventh Sun with a squirt gun."

"What can we do?" a voice called from the enraptured room.

Tony leveled a serious look at his adoring onlookers. "Perhaps nothing. Perhaps every-thing."

Another slide appeared, this one startlingly familiar. Tony's picture was an illustration, not a glossy photograph like Vilde Tanck had, but the book's cover was unmistakable.

"Here, you see Yiorgos Katopodis' *The Thirteenth Zodiac*. I share this because Katopodis–an astrologer that lived centuries ago–understood that ending the world is not the providence of the gods. Despite his profession, or perhaps because of it, he learned that the world's demise isn't resigned to fate, nor something to be predicted. It is something to be controlled."

The next slide appeared, this one showing an etching of a man in a pit covered in snakes.

"Yiorgos Katopodis died a very unpleasant death. He was an astrologer. Like other shamans and mystics and priests, he looked to the heavens to divine the future and steered people toward their heart's desire for many years. So good was he at his craft that he caught the notice of the queen herself. He was brought to her and commanded to predict her future. Yiorgos did just that, but his queen was displeased by his predictions. She was a Sagittarius. She was certain of it, and yet Yiorgos disagreed. He swore she was born in the thirteenth sign of the Zodiac; Ophiuchus, the serpent bearer. Ophiuchus," Tony repeated slowly and emphasizing the pronunciation: *oh-FEW-cuss*, "the impossible sign. Neither Scorpio nor Sagittarius but both and more. The queen was incensed by his obvious lies and excuses. With the venomous spite of a viper, she cast him into a pit with nothing but a stack of leather-bound parchment, a bone stylus, and a command for him to atone for his egregious affront by writing her a proper and true Sagittarius horoscope. Every day he did not give her what she demanded, she mocked his conviction that she'd been born under the sign of the serpent bearer and cast a snake down upon him. For eighteen days, from November twenty-ninth until December sixteenth–the days of Ophiuchus–he was bitten and poisoned but did not die. For eighteen days, he ate the snakes raw, cut his veins with the stylus, and wrote with his own blood. Yiorgos poured all of his sight into this book. All of his power. With it, he crafted a final horoscope, a divination so awesome that if someone were to read it, they would have the power to tear down the world and rebuild it to match their deepest dreams. All the stars and planets would bend to their will and grant them a future of their own choosing. And then, on the nineteenth day, the final day of the sign of Ophiuchus, he died."

The room was silent. Well, almost. You could actually hear the whisper of Sally Dupree's batting eyelashes.

"When I look out the window and see all of the so-called natural disasters rending this planet, I believe there is more at play than chemtrails and seismological disruptors on the International Space Station," Tony continued. "I believe that they—yes, *they*–have found *The Thirteenth Zodiac,* and the chaos we're seeing is their foolish attempt to control what they cannot understand. We all know that NASA has continually denied the existence of Ophiuchus and refused to add it to the Zodiac. I believe they do this to hide their hand while they secretly try to master Yiorgos' power and usher in their New World Order."

A forlorn voice called out from somewhere behind me. "How can we stop them?"

Sympathetic and angry grumbles filled the space. I hunkered down further into my chair, arms crossed so tightly across my chest that I was about to crack a rib.

The slide changed again, this one containing a URL. "Join my warlock workshop and contribute the Master-class amount, and you will learn all the secrets to master the elements yourself. Wield the wind. Hold the fire in your fist. Change the ocean's tides to ebb and flow at your whim. Buckle the earth beneath your enemies. You will learn how to resist your despot government and their ill-considered attempts to control things entirely beyond their control by learning mastery of the elements yourself."

As the room erupted in a standing ovation, I pushed myself to my feet and shoved past the people in my row. I heard Jay whisper my name loudly behind me, but was too disgusted to spend one more second in the same space as Tony. With a defiant cry of, "NASA doesn't have it! The joke's on you, douchebag!" I burst through the doors and into the hallway. Free of the stifling room, I leaned against a wall to catch my breath and let my blood pressure drop a point or two.

"I hate that guy," I gasped. "Hate. Totally hate. Hate, hate, hate. *Hate.*"

When my pulse had steadied and my vision was a bit less tinged with red, I pushed off the wall and headed for the nearest exit. Jay could do whatever he wanted. I was out of there; free beers be damned. I walked back into the vendor hall with every intention of getting out of Third Wall-Eye as fast as possible. I'd just made it through the vendor hall's Paranormal Abyss–the designation taking on a new and unpleasant significance–and crossed into the Ethereal Empire when someone called my name.

"Holy smokes! August? August Shade?"

I skidded to a stop and turned my head. There, between a table full of star charts and a banner with the words "Ope! It's Your Horoscope!" emblazoned over an image showing all the signs of the Zodiac was Clarissa thrice-damned Steyer. Despite the July weather, she was still wearing the same threadbare cardigan, skirt and stockings, and flannel earflap hat. A guy was sitting across from her, palms flat on the table and eager eyes looking up in supplication.

"What in the heck are you doing here?" she asked. "Although I shouldn't be surprised. You are in all of them, after all."

"Hey, get in line," the guy at her table complained to me.

"Sure," I agreed amiably. "Right after you get a life."

The oracle shushed me and waved me away. "Just, I don't know, go over there for a minute, August. I can't see a darned thing when you're around."

I held my hands up and took an exaggerated step backward. "Better?"

"No."

I took two more steps. "How about now?"

Clarissa squinted at me and then turned back to her customer. "I think... Maybe to the left a little? No, that's worse. How about to the right? A bit more? There! Don't move."

After being bent around like an old TV antenna, I shoved my hands in my pockets and stood awkwardly in the middle of the corridor. Con goers that might've jostled me noticed my scowl and thought better of it, leaving me in a bubble of my own making. With nothing better to do, I strained my ears to hear what Clarissa was saying to her customer. I heard her tell the guy that, sure, work is tough right now, and sure, he might feel like the can that everyone is kicking. The good news was that when people are playing Kick the Can, the can is actually what everyone wants.

"They're gonna be fighting over you; just you wait. All you have to do is be at the copy machine at two-thirty next Wednesday. Make a copy of... that last report you wrote up and give it to... Jim? John?"

"Jerome?" the guy asked, breathless. When Clarissa nodded vigorously, he leaned back in shock. "Seriously? Give him the report?"

The oracle smiled a wide smile. "Oh, you betcha. You do that, you'll be pushing up daisies. I mean coming up roses. Cripes, August. You moved," she accused with a glare in my direction. Returning her attention to the guy, she said, "Did I say next Wednesday? I meant Thursday. Okey-doke. Thanks for stopping by."

The guy shook his head, muttered something about wasting twenty bucks, and stomped off.

"I'm trying to work here, you know," Clarissa muttered when I walked back to her table.

By 'work,' I assumed she meant reading astrology charts for conspiracy nuts at twenty bucks a pop. The last time I'd seen Clarissa, she'd been talking about trying to keep the world from ending. I didn't know if oracles could get demoted, but this sure felt like one. The likelihood of The Third Wall-Eye convention having anything of cosmic significance going on was flimsier than the film showing Bigfoot in the woods. When I said as much, Clarissa rested her fists on her hips.

"Maybe something important happens here. Maybe not, but maybe. Crowds are tough. So many lives crashing together, intertwining and getting tangled up," she said sternly. "Tony said there could be some influencers in the crowd. Just gotta keep sifting through 'em."

"Tony?"

The woman scrutinized me before saying, "You know. That fella that kicked your keister at the bar. He helped get me a table here. Got me a discount."

Something twisted my guts and hunched my back. "Of course he did."

The oracle blushed and squirmed. "He's taken a real interest in my work. Asks all sorts of questions, and he knows a lot, too. Sheesh. I don't know if I've ever met anyone that reads as much as that guy. He has a podcast, too, you know."

I knew and mentioned I'd just come from his lecture.

"Jeepers. You were in that one, too?" she asked rhetorically. "I don't suppose you signed up for his workshop..."

I crossed my arms and lowered my chin.

"No, you wouldn't," she decided after an inward stare and nod of her head. "Well, I guess that closes off that branch."

"Clarissa, are you trying to see my future right now?"

She looked up, startled. "Yes," she admitted warily. "There was one where you did pretty good in his warlock workshop, and he had you as a guest on his podcast." She snort-laughed. "You. On a podcast. Cripes. I should'a known better."

Her words landed like a jab between my eyes. When she saw me react, she grimaced.

"Geez. I'm sorry, August," she apologized. "I honestly can't see crap around you. Too many possibilities that are just too darn bright. Speaking of, did you end up with that bartender lady? She seemed... fun," the oracle finished, blushing.

Memories of a certain breakfast surfaced. "Oh, her? Yeah. We're. Yeah. Totally a thing. Going great, thanks for asking. She, you know. Takes a real interest in my work. And stuff..."

For a long moment, we both looked at anything but each other. The uncomfortable bubble we'd suddenly found ourselves in burst when a young woman skipped up to the table and begged for her horoscope. Clarissa asked her a few questions: when was the woman born, was it morning or night, how close to water had she been, and whatnot. As she readied all of the materials, she glanced up at me.

"Well. Good to see you again," she finally said, intent clear.

"Yeah. Yeah, you too," I replied.

"Okay, then," Clarissa said.

"Okay, then," I agreed, and headed for the door.

# CHAPTER 10



*Ope! It's your horoscope, Libra!*
*Even the Biggest Ball of Twine in Minnesota will eventually unravel.*

---

"WHAT THE FUCK IS an álfablót?"

It was a fair question. Jay and I had finished a six-pack of Grain Belt and were playing paper-rock-scissors to see who'd buy the next when Tanckenstein had strolled into the art studio. Gone were the functional blue jeans and sturdy sweatshirt. Instead, he was dressed to the nines. Charcoal plaid sport coat over a crisp white shirt. Understated necktie with a shiny clip as big as my thumb. Freshly pressed black slacks. Patent leather shoes shined to a high gloss. The finery brought his mangled face and its assortment of staples, stitches, and scars into stark relief and revealed the most impressive surprise; he was flesh and bone again.

"Tanckenstein!" I'd hollered and surprised him–and myself–by giving him a hug. "Looking good! But how? How did she do it? How did she save you?"

The tall cadaver had ducked his head. "A spell. I'd tell you about it, but Ms. Tanck says I shouldn't dwell on the past. I guess that means I shouldn't dwell on being imprisoned in a stone body in her garden for weeks while birds pooped on me and then going through a very long, very painful spell to free me from the Gorgon's curse."

"Wow. Shit... Um. All's well that ends well?" I had tried and then sighed in relief when Stein had smiled in response. "Hey, you didn't bring beer, did you?" I'd asked.

The smile had dissolved into a random collection of stitches and scars, the large man's shoulders had slouched, and his hands had spread in apology. "No. Ms. Tanck says I should be more aware of the people around me and what they need. I'm sorry. I didn't know you needed beer. I can go get some."

I'd hastily told him that it was fine, he hadn't done anything wrong, that it was great to see him. Mopey crisis averted, he'd reached into the breast pocket of his sport coat and revealed the reason for the visit; a creamy envelope. Golden letters shone on the front as he'd passed it my way. I'd read my name in shock, opened the flap, and slid out a heavy card. A moment after that, I had to pick my jaw up off the floor and reattach it to my face. Once it was reasonably secure, the only possible words had been, "What the fuck is an álfablót?" followed by an equally reasonable question. "And you're joking, right? An invitation to a special evening with Vilde Tanck and Dieter Saint James? You have to be joking."

The big man turned his palms up. "If I was, you wouldn't laugh, anyway. No one laughs at my jokes. Ms. Tanck says it's my delivery. Too deadpan."

The large man stared. Jay and I stared back. Jay giggled, and then we both burst into full-fledged belly laughs. The stitches and staples holding Tanckenstein's face together stretched as a shy smile lit up his face.

"Ms. Tanck says I should look for the humor in situations. How am I doing?"

I wiped a tear from my eye. "Nailing it. You're absolutely nailing it." A few more laughs slipped out, and then I took a deep breath and let it slip out through my nostrils. "But seriously, what the fuck is an álfablót, and why would they invite me?"

"An álfablót is a Norwegian pagan elf thing, I guess. A kind of ceremony where people make a sacrifice to elves to seek their favor. It was Dieter's idea. Ms. Tanck told him she hadn't had a proper álfablót in ages, so he's throwing her one. You can go, too," he added with a nod at Jay. "August gets a plus-one, and I'm pretty sure there isn't anyone else for August to invite."

I gave him a look, and Stein responded with a shrug. "Ms. Tanck says to call a spade a spade."

While I stewed and tried to think of a snappy comeback, Jay was shaking his head vigorously while holding out his hands. "Sacrifice? No way. Leonard, I'm vegetarian."

The cadaver pulled a notepad from one pocket and a pen from another. "Vegetarian. Right. I'll make sure there's a veggie tray. Do you like Ranch or Bleu Cheese? Wait, do vegetarians eat cheese? There's going to be lefse too–lots of it–but that usually gets served with butter, and I think maybe there's lard in the lefse. I'm not sure about that last bit, though."

The artist rolled his eyes. "No, I mean the sacrifice. I am not going to watch some poor animal get killed. Sorry, but I can't. I just can't."

While Tanckenstein's purple lips made an understanding, "Oh," I told Jay not to sweat it. Honestly, I wasn't planning on sweating it, either. There was no way I was going to Vilde and Dieter's little pagan dinner party. The last time I'd seen Dieter Saint James, it hadn't exactly been a typical Minnesotan sit'n'visit. I'd trashed his place, broken out of his dungeon, bit his maid, and stole not only a book but his hearse and coffin. I held up four fingers and a thumb, then counted down those very specific affronts for Stein.

"After all that, why in the hell would he want me there? I mean, I get Tanck inviting me—sort of, not really—but Dieter? Unless he plans to sacrifice me at the afflebop."

"Álfablót. You have to stretch the A and the O, so they almost sound like long vowels." Dialect lesson apparently complete, he considered my question. "I guess Ms. Tanck wants you there to show her appreciation for bringing them back together. And Dieter? He does pretty much whatever she wants now, so if she wants you there, he wants you there."

I puffed out my cheeks and loudly exhaled. "So you weren't kidding. Those two are back together. What the actual fuck, Leonard?"

Vilde's henchman raised his palms and shrugged. "It's pretty much your fault. As Saint James tells it, after we got away with the book, he woke up and practically tore down his own castle in a rage. Then Ms. Tanck called him and said he owed her an apology and a way to lift the Gorgon's curse. He said she owed him a new library and a hearse. She said it sounded like a negotiation. He said he didn't negotiate with thieves. She said if anyone was a thief, it was him for stealing her heart all those years ago. Then more stuff like that. He drove across town that night, and she invited him in."

I'd never imagined someone with a face like Tanckenstein's being able to look embarrassed, but he was able to pull it off. After clearing his throat, he continued his recitation of the unmentionable events.

"He knocked on the door. She answered and said, 'Hello, Dieter.' After that, well... I was stuck in the garden, so I couldn't see them. I heard them, though. Night after night, I heard them."

I blinked. "Thank you, Leonard, for so effectively burning that image into my brain. If you'd be so kind, I'd like you to throw me off of the nearest bridge and into the river so I'll die and never have to imagine those two doing anything even remotely close to that ever, ever again."

"Like I said, it's your fault. If you hadn't grabbed that book, Dieter wouldn't have had the reason, much less the nerve, to show up at her front door like that."

"Hey!" I protested. "You were there, too, remember? Tanck only called him because you'd been turned into a doorstop for a really big door."

Tanckenstein held out his hands. "You can have all the credit. Two PNs like them getting back together? Forget the seven signs of the apocalypse. That one is more than enough, and I certainly don't want people blaming me."

"You're a true friend, Stein." The weight of what he'd piled on me was immense. I didn't want to be any part of the Lefse Queen of Minnesota hooking up with the Undead King of Midwestern Tanning Salons. "You know, I'm pretty sure I have a dentist appointment that day. I guess if you could just send Vilde my regrets…"

Stein held up a hand and stopped my excuses cold. "Not optional, August."

Jay gave me a nudge with his elbow and told me to look on the bright side; there would probably be free booze. When I gave Stein a skeptical look, he reaffirmed Jay's assumption.

"Well… if there's booze," I grumbled.

Tanckenstein took that as assurance enough that I'd be there. After a few parting pleasantries—or at least as close as the mopey cadaver was capable of—he'd headed out.

Barely a second after he'd vanished through the door, Jay snatched my invitation and instantly started *oohing* and *aahing* over it.

"I really wish they weren't going to sacrifice anything. I'd love to go. It's at Nicollet Island? Cool. That place is great. I wonder who else will be there? Knowing those two, it could be anyone, right? Or any *thing*. Whoever they are, I'll bet they'll be fancy."

"Shit," I blurted. "Do I need to wear a suit? I don't have a suit."

"You'll survive," Jay reassured me. "You've got some slacks and a white shirt, right?"

"No."

My friend's face squished up as he shook his head. "How tall are you? Never mind. We're close enough. Can you get your own sport coat, though? I think your shoulders are wider than mine." I nodded while he gave me a more than skeptical appraisal. "How about underwear and socks? Or should I get you those, too?"

I responded with a middle finger and then shooed him off. He took all the unwelcome sunshine with him and left me in a much more appropriate gloomy funk. An intimate evening with anyone was damn near the last thing on my want-to-do list. An intimate evening with Vilde Tanck and Dieter Saint James? Too unthinkable to even consider putting on a list. It was going to be awful—absolute hell—and I in no way whatsoever wanted to be a part of it.

But no one ever cared what I wanted.

My finger pulled at my shirt collar, and my other hand scratched at a trickle of sweat on my ribs. I was miserable. The only sport coat I'd been able to find at the thrift store was heavy wool–less than ideal for a warm summer night–and whoever had invented neckties was a sadist. In a vain attempt to distract myself, I looked around the river island while nursing a beer.

Nicollet Island was a small mound of earth sticking up from the Mississippi River. Its northern half held a few residential streets and a handful of old Victorian homes. Its southern half sported a fancy boutique hotel built in the late 1800s, an old boiler works building from the same era, and a small park in between. The boiler works had been converted into an event center with all the amenities today's hipsters had decided were chic. Exposed steel rafters, bare brick walls, Tungsten bulbs in wrought iron fixtures hanging down from a shadowy ceiling high above. It even had those annoyingly trendy rolling barn doors. Why, I had no idea. Apparently, cool people couldn't be bothered with pushing or pulling. Alongside the event center was a pavilion covered by a large, white tent. Tanck and Saint James had reserved all of it–and by that, I mean the entire lower half of the island–but the only seating was a small, round table under the center of the tent.

"Must be nice," I muttered.

Betty met the remark with a raised eyebrow.

"Being able to afford all of this," I indicated with an expansive sweep of my arm, "so a few people can have dinner and kill a sheep or something."

The succubus pursed her lower lip and puffed her bangs with a frustrated breath. "If I'd known you were going to be such a pain in the ass, I would've stayed home."

I was still more than a little surprised she'd agreed to come in the first place. For a day or two after Stein had delivered the invite, Jay had needled me relentlessly about a plus-one. It had been infuriating. Having a very solitary existence is bearable when you don't think about how completely single you are. That solitary existence becomes less bearable when your only friend forces you to try to think of someone–anyone–that might be willing to spend an evening with you, so you don't look like a complete loser at the party.

"Isn't there a client that you maybe hit it off with? Even a little?" Jay had asked.

"No."

"That werewolf you got the CD from a few months back. She might still be single."

"No."

"Clarissa?"

I didn't even bother to respond to that one.

Jay had scrunched up his face in thought. "What about the bartender? I mean, I know she was sort-of dating the Vortex Virtuo... I mean Tony the Douchebag," he quickly amended when I gave him a look, "but she also seems a bit... polyamorous."

I had to chuckle at my friend's blush, but the moment of good humor was gone a second later. I had told him about the night I'd spent at the succubus's apartment, but I'd neglected to mention the following morning. "I don't... I mean, that probably isn't a good idea."

"Why not?" he'd asked. "C'mon. The fear of getting hit is always worse than getting hit. Give it the old college try. Throw your hat in the ring."

"I, uh. I already threw... something. Didn't work out so good."

I should've kept my mouth shut. With a tenacity that professional interrogators at the CIA would have envied, Jay had wrung the details from me. After my grudging account of breakfast at Betty's, he'd stared at me aghast.

"And you haven't called her since?" he'd finally managed to ask.

"... No."

"August!" he'd screamed. "What the fuck is wrong with you?"

I'd rocked back at the outburst. Jay didn't swear often, and when he did, it was serious. After lighting the fuse on the F-bomb and lobbing it at my head, he had revealed an impressive arsenal of curses and let them all go in a brutal salvo. Ammo finally expended, he'd glared at me and had pointed at my office.

"Call her now. Apologize. Really, really apologize. Say you would've called weeks ago, but you were mortified and that you know that there is nothing–*nothing*–that could make it up to her, but you'd like to try."

The artist wasn't going to take no for an answer. I'd moped to my office, rummaged through my desk until I found her number, dialed, and almost hung up when I got her voicemail. Then my eyes flicked to see Jay standing sternly in my office's doorway, and my mouth-thing made word-sounds.

"Hey. Uh, Betty. It's August. So. About that night. Day. Morning. You know, when I... Yeah." I palmed my forehead, gritted my teeth, and forced the rest of the word-sounds in my mouth-thing to make noise-good. "Well, I'm just calling to say I'm really sorry and I should've called weeks ago, and I know there's nothing I can do to make it up to you, but

I'd like to try, so maybe you'd want to come with me to a dinner party with Vilde Tanck and Dieter Saint James on Nicollet Island. Call me. It's August. Okay, then."

And I'd hung up. And she'd called back.

Now she stood beside me, and she was stunning. Her dark hair was piled high on her head with an artful lock curling down one cheek, and a skin-tight black dress struggled mightily to contain her curves. The dress's neckline plunged down in a V low enough to convince me there was no way she had underwear on. A little garnet in her navel winked mesmerizingly when she walked. She exuded class, confidence, sexuality, and self-assurance. I, on the other hand, exuded a noxious blend of stale smoke and sticky pine. The previous owner of my second-hand sport coat had obviously enjoyed pipe tobacco, so I'd hung a bunch of car air fresheners around it in my closet. It had seemed like a good idea at the time.

Betty poked my middle-aged paunch with a finger. "C'mon. One smile. Please? I can't stand this."

"Can't stand what?" Tanckenstein asked as he joined us.

Betty pouted. "Poor widdle August isn't having any fun."

"And I can't seem to convince her that the not-fun feeling I'm having is completely appropriate. This," I said with a vague wave at everything around me, "is not fun."

Stein made a face, an impressive feat with a face like his. "Ms. Tanck says if you can only have one good thing, have a good attitude."

"Ms. Tanck talks too much."

There'd been no sign of Vilde or Dieter. When I'd rolled up with Betty in my bike's sidecar, there was only Tanckenstein waiting for us to arrive. He'd politely gestured to a freestanding bar near the boiler works and informed us to help ourselves to some drinks. We'd each had one and suffered through some awkward small talk with the bartender. Then we had another drink and suffered through some awkward small talk between ourselves. Then we'd just stood under the pavilion's tent in awkward silence. With no other entertainment besides my lackluster company, Betty was crawling out of her skin.

"Come on!" she cried, exasperated. "I'm about to die of boredom. Let's do something. Anything. Well, not anything," she amended, "unless you're certain you haven't eaten for at least two hours."

*Ouch.*

"I deserved that," I conceded. "I don't know what to do. Stein, how long until they get here?"

The big man looked at his wristwatch. "Maybe twenty minutes? Ms. Tanck said they'd be picking the other guests up along the way. Why don't you two take a stroll? The island is nice."

Betty clapped and exclaimed that she'd never been on the island at night. I figured that walking in silence would be better than standing in silence, so I shrugged and headed for the walking path.

The island was crisscrossed with trails that meandered through patches of native plants and wildflowers and plentiful trees. It gave the sense of being far from the hustle and bustle of the city across the water. Occasionally, the paths connected with the roads that provided access to the neighborhood on the north side. It was pretty neat, the experience of feeling completely lost in nature one second and then emerging into a quaint little village the next. Despite practically being in my backyard, I hadn't had many occasions to cross the bridge that connected the verdant gem to the river's east side. In my mind, the island was a place reserved for rich folks. While they might tolerate the occasional lower-class clod taking an afternoon stroll, that tolerance had limits. Rather than go where I knew I wouldn't be wanted, I'd simply stayed away. Now, as I let my feet follow a dark path while my eyes searched a cloudless and starry sky, I found myself questioning that decision. For a moment, I contemplated shifting so I could really enjoy the night. Only the fact that the succubus was with me kept me in check. She was plenty annoyed already. Watching her date turn into a coyote and slink off into the shadows wasn't likely to improve the situation.

"It's beautiful," Betty remarked, her displeasure eroding ever so slightly. Our path had taken us to one of the roads. A row of Victorian homes sat comfortably in the dark, their glowing windows adding an unexpected elegance to the already charming architecture.

"I guess," I agreed. "I haven't been over here much. A little foo-foo hoity-toity for my taste."

The succubus laughed mirthlessly. "A Burger King parking lot is probably too hoity-toity for your taste. Tell you what. For the next five minutes, you're only allowed to say nice things. Not crabby things, not snarky things, not grumpy things. Can you do that?"

I looked up and studied her face by the soft light of a nearby streetlamp. What I saw was something bordering on genuine hope. She was right. I was being insufferable. A jerk. I'd invited her and had been an ungracious twit the entire time. It wasn't right, and it wasn't fair. If I wanted even the slimmest chance of salvaging whatever there was between us, I'd have to do something really special. Really romantic.

"You ever see the Grain Belt sign?" I asked, then ducked my head in anticipation of the fiery response that was certain to follow such a stupid idea. Whoever said romance isn't dead has not had the pleasure of my company.

Incredibly, Betty's eyes sparkled with excitement. "You mean the giant lit-up bottle cap? Only from the bridge. Tony never brought me here, even though I asked like a hundred times. Can we get to it?"

In fact, you could. While Nicollet Island wasn't exactly my kind of place, it did have one redeeming feature: The Grain Belt Beer Sign. Easily fifty feet high and as many wide, it sat on the island's west side facing the river. You could see it from the far bank, and it dominated the view when you headed east over the Hennepin Avenue Bridge. I'd read once that it had 1,400 lightbulbs and who knows how many linear feet of red and green neon tubes. Like Betty had said, it was a gigantic bottle cap with the Grain Belt red diamond logo and the words "Grain Belt Beer" emblazoned across it. It was, in a word, glorious.

"Come on," I advised. Without thinking, I took her hand and was pleasantly surprised when she held mine tight.

We cut over to the aptly named West Island Ave and strolled hand-in-hand. In a few short minutes, the massive scaffolding supporting the sign came into view. Betty slipped off her heels, and we walked carefully through the scrub at its base until we were directly beneath it. I looked up at the closest thing to a worthy shrine to the almighty I could ever imagine and basked in the light and soft electric hum. The *Reclining Buddha*, sure. Rio de Janeiro's *Christ the Redeemer*, fine. For me, it was that sign, that big as the fucking sun bottle cap sign, that reassured me that something greater than myself might be at work in the cosmos.

"You must really like Grain Belt," Betty observed. "Geez. Need a tissue to clean yourself up?"

Her comment brought me back to myself, and I coughed with embarrassment. "Yeah, well. It's a pretty great sign. Anyway, I guess we should get back and get this over with."

She sighed and shook her head. "You, August Shade, need a lot of work."

The succubus led the way, and I followed. The road curved back to the island's southern half. We'd just crossed the small grassy park when I saw a pair of headlights flash from the nearby parking lot entrance. Tanckenstein was standing at the pavilion's edge, so we moved to join him. Three sets of eyes watched a black, shiny hearse swing into a parking spot. The purr of its engine blended with the crickets and cicadas, only noticeable when it was abruptly silenced.

"Oh good, they're here," Stein said. "Guess that means we can get started."

The hearse's door opened, and a familiar woman stepped out. After what Mona's boss had done to her partner, it was a bit of a shock to see her still among the living. Or undead. Or whatever. She'd obviously been patched up. As I watched her walk around the car to the passenger side door, I saw both arms swing easily. I recalled that she was every bit as badass as Tanckenstein and likely just as hard to kill. My shoulders tensed and fists clenched until I took a deep, steadying breath and willed myself to relax.

*It's a dinner party,* I reminded myself. *Nothing to worry about.*

"You know her?" Betty asked.

"We've met," I replied, my words eliciting a mirthless snort from Tanckenstein.

Mona pulled open the hearse's passenger door and out stepped Vilde Tanck. The huldra still wore a Norwegian bunad dress, but this one must've cost more than the property taxes on her North Loop bakery. I couldn't understand how a garment designed to be modest could make her look so unbelievably gorgeous. It hurt to look at her, but I simply couldn't look away. In a fuzzy sort of way, I realized I wasn't the only one caught up in her spell. The succubus' mouth hung open, and I heard her say in an awestruck voice, "She is definitely on my list."

With a slight curtsey, Vilde stepped to the side while Mona walked around the back of the Cadillac. A few loud clunks later, the revenant wheeled a gurney alongside the huldra. The casket was as familiar as the ride it had arrived in. I'd used it to transport a petrified Tanckenstein after escaping from Dieter's castle. Mona grasped the edges and lifted the lid. A moment later, Dieter Saint James rose up like every corny-ass vampire from every corny-ass movie you've ever seen. Plank-straight, arms across his chest and hands resting palm down against his shoulders, the old vampire rose up like the far side of a seesaw. Upon reaching his feet, he uncrossed his arms and leaped nimbly down from his coffin. With a sweeping bow, he took Vilde's hand and escorted her across the lot. The two of them made quite the pair. Her in that resplendent traditional dress that anyone else would look absurd in but on her was a festive wrapping on an unbelievably beautiful present and him in a classic tuxedo with long tails and a blood red cummerbund. One might've thought they were on their way to accept an Oscar rather than dinner with a shady shifter and his hot not-girlfriend.

"Welcome," the huldra exclaimed when they reached us, "and thank you so much for coming," she proclaimed, eyes on the succubus.

Betty was shivering. "Lovely to meet you," she said, her voice somewhere between a prayer and a purr.

"And I, you," Vilde replied. "August, I must admit you have exceeded my expectations. I did not think you capable of having such acquaintances. I assume this lovely creature has a name?"

My nature was wrestling with the eerie adoration Vilde's presence seemed to command. It had been a losing fight until she took her little dig and gave my innate temerity a booster shot.

"Vilde, Betty. Betty, Vilde," I growled. "You two have a lot in common. I got shit back from both of your shitty exes. Yay me."

"Thank you so much for inviting us," the succubus said in a throaty whisper. "I mean it. And if you aren't too busy later, I'm sure that hotel over there has an open room."

My elbow was about to make for Betty's ribs, but I checked myself when Vilde laughed a deep laugh. "Ja? Is that so? And this one would not mind?" she asked.

Betty rolled her eyes. "Being someone's plus-one doesn't mean they can tell you who you can or can't sleep with. I'd invite him to join us–he's actually pretty cute if you can get past the homeless look–but he's a buzzkill at best and an absolute horror show after a meal. How about your date? Want to share? I like experienced men. Even orange ones."

Dieter had been watching the exchange with a tolerant expression until that moment. His eyes widened and his jaw dropped, causing Vilde to laugh all the harder.

"Succubi," the vampire finally managed. "You certainly do make life more interesting. But let's set all that aside for the time being. Now, my dear, shall we gather our remaining guests and commence with our evening?"

In response, Vilde flicked a wrist at the hearse. Mona dipped her chin and headed for the other side of the car. When she reached the rear passenger door, she pulled it open and out stepped none other than Clarissa-fricking-Steyer. If I stuck out like a sore thumb in my ill-fitting excuse for finery, then Clarissa was all thumbs. The shapeless sweater, drab skirt, and wrinkled stockings made her look like a crumpled-up rag. It was actually a bit of a relief. Betty's homeless crack had stung more than I wanted to admit. It was nice having someone else around that lowered the bar a smidge.

Stein had noticed my reaction when the oracle stepped clear of the hearse. "You know her?" he asked.

I ducked my head and sidled behind him, hoping his wide frame would hide me from view. "Yeah. She's a client. Was a client."

"Ms. Tanck says it's a small world. I say sure, until you need to paint it," Tanckenstein cracked.

He wasn't wrong, and unfortunately, the world was about to get a little smaller. While Clarissa stood awkwardly in the parking lot's cold light, Mona had circled the hearse and opened its final door. The person that emerged had to be Clarissa's plus-one and, of course, had to be Tony.

Guests accounted for, the huldra and the vampire strode regally toward the large tent covering the pavilion, with Mona a step behind. Strings of cafe lights illuminated their path and bathed them in a warm, buttery glow. Tanckenstein gestured for us to follow, but Betty was rooted to her spot.

"Tony," she observed coolly when her ex drew near, and then she slipped an arm possessively through mine.

"Betty," he replied, nose high in the air. "You came here with that? And here I thought you had standards. It looks like disappointment in a cheap suit."

He was a fine one to talk. Tony was dressed like Tony. Stupid black fur vest over a stupid black silk shirt. Stupid black leather pants. Stupid black leather platform boots bedazzled with all those stupid metal studs.

"You look stupid," I shot back and smirked at the embers that sparked in his eyes.

Stein stepped between us and put a hand on each of our chests. "None of that," he cautioned. "I don't know what the problem is, but problems are not allowed. Not tonight. This is a special occasion, so you'd better behave."

Apparently satisfied that me and the warlock would keep the peace for at least a little while, he nodded to Clarissa. "Ms. Steyer? It's nice to meet you. I'm Leonard."

She turned, but her eyes were too busy darting everywhere at once to settle on his face. It was as if there were a thousand simultaneous things she was trying to watch and couldn't decide which was the most important.

"Cripes. You're dead," she finally observed when she managed to look directly at him. When Stein didn't disagree, she asked, "Do you know which one we're in? Heck if I know which one we're in."

"The Tank and Saint James álfablót," he answered, brow furrowed in confusion. "And look, here's August. He says you know him."

Whatever effect I'd expected her hearing my name to have, I certainly didn't expect her to cringe and recoil. Stein's tacked-on eyebrows furrowed, but I was too focused on Clarissa to try to explain things.

"Are you all right?" I asked the oracle quietly, even though I knew the answer. Whatever was going on with her, she was definitely not okay. The woman was shuddering.

"Uff da. Not really," she whispered back. "I can't see a darn thing. They're all too bright. So bright."

"Not nearly as bright as you, my darling," Tony crooned, as he put a possessive arm around her shoulders and tossed a wicked glance at Betty. "The stars that you read so well pale next to your beauty. Come along, now. We shouldn't keep our hosts waiting."

I startled as a pair of arms slid around my waist and two very full breasts pressed up against my back. Betty's breath was hot on my ear as she said a little too loudly, "Yeah, let's get this dinner over with so we can get to the fun stuff."

The sudden one-upmanship between the succubus and warlock didn't directly bother me. Anything that riled up Tony was generally A-okay in my book. Even so, knowing that I was nothing more than a tool for Betty to wield irked me. I guess she and Vilde had that in common, too. I let my feet drag me toward the tent where Vilde and Dieter stood by the round table. The succubus pressed against my side and curled her fingers with mine, but her eyes were fixed on Tony's back so intently that I was genuinely surprised when his fur vest didn't ignite. I turned to see if Clarissa was as put out as I was, but what I saw was even more worrisome. As she walked, she pulled at a loose thread on her cardigan's hem. When it gave, she worried at it with trembling fingers. If she kept at it, I didn't doubt that the sweater would be reduced to a pile of yarn before the night was over.

"They're all so darned bright," I heard her say to no one in particular. "All the pasts and all the futures, so bright. For Pete's sake, why can't I see?"

We finally arrived at the table at the center of the pavilion. Dieter and Vilde stood side by side, fully embracing their roles as the regal hosts of a very special evening. The huldra raised her arms and spread them wide to encompass us all.

"Din oppmerksomhet vær så snill," she proclaimed. Everyone blinked and looked around awkwardly until Vilde repeated her request in English. "Your attention, please. Now that we are all here, it is time for the evening to begin."

Dieter slid Vilde's chair back to allow her to sit. Betty took the seat to Vilde's left and scooted it a smidge closer to the huldra while Tony sat to Dieter's right and scooted it a smidge further away from the vampire. Stein and Mona stood behind their respective employers, apparently there in a work capacity rather than as guests. That left two empty chairs. Clarissa's eyes settled on mine, the frenetic energy from before gone. Only sadness remained. A deep and resigned sadness. Together but apart, we slid the remaining chairs back, seated ourselves, and hop-scooched closer to the round table's edge. There, under a tent over a pavilion on an island in a river shrouded in darkness, we braced for the unknown.

# CHAPTER 11

*Ope! It's your horoscope, Cancer!*
*When you're up against the Edmund Fitzgerald, be the Gales of November.*

---

"Velkommen, all," Vilde stated regally after we'd settled into our chairs. "Welcome to the álfablót. In my homeland of Norway, it was known since the oldest of times that the elven folk were to be respected. Sometimes welcomed, sometimes feared, but always, always respected. At the end of the growing season, the best of the harvest was given up to the elves, an offering to give thanks and beg for kind treatment through the coming winter."

She paused and looked around the table. Satisfied that all eyes were for her and her alone, she continued. "It has been many, many years since I was afforded a proper álfablót. I have missed it dearly."

"And as you're so fond of saying," Dieter interjected, "you simply will not tolerate something that you want being absent from your life. Well, my darling, tonight, that absence shall be filled. Tonight, you shall receive your sacrifice. First, though, you should eat!"

A string quartet had quietly set up where the large tent met the old boiler works building. Bows met strings, and the delicate notes of a lighter classical piece filled the summer night. On cue, a cadre of caterers emerged in a procession from the event center. Sadly, they didn't bring hotdogs. Instead, a bowl of fresh berries in a light cream paired with sparkling water appeared in front of me. Vilde explained it was the first course of five. I didn't really understand the concept. I had a deep distrust of so-called rules for the order in which you ate your food. Food went in one end and came out the other. That was the only order that mattered in my world. Stick to it, and you're good. Reverse it, and you're in for some unpleasant surprises.

I took measure of the table's reactions and realized that I was the only one that seemed put out. Churlishly, I spooned a few berries into my mouth. As I washed them down with sparkling water, I told my mouth it tasted awful and told my mouth to shut up when it disagreed. While I suffered through the experience of eating something healthy, I cast a glance at the vampire, curious about his reaction. Not surprisingly, he hadn't been served berries and cream. Instead, a waiter had delivered a stemmed wine glass roughly half full of a deep red liquid.

"Would you like a taste?" he responded to my questioning look. "It is a wonderful vintage that I believe you're familiar with: Chateau du Shane."

I shuddered and looked away. My arm moved mechanically and shoved another spoon-ful of berries into my mouth. I chewed, I drank more fancy water, and I said a silent prayer to whatever gods might be listening to just hurry the damned night up already so I could escape. The gods must have taken the night off. That, or they weren't listening to me, and why would they? I'd never paid them any mind, so it was pretty dumb to think they'd take much interest in my irreverent ass.

Small talk started the way it always does. Someone makes a little joke, and someone else politely laughs. An innocent question is posed for discussion, and a brave soul decides to weigh in. I should've known Betty would be the one to get things rolling. She was a bartender, after all, and half her job was chatting up patrons. I should've also known that her way of breaking the ice was going to be R-rated.

"Oh my god. This is so good," she moaned after spooning a boysenberry into her red lips with a small silver spoon. "Maybe it's just me being, you know, me, but a five-course meal is so," she paused, searching for the right word, "sensual. A courtship. The first course is like the first time your fingers touch theirs, and you start to imagine those fingers unbuttoning your blouse."

Mona was the first to laugh, a surprised, "Ha!" followed by a fit of coughing. The sound startled the others, which led to more embarrassed laughter. All it took was a little innuendo and an awkward laugh, and the entire mood shifted. Mona admitted she couldn't really taste things anymore, and Betty gasped in sympathetic shock. Soon the two women were discussing an assortment of topics: what Mona had liked to eat back when she could taste food, where Betty had found that dress, where Mona had liked to shop before she got cancer, died and was brought back to serve Dieter, how did Betty like bartending, and how did Mona like working in a castle. Vilde joined the conversation and shared the name of her personal tailor after Betty commented on the bunad dress and told her it was, "So hot, in a what's-under-all-of-that sort of way." Tanckenstein told Mona he was really impressed by her moves during the library battle royale. She said she was impressed when she'd learned he had thrown a car at Dieter, and damned if she didn't say it in a way that seemed like she was flirting with the big cadaver.

"I've been thrown," I declared, the proclamation bringing the comfortable banter to a screeching halt. "Many times, in fact."

Betty rolled her eyes. "It's true, you know. Tony threw him into some speakers once. Another time, he threw August through a door and into the street."

"I threw him into a bookcase and then into a dungeon cell," Dieter added as he raised a hand and then chuckled when he heard Tony laugh.

Stein chimed in and shared the story about tackling me when I was a coyote. Everyone laughed at that. Well, everyone except me and Clarissa. I glowered while she sat quietly beside me, eyes downcast and hands folded in her lap.

"I can't believe you brought Tony," I whispered.

Clarissa's eyes didn't leave her lap, but she answered. "He's never punched my eye out."

That stung. I shoved a few berries around their bowl with my spoon, pouting. When I noticed Clarissa hadn't touched her first course, I reached over and tapped her bowl.

"You don't like berries either?" I asked.

"Do I? Don't I?" she sighed without looking at me. "I don't think it matters. I don't think they matter."

I sympathized. I was waiting for the more substantial stuff, too. A noise caught my attention, and I saw the caterers emerge again with the next course. We were presented with a steaming bowl of stew and a warm roll. The stew smelled amazing, and by amazing, I meant like meat. My bowl had barely hit the table when I grabbed a spoon and gave it a good stir. Sure enough, I could see chunks of meat mixed in with what were likely potatoes and cabbage. I brought my spoon to my lips and let my tongue confirm what my nose suspected: it was delicious.

"This is what I'm talking about," I said to no one in particular, but Vilde decided it was a statement that merited a response.

"Fårikål," she informed us. "It is the national dish of Norway. Lamb, cabbage, potatoes. Peppercorn, sea salt. It is the quality of the ingredients and how they are introduced that results in the best flavor. It is good, nei?"

Others heartily agreed, and the dinner conversation resumed. The only difference was that slurps and exclamations were interjected between the questions and comments.

"I've been meaning to ask," Tanckenstein said to Tony, "how does one become a warlock?"

Tony smiled a crooked smile soaked in condescension. "The same way you get to Carnegie Hall. Practice."

"I've always had a natural aptitude," Dieter remarked with just a dash more smug than Tony had used. "Even as a human. Ah, those were the days. Angry wives asking for a curse on their unfaithful husbands. Angry husbands asking for a curse on their neighbor. I was so busy casting dark curses that I barely had a moment to myself."

"I've always found curses to be a bit of a bore," Tony rejoined with a dismissive wave of his hand. "The harnessing of the elements. There's a real challenge. To channel the storm's fury and bend it to your will. Command the raging fire to obey your commands, the tides to ebb and flow to suit your whims, the very earth to rise up and serve you. The dark arts come at a cost. Those that settle for the simple return of a curse..." the warlock sniffed. "Well, I suppose that has its appeal for some."

The vampire sat a little straighter in his chair. "I see. The elements, is it? And you've mastered all four, have you?"

Tony's dark eyes darkened more. "I have mastered the wind and studied the others. Mastery of all four elements is a lifetime's work."

"Ah," Dieter replied. "And such a short lifetime at that. Still, mastery of even one element is such an accomplishment. You must be quite proud. Compared to that, I would imagine that grasping a departed soul and coercing it back into its flesh must be a trivial matter."

"Necromancy? That's a little... cliche, isn't it?" Tony asked. When Dieter narrowed his eyes, the warlock held out his palms. "I don't mean to be rude, but let's be honest. You were turned. You died and now lived a cursed and soulless existence. The appeal of feeling like you have some control over death—especially when you had no control over your own—must be comforting."

"Not only a warlock but a shrink, too," Dieter said softly. "And you're so much more evolved that you don't feel the allure of control, of holding power over death itself?"

The warlock arched an eyebrow. "Of course I do, but why stop at dominion over a single soul? Eschatology. That's the real challenge."

Dieter snorted derisively. "Oh, you're one of those," he said. "End of the world. Been there, done that. When you've lived over four-hundred years, talk to me about the end of the world. I've seen this world teeter on the brink a dozen times. Nevertheless, here we are. Only a fool would believe that this world has some predetermined expiration date or–and this is even more absurd–that one person could determine when that date should occur."

"I'm a fool, am I?" Tony asked, a cold breeze quickening around the table and grabbing at the tablecloth's hem.

The vampire offered a wide smile, his teeth and two impossibly long fangs shockingly white against the spray tan orange around them. "The greatest fool is he who thinks he is not one and all others are."

"It is the peculiar quality of a fool to perceive the faults of others and to forget his own," Tony rejoined.

Dieter placed his palms on the table and leaned forward. Tony slowly raised a hand, and wind rippled the pavilion's tent. Mona's hand slipped inside her blazer. Tanckenstein's fists clenched, and he rocked onto the balls of his feet. The air practically crackled with pent-up violence, and then Betty grabbed me by my secondhand lapels and pulled me in for a wet kiss.

"August can change into a gorilla and an elephant," she gushed after letting me up for air. "Can either of you do that? I mean, I know Tony can change into a crybaby. How about you, D? Anything? Maybe a bat?"

Both men gaped at the succubus, their spat dissolving in the spreading puddle of their shared incredulity, while a wide smile stretched the succubus' lips.

"Leave me out of it," I whispered, but all I got was a terse, "Oh, shut up," from my shit-stirring date.

"How could you even?" Tony gasped. "How could you try to compare me to that?" A repulsed wave of his hand in my general direction made it pretty clear I was the 'that.'

Betty shrugged and twirled a lock of hair idly on her finger. "It just seems like you two have worked so hard, so very hard, to be so wise and powerful and *manly*, but you can't do what August here does so naturally." Her smile turned to a sympathetic pout, and she stretched an arm around my shoulders and drew me closer. "So sad," she opined.

Whatever this new game was, Vilde decided she wanted to play, too. "And all of your talk about power. That one sees the future," she remarked as her spoon tipped toward Clarissa. "Tell me, oh mighty dark lords, which of you can do that?"

The spray-tan coating Dieter's face looked ready to crack, his visage had gone so hard, and I could practically hear the steam whistling from Tony's ears. Meanwhile, Vilde's eyes twinkled, and the tip of Betty's tongue explored her upper teeth.

"Oh, look. Here comes the next course," I piped up. "Smells like fish. Is that fish?"

The caterer parade appeared again with dishes laden with battered fishcakes, asparagus, and garlic mashed potatoes. Large bottles of what we were told held lingonberry wine were placed within easy reach. Stemmed, crystal glasses were filled, and for a few moments, the only sounds were forks clinking against plates and throats swallowing food and wine and, in one case, Shane. Daggers were cast from warlock to succubus to vampire to huldra and back. If looks could kill, the dinner party would've become a homicide scene faster than you could say 'couples therapy.' Vilde coolly informed us we were enjoying hake, a whitefish similar but so much better than cod, because, of course, it was. Stein—too loudly—said it looked fantastic, and Mona said she used to love seafood. Betty decided it was a good time to share a story about a most unexpected but deeply satisfying encounter she'd had with a merman. Mona shared that she hadn't been laid since before she'd died. I'm not sure who else caught the look she gave Tanckenstein, but I did and spit out a half-chewed bite of hake.

"You haven't?" Betty exclaimed. "But you're gorgeous. Dead or not, you're a hottie. Don't let anyone tell you different. Hell, I'd do you. What are you up to later?"

I buried my head in my meal, lips mere inches from my plate as I forked bite after bite into my mouth. After what seemed like an eternity, waiters returned and cleared plates to make way for the fourth course. Mona was talking to Stein about how he liked being a revenant. Vilde and Dieter were enjoying their drinks, her sipping the pale lingonberry wine and him sipping what I really wished was just a cabernet Sauvignon. Betty found her way effortlessly into every conversation, adroitly adding a dangerous mix of insult and innuendo and adulation, while the other guests teetered on the razor-thin edges between. Clarissa and I just... sat.

"Fuck this," I muttered to no one. The caterers were diligently heading our way. I didn't know what the next course was, but I could smell that it wasn't meat. Suddenly suffocating, I shoved my chair back and stood up from the table.

"Bathroom," I muttered.

No one made an effort to stop me. No one but Dieter, that is. As I passed his chair, his hand shot out and grabbed my arm.

"You will return before the álfablót," he instructed quietly, tone pitched for my ears only. "And you'd damned well better start behaving yourself. At least pretend like you're having a nice time. Eat lots of lefse. Tell Vilde how wonderful it is. How charming this dinner party is. How glad you are that she invited you. Vilde's favor is the only thing keeping you alive. Don't disappoint her."

His eyes glinted dangerously and mine–hopefully–glinted defiantly. After a tense moment, his fingers relaxed, and I made good on my escape.

Heavy steps carried me from the pavilion and across the small park's grass. The sound of running water grew louder as I stepped from the grass and into the brush and trees that ringed the island like a living fence. The remains of an old concrete piling stuck up from the river's black water invitingly, so I hopped onto it and then sat with my knees pulled up tight to my chest. The sky above was dark, the twinkling of stars erased by the city's light pollution. I resigned myself to looking at the skyline rising up from the far bank. It was my city, my home, but it felt very far away.

"Pretty," a familiar but wholly unexpected voice remarked.

"It is, Canute. It certainly is," I said carefully and forced myself to stay very, very still. "Um, what are you doing here? Your bridge is further up the river."

I squinted my eyes to better see the old troll. What I'd thought was a misshapen boulder by the water's edge uncurled, and Canute's silhouette appeared, backlit by the brightly lit buildings across the water.

"My river. My bridges. Me and Yrsa."

"Of course they are, Canute," I soothed, all the while wondering if the other trolls rumored to lurk under the nearby Stone Arch Bridge or Hennepin Avenue Bridge had gotten that particular memo. Then something hit me. "Yrsa? Is that, I mean... did you? Are you dating someone, Canute?"

His granite features split in a slow smile, and a thick finger crept up to a nostril. Who'da thunk trolls could look bashful? It was almost cute. Almost.

A slow whistle escaped my lips. "You dog. Regular lady killer, aren't you?"

I'd forgotten that trolls don't have a sense of humor.

"Yrsa strong. Mean. She'd kill Canute," the troll proclaimed, and again that little smile pushed his cracked lips into unfamiliar shapes.

*Or maybe they do,* I amended.

"I suppose you're right," I placated. "What are you doing here? Were you invited to the álfablót, too?"

"Alpaplop?" he asked, working on each syllable like it was a Rubik's Cube.

"Yes," I agreed, keeping my voice as calm as possible and considering my options, which were few. "A huldra and a vampire are having an intimate evening and a sacrifice tonight. Isn't that nice?"

Canute snuffled. "Dunno."

I waited for a few more breaths, then asked tentatively, "You aren't hungry, are you?"

"No," the troll replied, still looking wistfully at the dark water. "Ate. Full."

I didn't want to know what—or who—had satiated the large troll. I just wanted to get as far away as possible before he started to feel peckish again.

"That's good. That's real good," I offered agreeably. "It's nice to be full. So, if I just, you know, left... That'd be okay?"

The dark, lumpy shadow near the water *hmph'd*. "Eat you later," the troll said. Whether it was a threat or a joke, I couldn't be sure and didn't plan on finding out. I slid backward, gained my feet, and then ran.

I'd pushed through the trees and back into the park's edge when I heard Tanckenstein's raspy voice. I followed the sound and found the tall cadaver chatting with Mona a few paces from the table.

"Hey Stein. Stein!" I gasped. "There's a... there's a tr..."

"Not now, August. The álfablót is about to begin."

"But it's a..."

The big cadaver held up a hand. "Ms. Tanck says patience is a virtue. I guess that means you'll have to wait to tell me whatever it is you want to tell me until after the álfablót."

I tried again, but he'd already dismissed me. All I could do was cast a nervous glance over my shoulder, hunker down, and hope Canute stayed put.

I hadn't needed Dieter's stern encouragement to enjoy some lefse. I'd missed the fourth course but returned in time for the fifth and final: Potato flatbread with hand-churned butter and real cane sugar. Vilde's secret recipe was—in a word—amazing. Not only was it delicious, but it seemed to have brought the boiling dinner conversation down to a warm simmer. I had shoved two rolled-up pieces into my mouth, washed them down with a healthy swig of lingonberry wine, and was munching on a third when Vilde gracefully rose from her place and spread her arms to encompass the small gathering.

"Takk skal du ha. I am so pleased that each of you is here. Now, I would like to take a moment to recognize two very special people," Vilde continued. "Clarissa Steyer, your clear interpretations of the celestial design have long guided my steps. It was you that told me what had to be done and who had to be the one to do it."

The oracle looked up from her musings, apparently confused. She blushed and waved a hand and muttered, "Shoot. I was just. Oh boy. I don't know. Too bright. Just too darned bright."

The huldra smiled a patient smile for her muttering guest and turned her eyes on me.

"August Shade, you fulfilled your purpose wonderfully. Because of you, Dieter and I are reunited. Because of you, I have my book."

"Because of him, I've lost a very capable servant, my library is a disaster, and my maid is still too distraught to clean it up," Dieter added bitterly.

The huldra tsked. "Don't pout, Dieter. This is my álfablót, not your pity party."

I'd never have thought that a centuries-old vampire could look chastened, but Dieter surprised me.

"Apologies, my dear. You are quite right. As you say, the heavens will illuminate the path, but that path may not be easy."

The huldra placed a hand on his shoulder in benediction. "I know how much it has cost you to relinquish the book. As this is an álfablót, consider it a fitting sacrifice. Speaking of which... Leonard, would you be so kind?"

The big man stood and headed to the boiler works. A few moments later, he returned with a rough wooden plank held between his hands. On it, *The Thirteenth Zodiac* seemed to suck in all the light from the strands of bulbs crisscrossing the pavilion's tent like a rectangular black hole. As before, it looked old and serious and as before, just looking at it turned my stomach. Stein didn't seem any happier about being so close to it. With the level of care normally reserved for handling fine crystal or doing surgery on a really important person's brain, he set the plank in front of his master.

Vilde caressed the cover with a slender finger. "This book. This extraordinary book," she crooned. "Dieter, do you remember when you first gave it to me?"

The vampire's unnaturally orange face folded into a reasonable facsimile of a genuine smile. "Of course. You'd been talking about it incessantly. For so long, we'd whispered all of our plans, our aspirations, our dreams as we laid in each other's arms. Such bold dreams. So audacious. Tanning salons were child's play by comparison. Together, Tanck's Tasty Treats would be in every city in the state. The whole Midwest. The whole world. Together, we'd amass riches beyond any this world has ever known. Together, we'd rule."

"Ja, such dreams," Vilde agreed. "But dreams do not always come true, do they? Nei, they do not. I wanted more than dreams. I wanted certainty. When I learned of this book, I knew it had to be mine."

"And I knew I had to be the one to find it for you," Dieter said with a proud smile.

I shoved another lefse tube into my mouth and chewed. The huldra and vampire basking in the glow of their shared narcissism was threatening to send my four-fifths of a five-course meal up my throat and all over the white tablecloth. My only hope was to build a potato flatbread wall in my gullet to keep the rest down. After swallowing hard, I raised a hand.

"Still not sure what an old book has to do with building a lefse empire," I stated. "Not that you don't have a really swell goal. World domination by selling potato bread. That's plenty stupid already. Do you really need to make it stupider by tossing the book on top?"

"August," Tanckenstein warned. "I know you're just being you, but maybe this is a good time to shift into someone else."

Betty laughed. "Good luck with that."

I ignored my date–she'd already made it clear that my sidecar would be empty on the way home, anyway–and ended up looking straight at Tony. The warlock's face was expressionless, eyes unreadable as they stared not at me, not even at Betty, but at the book. The tiniest of breezes, barely more than a breath, rustled the air, and then it was gone.

"Mr. Shade," Vilde snapped. "August. Please. You are my guest. Behave as such, and I will answer your question."

I folded my arms across my chest. "Fine. Just, you know. Get on with it."

Dieter showed me his fangs, but Vilde placed a restraining hand on his shoulder. "Tålmodighet er en dyd, my dear. Patience is a virtue." A slow, steadying breath filled the huldra's lungs, followed by a slow exhale. "This book was written by a powerful oracle. Yiorgos Katopodis wrote of a thirteenth sign of the Zodiac called Ophiuchus and wrote it with the blood from his veins..."

"I know, I know. I was at his stupid lecture," I interrupted. "And it really was stupid," I piled on with a salty glare at Tony.

The warlock bridled. "That was you? Of course, it was. If I'd known you were there..."

"How would you have known?" I shot back. "You were too busy looking at Sally Dupree's magic orbs."

"Who's Sally Dupree?" Betty and Clarissa asked in unison.

Tony squirmed. "A colleague. A professional colleague. Really, that's all..."

The succubus' skin flushed, and her eyes narrowed to dark slits. Clarissa's eyebrows drew closer together.

"You work with magic orbs?" the oracle asked. "Wait... Ohhh."

Ignoring the burgeoning three-way argument, my finger jabbed toward the book.

"The Vortex Virtuoso was going on and on about that book," I told Vilde and then snorted. "He said the government had it. Dumbass. But seriously, what is that book?"

My question yanked everyone's attention back to me and the huldra. "Power," she finally sighed. "Such complete and total power."

"That you're going to use to build a lefse empire?" I asked again, genuinely flummoxed.

It was Dieter that answered. "If only it were that easy," he sighed. "Alas, the book is incomprehensible. Yiorgos knew that others would covet the book and all that it reveals, so he laid a final trap as he wrote it. The pages are not just full of his power. They are full of his madness. Those who have tried to read its words have, like poor Yiorgos himself, gone quite insane."

"So it is poetry," I confirmed. "I knew it."

Vilde ignored my commentary. "Through the ages, people have found the book and tried to claim its power for themselves. Each met their demise, starting with Yiorgos' own queen. She tried to read his words. It is said she was still screaming as she leaped from the highest tower's only window. Can you imagine? Well, I shared the tale of the book with Dieter and my suspicions of where it might be. My darling turned his not inconsiderable talents to its discovery. It was a gift without equal."

I shook my head. "I still don't get it. What good is a gift like that if you can't use it?"

The huldra was watching me closely. "You are... familiar... with the book. Tell me. How did it feel to touch it?"

As the table turned to look at me, I realized how every muscle in my body had tensed. Just watching her fingertips brush the book's cover had set my teeth grinding and the hairs on the back of my neck on end. My stomach was considering returning all the food I'd eaten, and my feet had slid back under my chair in an effort to drag me away from the table.

"Not good," I finally managed.

"Ja. Not good," the huldra agreed. "Most cannot tolerate even touching this book." Her hand reached out to caress the book yet again. "Those that can inevitably try to read it and, as has been explained, go insane." Her slender fingers slid around the Zodiac signs circling the sun and moon. "I am not so frail. I can look upon this book. I can touch it. I can open it and not succumb to its lure. Oh, ja. I do wish that I could unlock its secrets, that I could take the thirteenth Zodiac and wield its power for myself. Sadly, I know that I cannot, and so I do not try."

"So why in the hell is it so damned important?" I asked again.

Her fingers continued their exploration of the book's corners and contours and then slipped down and across the edges of the pages. Sensing what they were searching for, she opened the book somewhere near the middle and retrieved a small sheet of paper pressed between its pages.

"It is a good place to keep recipes," she remarked. "Julekake. You might call it fruit-cake." More pages were turned, and another loose sheet was revealed. "Fattigman. Simply delightful." Again, she flipped through the pages and retrieved a piece of paper covered in neat, scrolling words. "Krumkake. So fragile that to look at them is to risk their destruction, but to taste... Ah! The world has not known such pleasure. An empire is not built on lefse alone. An empire is built on the best Norwegian baked goods in all the world. And those recipes must be kept safe, nei?"

My jaw ached from pressing my molars so tightly together. I pried them loose and asked, "You had me storm his castle, get my ass kicked six ways to Sunday, and then thrown in a dungeon for cookies?"

"Not I," Vilde said with a slight shake of her head. The movement sent her lustrous golden locks swaying. "It was her. Had she not divined the true intent of the stars and planets as they danced their infinite dance, I would not have known of my need for your services."

I turned my head and looked at Clarissa. She looked miserable, but I was too caught up in my own misery to worry much about hers. I'd known it was going to be a long night. If I'd known it would be a pissing contest, a romantic fencing match, weird food, a bunch of horoscope talk, and the revelation that I'd almost been killed for a recipe box, I'd have let old Canute eat me when I'd had the chance.

"I didn't think they were real," the vampire remarked with just a hint of sour grapes in his voice. "Horoscopes. Malarky."

The huldra's surreally beautiful face made smug look gorgeous. "Or so he thought until I introduced him to your work, Ms. Steyer. It did not take long to convince him of your power. Our parting was all the more bitter, as it was a disagreement over our horoscopes that led us to believe our time together had come to an end. And yet..." The smug look turned triumphant, "here we are."

Dieter stood and took the huldra's hands in his own. "And yet, here we are," he agreed. "And since tonight is all about sacrifices, I'd like to offer one more."

The vampire tilted his head, and Mona strode off for the boiler works building.

"You know I'm a Capricorn," he continued after his servant had left. "The goat. It seemed only fitting that for your álfablót, I should give you... myself."

I heard the worried bleating a moment before Mona emerged with a small goat in tow. The little brown and white beast was pulling against a rope that had been looped around its neck to fashion a crude leash, but Mona was–as I knew from very personal experience–the stronger.

"One sacrificial goat," Dieter's henchwoman proclaimed when she reached the table and tied the leash to her chair.

Vilde squealed in delight while Dieter's eyes twinkled at the joke. I sighed and flopped back in my chair. The fact that the poor thing was going to get its throat cut for the sake of a bad pun hurt me more than I would have imagined. Had I known what was to come, I'd have traded places with the goat willingly. Unfortunately, I didn't. I wasn't the oracle.

# CHAPTER 12



T HE WARM NIGHT AND promise of bloodshed had me sweating profusely. I squirmed in my ill-fitting trousers and reached for my wine. As I tipped the glass up, I took some comfort in the fact that I wasn't the only one in need of a drink. Tony had drained his glass, refilled it, and drained it again so many times that I'd lost count. I only knew that the caterers had brought more bottles.

A moment of sympathy tugged something inside of me. I'd spent time with Clarissa. Not much, granted, but enough to know how annoying she could be. I'd also spent time with Betty. Again, not much, but enough to know how annoying it was to want her attention and simply not get it. Sitting beside Betty, seeing her lean toward the huldra like a sunflower toward the sun, her chest practically heaving with unfettered desire, was driving me nuts. I couldn't imagine what it was doing to him.

"So, how does the sacrifice work?" Betty asked the huldra.

"In the olden days... Ah, it was quite a spectacle. Entire households, even villages, would bring the best of their harvest and lay it all at my feet. The crops would be burned, and the animals slaughtered, for what need did I have of their bounty? It was not their food or their dumb beasts that I needed. It was their *sacrifice.* The knowledge that they would give up the best of their harvest and risk a hard and hungry winter to appease me. That is what made it so splendid."

Betty's hand found Vilde's and squeezed. "That is so primal. So hot. I would give you everything I have. Everything."

"And she'd still want more," Dieter remarked affectionately. "It's a good thing I'm already dead, or this one would drain me dry instead of that goat."

Vilde still held Betty's hand, but reached with the other for Dieter's. "Hysj, hysj. Hush, now. I would do no such thing." Returning her attention to the rapt succubus, she explained the rite. "It is simple. Dieter will proclaim it is the best goat. Fat and loud. He will open its throat and spill its blood at my feet. I will dip three fingers in the blood and bless his brow."

"And mine?" Betty asked, ensorcelled. "You don't need to stop at my brow. You can bless every last inch of me."

I found myself remembering my early days in Minneapolis. I'd scrounged up enough money to afford maybe one drink at a shitty bar. There was a dingy little pile of cinder blocks in the neighborhood that had live music on the weekends, so I'd decided to give it a shot. A grunge band was on a small stage in the back, pounding out chords hard enough to rattle the walls. It was the first time I'd seen music live, and it had been glorious. The sound. The energy. There was this crazy feedback loop between the band and the crowd on the floor below. The louder and faster the band played, the harder the crowd gyrated and thrashed. The harder the crowd gyrated and thrashed, the louder and faster the band played. I'd been frozen in place, completely transfixed by the escalating energy and its mad, self-perpetuating spiral.

By comparison, what was happening between Vilde and Betty made that crazy night at the bar feel more like a smooth jazz jam session after everyone had popped some quaaludes.

I tore my eyes away from the scene and looked at Tony. Vilde's effect on Betty's already-supercharged libido was like gas on a fire, and the heat had turned the warlock's face a red so bright it rivaled Dieter's orange for the least-natural color award.

"It seems like the only sacrifice that matters has already happened," Tony suddenly proclaimed. "You've ripped my heart still beating from my chest and cast it aside. Stepped on it and ground it into the dirt. You've killed me, Betty." When the succubus returned his melodramatic tirade with a confused look, he shook his head angrily. "Bad enough that you came here with him. That abomination. As if that wasn't enough, you're throwing yourself at her. That, that... cow! Why do you torture me? Does hurting me cause you that much pleasure?"

The succubus smoothed a strand of dark hair that had pulled loose and crossed her arms across her chest. "You love it, and you know it."

"I do not!" Tony cried as he slammed his fist on the table. "I am everything you need. All that you need, and yet you treat me like some second-hand playboy. A passing fancy. Nothing more than a booty call."

The huldra watched the exchange and then took a deep, shuddering breath. An eerie calm settled over her.

"Cow? You must be a Cancer," she observed when she'd regained some measure of control over herself.

The warlock glared. "So?"

Vilde nodded slowly. "A sign not without its redeeming qualities, but also so emotional. So temperamental. So rude." The huldra clucked her tongue. "You come here on this night as a guest. Not only a guest of mine, but of a powerful oracle who deserves every drop of reverence one could muster. And yet you behave like a spoiled child. You insult your host. You ignore your companion completely and instead fawn like a lovesick puppy over this one. I wonder. Will you realize the errors of your ways?"

As she spoke, voice soft but impossible not to hear, Vilde's face had taken on a new aspect. She was beyond beautiful. Her beauty had become terrifying.

"Clarissa," the huldra asked, "do you truly care for this one?"

The oracle looked up, for the moment fully in the present. Her eyes shifted from Tony to Betty and back. "Care for him? I don't know. I might have. I think I did, but what's the point? When he's not falling all over her, he's chasing magic orbs."

Vilde's face turned sympathetic. "Uheldig barn. You poor, unfortunate child. That is all I need to know from you."

With an air of ritual, the huldra turned to look down at the succubus.

"And you, Betty?" she asked. "You find me beautiful, nei?"

The succubus lifted her hungry eyes to the huldra and responded with a throaty, "Oh god, yes."

"Your warlock lover was correct. This is an álfablót, and sacrifices are being made. I will accept him as your sacrifice. If you agree, you may lie with me tonight."

Betty trembled and chewed on her lip. "Ex-lover," she clarified, "and sure. He's all yours. Sacrifice away." The succubus gave an almost-guilty look to Tony. "Sorry, babe."

Vilde nodded, and Tanckenstein stepped forward, and I found myself anxiously looking around for a woodchipper. The revenant had only made it halfway around the table when a sudden gust lifted him from his feet and sent him sailing backward. I heard him land heavily with a curse, and then curse again as he pulled himself unsteadily to his feet. Dieter pounced, but like the revenant before him, he arced across the pavilion in the grip of a strong and sudden wind. Mona drew a pistol, Dieter crouched for another leap, and Stein took a menacing step. Betty was on the edge of her seat, large eyes drinking in every tense moment. Meanwhile, Tony looked at them all through narrowed eyes under dark eyelashes. A dark cloud swirled just over his shoulder and blinked its glowing red eyes.

"Kill me," he warned, "and you'll never be able to read that."

"Stoppe!" Vilde commanded. Dieter, Mona, and Tanckenstein all waited while the huldra and warlock engaged in an uncomfortably long staring contest.

Dark specs floated in front of my eyes, and I realized I'd stopped breathing. My sudden gasp broke the silence, and suddenly everyone was looking at me.

"What? This is stressful," I complained. "But don't let me stop you. Everyone go back to being all violent and scary."

The huldra ignored me. "Explain yourself," she demanded of the warlock.

"That," Tony repeated. "Yiorgos' book. You can't read it. I can."

I heard a whimper beside me. Clarissa had buried her face in her hands. I put an awkward arm across her shoulders and felt them shake. I had no idea what was going on, but whatever it was, she clearly wasn't a fan. I whispered that she didn't need to worry; everything would be fine. They'd all kill each other, and we could nab another slice of lefse and be on our way. Either she couldn't hear me, or my words weren't as comforting as I'd thought they'd be because her shoulders just shook all the harder.

The warlock didn't bother to refill his glass. He rose to his feet, grabbed the wine bottle, and brought it to his mouth. His Adam's apple bobbed a few times, and then he wiped his lips on his sleeve. A moment later, he burped.

"The thing is," he started with a bit of a slur, "I don't think you know the whole story. Yiorgos' story. I do. Eschka... Eschatology," he pronounced carefully, "is my area of expertise. I have studied it for years. The Bible's *Revelations*. Vaishnavism's *Kali Yuga*. The Buddhist's *Seventh Sun*. The Norse *Ragnarok*. And Yiorgos Katopodis' most incredible book. I know things. I have a podcast," he proclaimed, and a powerful gust rippled the pavilion's tent and set the strands of cafe lights swaying.

Certain that he had everyone's attention, Tony continued in a lecturing tone. He might have sounded a bit more authoritative if he hadn't downed at least a bottle and a half of lingonberry wine, but the wine had also made him immune to that particular fact.

"Yes, Yiorgos angered his queen. Yes, she tortured him. And yes, he wrote that book. It wasn't for vengeance, though. It was for love. He loved her. Loved her," he repeated after another swig and burp.

The warlock swayed like a lingonberry tree in a summer breeze. His arms splayed and seesawed until he'd regained his balance, and his eyes cast suspicious glances.

"Love," he continued, "is written in the stars. It is preordained. It is eternal. As timeless as time. It is also torture. Tribulation. An endless struggle. As it should be. Nothing worth giving your entire soul for should be easy, should be free." The warlock hiccupped loudly and looked accusingly at the wine bottle. "Yiorgos knew that. He knew. When he drew his last breath, it was to profess his love for his queen despite every hurt she'd visited on him. It was to give her the power to write her own future. He only hoped he would be included. He didn't know it would drive her mad."

"Indeed," Dieter said in a low voice dipped in a promise of blood and pain. "Thank you for that most excellent interpretation. Now, if you don't mind…"

"I mind!" Tony screamed, and a fresh gust buffeted the tent. More stemmed wine glasses tipped over, cloth napkins fluttered off the table, and the poor goat bleated. "I mind very much. I was telling a story. The story of how someone in love gave everything–every single thing he had–to the one person, the only person, that deserved that love."

"And drove her mad," Betty sighed, hands pressed to her heart and eyes heavy with unshed tears as she gazed lustfully at the drunken warlock. "That's so sad. So incredibly beautiful and sad."

I was trying to figure out how anything Tony was saying could be a turn-on but was coming up short. My lack of comprehension didn't matter, though. The succubus was looking from warlock to huldra and back, practically panting with indecisive desire. Meanwhile, the wind was getting stronger. What had started as a gust became a steady, stiff breeze. Only Betty and Tony were spared its rough touch.

"A madness I now understand all too well," the warlock stated.

The wind ripping through the tent grew stronger. Tony's hand patted his chest and then fished inside his vest. A moment later, he withdrew a folded sheet of paper. After opening it, he grasped the wine bottle and raised it high. As if toasting the strong wind, he read the scrawling ink that covered the page:

"Night's mistress, winged desire

Sweet release of passion's fire

On my lips, Betty's name

Consume me with your passionate flame.

The seas will boil, the land will crack

The skies will fill will clouds of black

One caress will set us free

No one left but you and me..."

When Dieter's patience snapped, it was almost audible. It surprised me to have something in common with the orange vampire, but I sympathized with his sudden and violent reaction to Tony's words. I hated poetry, too. The vampire crouched, leaped... and sailed sideways. The gust of wind that knocked the vampire aside upended the table and sent Vilde tumbling. I dove to the ground and covered my head with my hands. When I looked up, Dieter had regained his feet and was trying to get to Tony, but was forced to push against a gale-force wind. A dark cloud swelled as Tony's pet elemental grew and grew. When it reached Tanckenstein's height, it lumbered off to confront Vilde's man. Stein had pulled his own gun and fired off a few shots, but each bullet's path was bent by the wind and sent whistling into the night.

"Dieter!" Vilde screamed. "You will stop him now!"

The vampire leaped again and, again, was cast aside. "Trying, my dear. Trying..." he complained.

The huldra spat some angry Norwegiany-sounding words and then composed herself. Her eyes shimmered as they sought the warlocks. "Human," she commanded. "You will stop."

She wasn't looking at me, and thank goodness. If I'd been forced to bear the full brunt of her command, I've no doubt my lungs would've simply stopped breathing, my heart, beating. Even so, I stopped moving and stared, every bit of me waiting for her to tell me what to do next. Tony, however, had no such compulsion.

"Spare me," he muttered and flicked his wrist. Like her vampire lover, the huldra was violently tossed backward by an unnatural gust. "I could never love another, so your wiles are worthless. Much like Yiorgos' book. It is said that madness waits for any who try to read it, but that is not my fate. That is the secret of *The Thirteenth Zodiac*. It cannot drive you mad if you already are, and I am mad. Quite mad. Madly in love."

The warlock stepped to where Vilde's book had fallen to the ground. While his lips sounded out whatever spells were needed to keep the winds blowing and his elemental doing his bidding, his hands lifted the book and opened the cover. He balanced the book in one palm and turned to the first page. The shape of his lips changed as he sounded out the words before him, but the howling wind kept them from reaching my ears. All I could do was watch the warlock's face, and what I saw was terrifying.

Maybe Tony had been right. Maybe his obsession with Betty had already sent him halfway to the loony bin before he started to read *The Thirteenth Zodiac*. That, or the first page of that damned book was everything the legends warned about and more. The warlock looked up from that page and screamed into his own personal storm.

"I see! I cannot see! I must be able to see!" he cried in revelation. "Every future must be obliterated, burned to ash, ground to dust. There can be only one future. There must be only one future!"

The warlock began to pace anxiously with short, uneven steps. He returned his attention to the book, read another page, and raged again at the heavens. A third page, and he fell to his knees sobbing and cackling. A fourth page, and he was on his feet again, pacing. All the while, the storm and the elemental made sure Tony had plenty of personal space for his rapid descent into madness.

I've never watched someone go insane before. Like, literally go bat-shit crazy before my very eyes. How could I tell he was going totally 'round the bend? Call it an educated guess. When someone stomps and screams and yells to no one but themselves, and when their eyes go so wide that their irises look like dark specks in a milky white sea, and the corners of their mouth pull back so far in a demented grin that their jaw looks ready to fall from their skull, and the muscles in their cheeks writhe like ornery eels beneath the skin as they still try to make the mouth read words out loud despite the face-splitting grin... Yeah, that meets my definition for going bat-shit crazy. Well, that and what he did next.

Tony spun and twisted in his agonized contortions, and landed on his knees. When he raised his face, his eyes locked onto Clarissa. The oracle huddled on the ground while heavy sobs shook her shoulders. When she raised her face toward her really bad choice for a plus-one, Tony's eyes widened even further and cast about in sudden indecision. Finally, they settled on an unlikely object: a silver spoon. It had served one of the guests well back when we'd had the silly berries and cream and must've been missed by the caterers when they'd cleared the remnants of each course. I made a mental note to complain to the management: Don't leave spoons lying around when there's a crazed warlock that might decide to read a magic book that drives you nuts. Otherwise, that warlock might just reach for the spoon, grasp it tightly in their hand, and gouge out their eye.

"Oh, that's gross!" I screamed involuntarily, unable to look away as a geyser of blood erupted from the deep wound. "What the actual fuck?"

The whipping wind ripped my words away and flung them into the night. At the same time, it gripped the oracle in an invisible fist and lifted her high above the ground. She floated for what seemed like an impossibly long amount of time, and then violently crashed back to earth. I didn't hear the back of her head hit the ground, but I felt it all the way down to my toes. A tiny spark of the escalating lightning's sky-rending bolts was caught in a small, glass orb that arced away from Clarissa's head. The glints continued–minuscule parodies of the light show above–as it bounced, then rolled toward the warlock's outlandish boots. Letting the spoon fall, he grasped the oracle's eye, held it up to the tumultuous heavens, and then shoved it into his raw and bloody socket.

With a mean and maniacal grin, Tony turned his eyes–one wide with madness, the other ringed with blood–back to the book. A finger turned a page, and his lips continued to move in recitation. Storm clouds piled up in what had been a cloudless night, and more lightning flashed. The earth bucked, and the smell of sulfur burned my nostrils. The loud cracking of tree trunks split the air.

Tanckenstein had tried to reach the madman again, but Tony's elemental took Stein by the wrists and tossed the large man aside. Having been on the receiving end of the elemental's wrath, I felt every bump, scrape and jar as Stein tumbled and rolled across the concrete. The elemental then pivoted to face Dieter, and the two traded blows. The vampire attacked with an apex predator's ferocity, but basketball-sized fists of semi-solid air blocked his repeated strikes.

Still, Tony's lips moved. The large tent that covered the pavilion–anchored by strong nylon straps to steel pegs embedded in concrete–ripped free and sailed into the night. I heard windows shatter in the boiler works building. I felt another tremble and heave of the ground under my feet. The world was chaos except for an eerie calm around Betty and the space around Tony. He flipped another page, read on, and a cold rain hammered down.

I belly-crawled through the storm until I reached the fallen oracle and took her wrist. Rainwater poured down Clarissa's face as she looked up, eye naked and imploring.

"I think I know who has your glass eye," I yelled, voice straining to be heard above the winds, "and you're definitely post-relationship now. Regrettably, I can't get it back for you. Want a refund?"

"I said you could keep it for your troubles," she screamed, "and I'm still willing to pay you the rest when you return it."

"How?" I screamed back.

"In cash," she replied.

I palmed my face in frustration. That wasn't at all what'd I'd meant, but the rushing wind made any more talk worthless.

As I ground my teeth, the others were still doing their damnedest to get to Tony. Sadly, exactly none of them were having any luck. Dieter and the warlock's air demon battled on. The vampire tried again and again to break through the elemental, get around the elemental, go over the elemental, but every attempt was rebuffed. Frustration was clear in every line of the old bloodsucker's visage. With an enraged cry, Dieter charged and tried to tackle the semi-solid monster head-on. I winced involuntarily, then grinned. Having fought the vampire myself, I knew how strong he was. Certain I was finally going to see the end of Tony's pet, I was instead treated to the end of a centuries-old tanning salon mogul. The elemental grabbed Dieter's wrists, spun around like an Olympic hammer thrower, and sent a very surprised vampire over the trees and into the river. Vilde's wail confirmed what I already knew: vampires can't swim. Mona had managed to keep her feet and draw a pistol, but the bullets she fired veered wildly off into the night. I startled when one hit the concrete at my feet and saw the henchwoman mouth the word, 'Sorry!' Vilde was on her knees, eyes wild and cow tail thrashing. Tanckenstein was huddled in front of her, his back to the warlock and arms wrapping her up in a protective embrace. And then there was me, August Shade. What could I do? The warlock's elemental was tossing aside its assailants like leaves before a leaf blower. The sky flashed with lightning so bright I could barely see. The earth bucked and twisted. Rain pelted down hard enough to sting bare skin. What good could I possibly do?

"Get my eye!" Clarissa screamed. "Maybe I can see something. Maybe I can change it!"

An ear-splitting sound momentarily deafened me, and a crack opened across the pavilion's concrete. The world was about to be ripped in two, and she wanted me to get her eye out of the skull of the nutso warlock that was pulling it apart.

*Fuck it,* I decided, fatalism darkening the thought to match the storm-whipped night. *I get things back for people after a break-up. Might as well die doing what I do.*

A giant gorilla and a pile of shredded clothes occupied the space where I'd been a second before. I thumped my chest, roared, lunged for Tony, and sailed backward. An elephant rose on four legs, each thick as the trunk of a young tree, and galloped forward only to be sent skittering to the side as a wall of air slammed into my ribs. A turkey flapped its near-worthless wings and rode the storm's vortex high into the sky. Once it had reached a height that other turkeys would whisper about for ages to come, it turned into a Maine Coon and dropped like a furry little meteor. I was scant inches from Tony's head when another gust sent me tumbling to the grass. A wolverine growled, shook its displeasure, and marched deliberately toward the warlock, belly low to the ground in an effort to stay below the insane magical wind. That tactic might have worked had the air elemental not noticed. It plucked me from the ground easy as picking daisies. Again, I found myself airborne and again landed in a heap beside the oracle.

"Sorry, lady, but there is no way I can get that glass eye back," I gasped after turning human again. Waves of violent nausea from all the shifts forced me to spasm and convulse while a handful of yards away, Tony was bringing on the apocalypse one page at a time. "And that future you're always talking about? You don't need a magic eyeball to see that it's pretty damned short. Nothing's gonna change that. Not you, not your horoscopes."

Clarissa stared at me, one eye wide and wild, and a pit of pink flesh where the other should have been. "You're right. Holy crap, August. You're right. Not me, not my horoscopes. He's rewriting the future. Making anything possible. Making everything possible. I don't matter anymore. You, though... When is your birthday?"

The sudden change in the conversation's direction almost gave me whiplash. "My birthday? Why would that matter? I'm not going to live long enough to celebrate."

"When is it?" she begged. "It's in November, right? When in November?"

Her intensity was stupefying. I couldn't think of anything to say, so I simply answered her question. "November thirtieth."

The oracle's face transformed from terrified to transcendent. "That's it. Cripes. That's it! You can change it. You can change all of it!"

"I tried," I practically sobbed. The bone-deep weariness of trying so many shifts in such a short time was dragging me down to the bottom of a deep and dark pit. "I changed in to damn near everything I could."

"Don't you see? You're Ophiuchus! Not Sagittarius, Ophiuchus! The thirteenth Zodiac. You are the change. You can be the change. You are change."

What she probably thought was a pretty good motivational speech was cut short by a loud bleating. A few yards away, the little sacrificial goat was on its knees, scared half to death.

*You and me both, little buddy,* I thought, as the world around me was being torn asunder. *Death by douchebag. What a way to go. I should have let Canute eat me when I'd had the chance. Poor Canute. No goat in his future now.*

The dark thoughts snagged something in me and yanked hard. I'd told Canute that he'd get his goat back, and I should've let Canute eat me when I'd had the chance. I'd told Clarissa I'd changed into damn near everything I could. Damn near everything, but not *everything*.

A plan exploded behind my eyes, brighter than the lightning that was sending iridescent cracks across a pitch-black sky. I dug deep, as deep as I could, and then dug deeper.

Maybe I found some untapped reserves. Maybe I found a new resolve. Maybe I just found that fatalistic space where we finally accept death and all fear and weariness and heartache ceases to exist. Whatever it was that I found, I grabbed it and held it tight. A moment later, a coyote leaped up from where I'd been huddled on the ground and charged the goat. Fear of a natural predator trumped fear of the storm, and the little beast broke its restraint and took off into the night. I stretched my gait and swung wide, attempting to herd the goat. It worked, but a little too well. The damned thing went in a circle and raced off in the completely wrong direction.

*Just run for the douchebag, you little shit!* I thought furiously while again trying to both catch up and redirect its path. *The douchebag!*

The goat zigged when it was supposed to zag, zagged when it was supposed to zig. The coyote looked frantically at where the warlock stood in the eye of his own world-rending storm. Non-stop lightning illuminating his demented features like a constant strobe, the reflected light in Clarissa's stolen eye making it look like a halogen light was shining from the side of his nose. My future and everyone else's were dwindling to seconds. Even so, I ran, cut, barked, and growled. Inch by haphazard inch, I corralled the little goat closer and closer to where I needed it to be.

And then it happened. The dumb little shit finally went the right way and burst through whatever magic bubble had been protecting the warlock. Suddenly free from the wailing winds and pounding rain, the goat skittered to a stop, its legs splayed and head down. I stopped running, too, and simply stood with my tail hanging down and tongue lolling as I tried to catch my breath. A moment later, I shifted again and fell hard to the ground.

Meanwhile, Tony had noticed the goat.

"What have we here?" he cried as he reached down and grabbed the goat's scruff. "A sacrifice for me?"

Somehow, amidst the wind and the rain and the lightning and thunder and buckling of the broken earth, I found my feet and yelled the only words I had left.

"That's not your goat, you douchebag!" I screamed. "It's Canute's!"

At the end of my strength, I managed to shift one last time. The doctors had forced me to shift into a lot of things. Oddly, the one that best fit my disposition was the one I hardly ever became. A goat, similar but not quite the same as the one Tony was lifting into the air, ran for the river. I just hoped that both me and the real goat looked at least a little like the one poor Canute had given to Urmalena right before she broke his heart.

*Look at me! Fat!* I bleated desperately. *Fat! Noisy!*

Goats have excellent vision; exactly what prey needs to avoid the predator. And when the goat saw a large, lumpy shape lumbering up from the riverbank at an impossible speed, it did what prey does; turned and ran like hell. I went straight for the warlock, sharp little hooves kicking up clumps of earth. Behind me, the troll's feet were shaking the ground with a ferocity to rival the warlock's magic. I leaped for Tony and shifted mid-air. He turned, shock plain in the lightning's constant flashing as a fiercely grinning, middle-aged, buck-naked guy literally streaked across the pavilion. His elemental stepped into my path, and I felt a wrecking ball hit me. I careened off to the side, but I didn't care. I knew I'd never be able to get to Tony, but I didn't need to.

"My goat!" I heard Canute scream. "Fat! Noisy! My goat!"

Too late, Tony realized his peril. The dark, vaguely humanoid cloud that obeyed his commands whooshed toward the troll, but the elemental was no match for the quarter-ton of stupid on a mission. Canute smashed through the elemental and shattered it into a hundred swirling dust devils. Three more steps and Canute reached the warlock. One hand grabbed the goat and pulled it from the warlock's grasp. The other took the front of the warlock's vest, wrapped it up tight in its thick troll fingers, shook him like a rag doll in the hands of a tantrum-tossing toddler, and then whipped around and sent the warlock flying. I watched Tony's silhouette arc across the stormy night sky and slam into the Grain Belt beer sign. Sparks flew, pyrotechnics joined the lightning to fill the sky with eye-searing light, and then all went dark.

Instantly, the wind stopped. The lightning stopped. The rain stopped. The clouds evaporated. The violent heaves breaking the earth stopped. All that was left was a ruined wasteland, a succubus without a stray hair on her gorgeous head, a disheveled huldra, two worse-for-wear revenants, a pair of galoshes connected to a mismatched bundle of second-hand clothes, a naked shifter, and a troll holding a little goat.

"Fat. Noisy. Yrsa like you," Canute crooned as he tucked the little beast under an elbow and lumbered off into the night. "Future happened. Thanks, wizard," he called over his shoulder.

The troll was a shadow blending with the darker shadows as he lumbered toward the now-dark Grain Belt sign. The night was so still that I clearly heard the snap of a branch and Canute's surprised exclamation of, "Oh! Crispy douchebag. Yrsa like goat. Canute like crispy douchebag."

There were a few more snaps as the troll pushed through the trees and I heard what I could've sworn was a happy tune hummed by a tone-deaf troll, and then he was gone.

I inched myself up from the pavilion's broken concrete. The world had stopped ending, but, at least for me, it was still tilting and wobbling something fierce. Staggering and stumbling like I was at the bottom of the seventh during the World Series of benders, I cast about for something akin to clothes. The best I could see was a torn section of table cloth that the warlock's storm hadn't managed to send into the night. As I crossed the short distance, I didn't even bother to hide my nakedness. After the night I'd had, someone seeing my schlong swaying in the breeze was the least of my concerns. Not that there were many people left to see anything. After reaching the toppled table, I fashioned the ragged piece of fabric into a sort of toga and decided it would have to do.

Modesty preserved, I turned in a slow circle to take in the destruction Tony had wrought. The pavilion's large tent was gone, reduced to another piece of trash in the river. Its posts and stakes stuck up from the ground like broken fingers grasping at the sky. The attached event center was solid brick. It had been around for decades and would likely endure many more, but it would definitely need some new windows. Easily a third or more of the trees ringing the park on the island's southern half had been felled by the strong gusts or torched by the pyrotechnic lightning show. Those left standing had lost a good number of branches. The wide concrete slab alongside the event center and asphalt walking trails, even the good old-fashioned grassy park, were crisscrossed with cracks and buckled earth. It was amazing to see what a pissed-off douchebag is capable of, especially if he's a warlock.

I continued my slow inspection until a glint of light caught my eye. A few short steps, a lean at the waist, an outstretched arm, and a gentle pinch of my finger and thumb later, I'd picked the source up from the rubble. Not to brag, but I'm a bit of an expert on glass. The small orb I held in my hand was the real deal, not plastic or whatever they probably made prosthetic eyes out of these days. A keen eye could tell the difference. I didn't have that keen of an eye. I just knew a fake eye when I saw one.

"I got your eyeball!" I called out.

The oracle's head popped out from under a twisted cardigan. One eye was squeezed shut, and the other took in the surrounding devastation. "Is it over?" she asked.

I considered the ruined ground between her and me and shrugged. "You tell me," I groaned. "You're the oracle."

"No, she is not!" an angry voice spat. I saw the succubus and Stein helping Vilde to her feet. Where Betty had escaped the magic storm's wrath, Vilde had borne much of its brunt. The huldra's gown was twisted and skewed, her perfect hair was a rat's nest, the rain had turned her mascara into soupy mud puddles below her eyes, and the rest of her face was cut and bruised. "Faen i helvete," she said, intonation making it clear that I'd just heard a Norwegian curse. Clarissa had found my side and Vilde's anger found a mark. "This was not in my horoscope, young lady. This most certainly was not."

The oracle squinted, her good eye managing a glare that most folks with two could never surpass.

"As your late husband's late familiar would have said, *Metro Pages* is in no way, shape, or form responsible for what may or may not happen to individuals that read its horoscope section."

The two women took each other's measure, and something like understanding passed between them.

"No matter," Vilde muttered as she twisted her gown into some semblance of straight again.

I gaped. "That's all? 'No matter?' Look around. This is a complete shit show. The cops—hell, the National Guard—are going to be here any second. You've got hundreds of thousands in damages, and your recently-deceased-again boyfriend is probably halfway to the Gulf of Mexico by now, and all you can say is, 'No matter?'

"That is correct, Mr. Shade. All of this," she waved an idle hand to encompass the destruction, "truly is no matter. There is only one thing I require, and then I would suggest you all be on your way."

The huldra's arm raised, and a finger extended to point at my hand.

I lifted it in confusion. "What? This?" I asked.

"Yes. The eye. That wondrous eye that revealed the secrets of *The Thirteenth Zodiac* by Yiorgos Katopodis. I want that eye." The huldra patted her dress and shoved a hand into a deep, hidden pocket. "Here. Here! Take this. There will be more. I promise, there will be much more."

Clarissa reached out and took the neatly folded bills from Vilde's hand.

"... Three, four, five hundred," she counted. "Five hundred dollars."

She looked from me to Vilde and back. After a long moment, she took her eye from my lax grip. In its place, she pressed the five crisp Benjamins.

"The other half after you return it," she reminded me with a solemn smile.

Vilde Tanck watched the exchange avidly. She licked her full lips, and the tip of her tail swished eagerly. The oracle held out her hand, the small orb resting in her palm. With the softest of sighs, she dipped her hand and let it fall to the ground. A galosh-clad foot raised up and stomped down before it could roll away, and a small crunch filled the night.

The huldra's face turned into a mask of fury. She threw herself forward–hands outstretched and fingers clawed–but her sudden lunge was brought to an abrupt halt when she reached the end of Tanckenstein's arm. He'd grabbed the back of her gown and held her while she spat and flailed.

"Ms. Tanck," he said firmly, "you always say I should learn to accept my fate. I think it's about time you did the same."

"Thanks, Tanckenstein," I breathed in relief while the huldra screamed.

The large cadaver nodded. "Dieter's dead, so I don't have to work for her anymore. You can call me Leonard now."

"Thanks, Leonard," I amended.

The big undead dead guy nodded, lifted his former boss like a petulant child, and slung her over a shoulder. Her legs kicked, cow's tail flailed, fists pounded his wide back as he stepped carefully over the buckled concrete of the pavilion. He was clearly looking for something. When he found it, my blood ran cold... until he swung a leg back and forward and kicked *The Thirteenth Zodiac* into one of the deeper cracks in the earth. Vilde screamed all the louder, but Leonard just turned and headed toward the parking lot with Betty hurrying to follow. Mona appeared and walked at his side, a slight limp the only indication of what she'd endured. A moment before I lost them to the dark, I saw her hand reach for his.

A moment later, I startled as someone's hand found mine.

"I think this is yours," Clarissa said, looking up into my face.

For a moment, I thought she'd pushed more money into my hand. When I opened it, I saw a small, bent card instead. I unfolded it and saw its familiar words, words that Clarissa recited out loud.

"August Shade. Post-relationship personal effects repossession specialist. Some pets. No kids. Satisfaction possible," she finished with a smile. "Guess you need to get new cards."

I frowned while trying to make sense of her words. I played the last few moments back through my mind... and slapped myself on the forehead.

"The goat. The little goat. A kid." I shook my head and threw my crumpled business card to the ground. "That's even cornier than your horoscopes."

There were sirens in the distance, but I knew they wouldn't be distant for long. Grasping her hand, I led us back to where my beat-up cafe racer and its ragtag sidecar had miraculously stayed upright throughout the night's events. I gave her my helmet and buckled it under her chin before mounting the bike, rearranging my tablecloth toga, and kicking the reluctant engine to life. We'd just crossed the bridge with a silent nod to old Canute when the first fire truck came screaming down the road in the opposite direction. I turned at the first available corner and weaved us into the late night's protection. After a few blocks had passed, I asked if she was all right, my voice straining to be heard over the engine.

"I'm not sure," she yelled back while yanking hard on her cardigan's hem. When she'd pulled a length of knitted yarn loose, she tied it around her head and covered her empty socket. "I think so. For so many years, I've been trying to steer the world clear of disaster. That's all that there was. All that there could be. I had to focus so darn hard on everyone else's futures that I couldn't have one for myself. Now, thanks to you, the earth will keep circling the sun, and all of humanity is still along for the ride. I don't think it needs me anymore. I think I'm free."

I watched something change in the woman beside me. A weight seemed to lift. Tiny creases around her eyes and mouth smoothed, and her spine straightened.

"What will you do?" I asked.

"Besides get an eye patch? I have no idea."

I twisted the bike's throttle. "Well, I don't know about you, but I'm still hungry. Want to grab some food?"

Clarissa's lips parted in surprise. Honest, genuine, one-hundred percent real surprise. "Hot dogs?"

"Not at this time of night," I complained. After wracking my brain, I remembered a little pizzeria near my place that stayed open late.

"You like pizza?" I asked as I checked my blind spot and changed lanes. "We'll have to get takeout. I don't think they want half-naked guys dining in. That okay with you?"

When she didn't respond, I turned my head back to look at her and found her looking at me curiously. "You might spill sauce on your shirt," she said with a smile.

As it turned out, she wasn't wrong. We sat side by side on my couch, a large pizza on the coffee table. I'd lifted a second slice, and the cheese slid off right before I got it to my mouth. It landed wetly on the mostly clean shirt I'd pulled on after we'd arrived and left a saucy, greasy mess. We both laughed and looked into one another's eyes. Well, eye...

# CHAPTER 13

...

———◊———

"Clarissa's were way better," Jay proclaimed as he folded up the horoscopes and used them to wipe paint off a brush. "I can't believe she quit. Their new guy sucks."

The rest of the *Metro Pages* was folded in my lap. I'd wondered if the sudden disappearance of their managing editor might be the final nail in the paper's not-so-metaphorical coffin, but apparently no such luck. The opening letter from the new editor, one Todd Betzold, offered enthusiastic reassurance that the Twin Cities wouldn't lack for its monthly mishmash of amateur journalism, horoscopes, and all the other worthless crap in between. I'd picked up a copy during a quick beer run. The only reason I'd even considered dirtying my fingers with its pulpy pages was a story about a freak summer storm and the first earthquake in Minnesota since 1975 that had combined to wreck half of Nicollet Island.

Someone had found my card in the detritus, and a reporter—or as close as the *Metro Pages* had to offer—had called my office. After a brief interrogation, I'd bribed her to keep my name out of the article by promising to get her rice cooker back from her ex for free. She'd kept her word. The story's only 'first-hand witness' was an anonymous and fortunate soul who'd taken a late-night stroll in the park and somehow survived the dual natural disasters. The rest of the article detailed the damage with clumsy attempts at profound metaphors, offered what I supposed was a cautionary tale about climate change, and speculated on whether the Grain Belt Beer sign would be restored. It was a half-page spread of crap, but at least my name wasn't in it.

I leaned back in the beanbag–the move eliciting a familiar farty noise–and wondered again at the normalcy of my post-dinner party life. Jay was still subversively challenging popular narratives and resisting 'the Man.' Betty was still tending bar, although I didn't drink there anymore. Leonard and Mona had moved into a recently vacated castle on a nice piece of lakefront property. He'd called to let me know I was welcome to visit his new place anytime. I had promised I would, even though we both knew I was lying. And me? People–human and otherwise–were still falling in love, breaking up, and calling me to get their shit back. The world was as normal as normal could be. With a rueful smile, I realized it was precisely what Clarissa had been fighting for.

"It's done," Jay announced. "Want to see it?"

I pushed my way up from the beanbag and moved closer to the studio's windows. The slight change in perspective brought his current project into my line of sight. The wooden case sat on top of a worktable. From my current distance, it was just a box stained a blue so deep it was almost black.

Stepping closer, I observed that the box was probably a foot long, a half-foot deep, and maybe eight inches high. The top had stylized illustrations of a sun and crescent moon, both in a light periwinkle that practically shined. Around the lid's edges was a series of constellations.

"Open it," he encouraged. "The top lifts up, and there are two drawers to pull out. Careful, though. There are still a few spots where the paint is wet."

I set a finger to each corner of the lid and lifted, then delicately pinched the little knob on the front of each drawer and slid them open. Inside the case's top layer were six pairs of glasses. Beneath it, the first drawer was only about half as deep as the case itself and held three more pairs. The bottom drawer was designed to extend past the first drawer's end and show an additional three pairs. The final effect was a three-tiered terrace that put all twelve pairs of spectacles on display.

"Look closer," Jay encouraged.

I followed his suggestion. The inside's soft velvet lining was the blue of a dusky sky. Each pair of glasses was unique in both style and hue, with fine detailing along the rims and stems. On the bridge of each pair, Jay had painted a small, squiggly symbol. After double-checking, I confirmed that no two were alike.

"Signs of the Zodiac," he said. "See that mirror inside the lid? When you put the glasses on, look in the mirror and you will see your own future. You don't need planets or stars to know what your future holds. You just need to look inside yourself."

"Clever," I remarked, but before I could say more, Jay held up a hand. With a show-man's panache, he slipped a fingernail behind the mirror's upper edge and gently pried it loose. Its bottom edge concealed a hinge that let it fold down. Hidden behind the lid's mirror was a thirteenth pair of glasses. With a sly wink, Jay flipped the mirror back into place.

"Shhh," he advised with a finger pressed to his lips. "No one's supposed to know about that pair."

I barked out a surprised laugh. "Clarissa would've loved this," I told him.

My friend waved off the compliment. "You still haven't heard from her? It's been days. I wonder where she's gone."

I didn't know and didn't want to wonder. Clarissa and I had briefly dated after that fateful night. It had gone about as well as could be expected given the natures of the two parties involved. When I'd woken a few days earlier and found her side of my bed empty, I'd sighed at the inevitably of it all. Some futures were simply too predictable to not come true.

The beer I'd picked up was calling, so I passed a cold can to Jay and opened one for myself. The rim had barely touched my lips when he recalled that my phone had rung while I'd been out.

"Seriously? I was only gone for like five minutes," I muttered to myself. "Wonder who it'll be this time? A pissed-off mermaid? An angsty leprechaun? Or worse, a human hipster? Ugh. I hate hipsters."

My desk chair creaked as it took my weight and swiveled toward my old-school digital answering machine, where a red '1' blinked. I hit play and reached for a pen and notepad.

"Hi there, August," she said, her words knocking the pen from my suddenly numb fingers. "I hope this finds you doing good. I'm sorry I didn't say goodbye in person. I didn't know if you'd be sad or happy or angry, and I'm still not sure how to handle all of this... uncertainty. There's something unexpected around every bend, and cripes... Welp, I'm more worked up than a walleye at a fish fry. It's scary and exciting, and I honestly don't know how people endure it. I only know that I have to do this alone."

Jay had come to my office when he heard her voice and eased himself into the spare chair.

"I don't know what the future holds," she continued. "Not anymore. When I look up into the sky at night, I just see the stars. Even so, I'd like to think that if I could still read their secrets, they'd tell me I may need your help again one day. You see, I was in a relationship with someone, and they still have something of mine: a piece of my heart."

The answering machine beeped. I sat with my fingers steepled under my chin, not trusting myself to speak. Jay had wet streaks on his cheeks, the big softy. After a long moment, I let the breath I'd been holding go in a long sigh... and then the phone rang.

"Clarissa?" I asked as I snatched it up.

"August... Shade?" a voice that wasn't hers replied. A voice I almost recognized. A voice I almost knew.

"Yeah," I confirmed. "Who's this?"

In response, the line disconnected.

"Who was that?" Jay asked.

I considered the phone in my hand. Not to brag, but I'm a bit of an expert on glass. I've gone through enough windows, bounced off of enough windshields, been hit over the head with enough vases, and broken enough mirrors to know a thing or two. Like how easily something can shatter when it's violently flung to the ground, which is exactly how that voice left me feeling. I picked the jagged little pieces of myself up and fitted them back together as best I could.

"Wrong number," I said with what I hoped was a convincing nonchalance. "Now... Didn't your horoscope say you'd be having another beer?"

We sipped on our cold pilsners and talked about the usual stuff: conspiracies, the worst bands from the nineties, annoying PNs, and the crap they just had to get back from their exes. All the while, a voice saying my name echoed in my skull. A voice I'd almost recognized. A voice that brushed at the heavy layers of dirt that I'd shoveled over my past.

And to think that I'd been worried about my future.

## AUTHOR'S NOTE

*Thanks for reading! Poor August, right? Mysterious phone calls are the worst. After all the guy's been through, he needs a break. Unfortunately, he isn't going to get one.*

*The misadventures continue in **A Scarecrow Wins an Award**. August heads to Minnesota farm country—definitely not his natural habitat—and gets mixed up with two feuding hag sisters, a loan sharking coblyn, and a mysterious woman with a very scary ex. Jay's latest art project lands August in a heap of trouble, and the shapeshifter's efforts to keep a low profile fall apart.*

*It's life or death for August Shade, and the scales keep tilting toward the latter. No one said being a paranormal post-relationship personal effects repossession specialist was easy.*

---

*If you like paranormal comedy, sign up for my once-a-month newsletter,* **The Paranomedy Pint***, and get a FREE short story! Each month, I share a great book to read, a fun show to watch, a tasty drink to drink, and a little paranormal weirdness, too.*

---

THE END

# Did You Have Fun?

I HAD A HECK of a good time writing this book. If you enjoyed reading it, I hope you'll take a moment to share a rating or even a review! Ratings and reviews for authors are like tips for bartenders. We love 'em. They also help others who stumble across the book decide if they should give it a try.

Use these QR codes to easily post a review on your preferred site(s):

**Amazon**

**Goodreads**

**BookBub**

# A Post-Relationship Personal Effects What Now?

⟡

The funny thing about authors is that there's a story behind every story. We love to call it by the flashier names like *inspiration* or *muse*. End of the day, though, it's just a story. An experience we had at some point in our lives. An experience that stuck with us. Then one day, that experience becomes the seed that sprouts that next book.

So there I was, driving from Minneapolis, MN to Chicago, IL with my buddy. It was the late 90s. He'd gone to college in those parts. We were going to see some of his friends and have a little fun. It's anywhere from a six to an eight-hour drive, depending on things like the weather, the car, and how much Coke you drink (and how many times you have to pee). Suffice it to say that we had a lot of time to fill on that drive. Seeing as how we were in our early twenties, we spent a lot of that time talking about girls. On this particular trip, one of us had recently been dumped. I don't remember which one, but odds are good it was me. My buddy was a little better at maintaining relationships, where I was prone to being the oil to someone else's water. Anyway, the conversation had meandered to how annoying stuff was, especially stuff that you liked that your ex wouldn't give back. We figured there were a lot of people in that situation. Being the ingenuitive types, we also figured we were the best ones to help.

So there we were on the Illinois tollway, cooking up a new business venture. The car needed gas, or we needed more Coke, or one of us had to pee. Who knows, and it's not important. What is important is that we pulled off to an Oasis. Those are travel stops on bridges that span the freeway. They've got a gas station, a variety of fast food options, restrooms, a few picnic tables, and a sad patch of grass for your dog to do its mid-road trip business. They also usually have some random kiosks where you can find exactly what you hadn't realized you needed until that moment. In our case, it was a business card printing machine. It had a little black and white electronic screen and a sticky keyboard. You typed in what you wanted on your card, slid in a few bills, and waited. After ten minutes and some whirring sounds, a small cardboard box would appear with your newly printed cards.

Any fool knows you can't have a business and not have business cards, so we had a quick brainstorm, slid in a few bucks, and waited anxiously for the next chapter of our lives to begin as Post-Relationship Personal Effects Repossession Specialists. It was brilliant, it was necessary, and—because we had business cards—it was totally legit.

Spoiler alert! We became neither rich nor famous. I don't think we booked a single job. That silly idea became nothing more than a fun story, but it was a story that stuck with me. For years and years, it was tucked in the back of my brain. Faded with time and buried under a myriad of other moments, other experiences, other stories, sure, but still there.

Then came the day when that old buddy of mine was moving from somewhere to somewhere else. While packing for that move, he unearthed a box of business cards. My god, how we laughed. Those stupid cards were the key log for a bunch of memories and pulling one out of its old box cleared the jam. We reminisced on those days gone by. We talked about those girls we'd dated, talked about how one still had his favorite sweatshirt, another still had my favorite flannel, and on and on.

So there I was, trying to think of a new series to write. After finishing my third book, *Undead Cheesehead,* I was having a hell of a time coming up with that next story. I tried hard scifi. I tried a spin-off of my earlier books. I even rewrote *The Breakfast Club*—scene for scene, line for line—but with monsters. Claire was a fairy. Andrew was a werewolf. Brian was a mad scientist. Allison was a banshee. Bender was a goblin. Principal Vernon was a skunk ape. You get the idea. I had a lot of stuff sloshing around in my brain, but nothing was working. Nothing felt right. And then...

I thought of those business cards. I thought of how hilarious it would have been to be a Post-Relationship Personal Effects Repossession Specialist. I thought of all the people I would have met and all the messes I would've gotten into. And just like that, I thought of my next book. All I had was a story, an experience, a little spark of inspiration, the faintest whisper of a muse. It was enough, though, and August Shade, the Paranormal Post-Relationship Personal Effects Repossession Specialist, was born.

I hope you enjoyed the book and are looking forward to more of August's misadventures. Also, if you're in a relationship, and things go sideways, and that not-so-significant-anymore other keeps the book and you want it back...

Here's my card.

# A Bit About Scott

People say you should write what you know. That's damned good advice, so Scott writes about ordinary Midwesterners making an extraordinary mess of things. Hey, if the flannel fits...

Oh, one more thing. "Ordinary" totally includes vampires, werewolves, zombies, witches, shapeshifters, aliens and more!

Find Scott on:

**www.swbauthorblog.wordpress.com**
**www.facebook.com/swbuthor**
**www.instagram.com/swbauthor**
**www.goodreads.com/swbauthor**
**www.bookbub.com/authors/scott-burtness**
... and in bars and bowling alleys up in the Midwest.

# FREE SHORT STORY

Get *Five Stars*, a FREE demonic horror comedy short story, when you sign up for **The Paranomedy Pint**, Scott's once-a-month email featuring a great book to read, a fun show to watch, something terrific to drink, and a little paranormal weirdness to enjoy!!

# BEER-FUELED URBAN FANTASY BY SCOTT BURTNESS

THE MISADVENTURES OF A PARANORMAL
POST-RELATIONSHIP PERSONAL EFFECTS
REPOSSESSION SPECIALIST
*An Oracle Walks into a Bar*
*A Scarecrow Wins an Award*
*A Siren Sings Her Heart Out*

MONSTERS IN THE MIDWEST
*Wisconsin Vamp*
*Northwoods Wolfman*
*Undead Cheesehead*
*Monsters in the Midwest: The Complete Trilogy*
*Bjørn Again: A Monsters in the Midwest short story*

ODDS 'n' ENDS
*A is for All the Monsters We Can't Stand: A Hilarious Monster-Themed Coloring Book for
Grownups*
Story and poems by Scott Burtness | Illustrations by Harold Torres